NEVER COME BACK

BOOKS BY CARA REINARD

The Wife at the Window
The Clinic

Pretty Dolls and Hand Grenades
Last Doll Standing
Sweet Water
Into the Sound
The Den

NEVER COME BACK

CARA REINARD

Bookouture

Published by Bookouture in 2025

An imprint of Storyfire Ltd.
Carmelite House
50 Victoria Embankment
London EC4Y 0DZ

www.bookouture.com

The authorised representative in the EEA is Hachette Ireland
8 Castlecourt Centre
Dublin 15 D15 XTP3
Ireland
(email: info@hbgi.ie)

Copyright © Cara Reinard, 2025

Cara Reinard has asserted her right to be identified
as the author of this work.

All rights reserved. No part of this publication may be reproduced, stored in any retrieval system, or transmitted, in any form or by any means, electronic, mechanical, photocopying, recording or otherwise, without the prior written permission of the publishers.

ISBN: 978-1-83618-353-2
eBook ISBN: 978-1-83618-354-9

This book is a work of fiction. Names, characters, businesses, organizations, places and events other than those clearly in the public domain, are either the product of the author's imagination

All human beings, as we meet them, are commingled out of good and evil.

> Robert Louis Stevenson

ONE

ROWAN

The bags are packed by the door, one laptop backpack looped on top of a suitcase.

He's leaving her.

Not for good, of course, but the bags are a trigger, and she can't help but think he shouldn't be going at all. Not now. She rubs the swell of her lower abdomen thinking about how they made love last night the way she likes it.

The way he likes it too...

It might be for the last time. Everything on her body is changing faster than the previous pregnancy.

"Don't worry, I'll be back before you know it." Wyatt stands at the door in his airplane clothes—jeans and a tailored button-down shirt, new sneakers, trendy sunglasses. He screams hot-tech guy, and that's exactly her worry. She'd rather keep him to herself instead of releasing him into the wild. She remembers in their early years of marriage how she had to tame that wild; and take out a few thirsty interns along the way.

"I know. I just don't like you traveling internationally by yourself. I wish you had another colleague going with you."

His soothing expression could calm a bear. "Rowan, this is a one-man job. It won't even take me that long. Back before the end of the week." He kisses her on the cheek. She brushes the wide expanse of his shoulders, trails her fingers over his nicely formed biceps. *Mine.*

Rowan's aware females ogle her husband.

Women would walk right up to her and say, *You're so lucky.*

You're so lucky to have such a good-looking, dedicated husband...

There's responsibility to uphold with that statement. Pressure to be Wyatt's equally indelible plus one. When they lived in the city, she felt like his match. Before kids they were a power couple who could rule a kingdom. Once they had Landon, though, she felt herself slide.

The dark circles beneath her eyes became a constant placeholder. Her body shape changed significantly after childbirth, and even though other women swore if she did the right exercise routines, she'd return to her pre-baby size, she never did.

Once they moved from Philadelphia to Bryn Mawr, she felt at one with some of the other suburbanites, young couples like them, and her contentment returned.

Bryn Mawr was quiet. Subdued. *Safe.*

Wherever Wyatt's heading now might not be. Growing up in a broken home left her constantly aware of anything that might threaten hers.

Landon tugs on Wyatt's leg. Their four-year-old has sandwiched himself between them, one of his favorite places.

"Flute, Daddy?" Landon glances up, expectantly. Every time Wyatt goes away, he and Landon pick out a gift he'll bring back for him, something indigenous to the area he's visiting. This time they've chosen a Mexican flute.

"That's right, buddy. I'll try to find a hand-painted one, like the flutes we saw online," he says. The promised gifts smooth over the passage of time when Wyatt is gone.

"Yeah!" Landon cheers and hugs his daddy tight.

Rowan both loves and hates the notion. In one instance, he's giving Landon something to look forward to upon his return. In another, he's paying him off for his absence in the form of a bribe. It's more than her father ever gave her when he worked overnights. At least Wyatt has the decency to pretend like he misses them. But what really bothers Rowan is that she fears he enjoys it.

Venturing to new destinations—without her.

Wyatt offers her one final tight squeeze before he heads off, and she's sure everything will go smoothly, like every other time he's traveled for work.

She's just vividly aware of how much more there is at stake now that she has another human growing inside her body.

She watches Wyatt's SUV pull out of the driveway. He traded in his sports car for the Highlander, a family car, the practical choice. Wyatt's a good husband, and a kind man— maybe too kind. It's everyone else she worries about.

Landon turns on the television, flips to a cartoon featuring zany characters in vibrant colors; a brighter world than the one she's living in now. Rowan pulls out the prescription from her purse for an anti-depressant the doctor said is *fine* to take with pregnancy, although when she read about it, the language—*the potential benefits of the drug may outweigh the risks*—made her queasy. It didn't sound fine.

So... there is some risk? Or they don't know for sure if there is?

Rowan didn't bring up the subject with Wyatt to get a second opinion on the matter. She doesn't want him to know she's struggling. She also doesn't want to put her unborn child in harm's way. She crinkles up the paper and places it back in her purse.

Her fear of being alone stems from growing up in a suburb southwest of Philadelphia. The week after her father moved out, they had a break-in at their walk-up rowhouse, same as all the others on the block. She never understood why the thief marked theirs. The cops said end units were a prime target because they offer easier access, but Rowan didn't buy it.

No one was injured, but they were burglarized. Rowan was half convinced her father committed the crime himself to get back at her mother, but when she saw that they'd stolen her golden crucifix her grandmother had gifted her, she knew he didn't. He'd never do that. A stranger had broken into their house, gone through all their things, and taken what they wanted.

Even though they lived in a super safe neighborhood now it wasn't enough to calm her nerves. Rowan retreated to her bedroom, and into her walk-in closet.

She kneeled on the floor, used her fingerprint to open the gun safe, took out the pistol. It felt good to hold the weapon in her hand. The weight of it.

Wyatt didn't know she did this sometimes when she was scared. It was sensory, the metal to her skin, giving her strange comfort. Her mother never let them keep a gun in their house. Even after the break in.

Wyatt didn't argue with her when she wanted to buy a firearm. They'd even gone together to the shooting range to practice. Wyatt was a good shot.

Rowan was better.

And nobody would ever take anything from her again.

TWO

WYATT

Mexico City

Wyatt's eyes are drawn to the gold pendant lights hanging like rheumy teardrops from the wood-paneled coffered ceiling. One of the nicest hotels in Mexico City, he's surprised his boss sprung for the Marriott. He leans on the retractable handle of his suitcase as he waits in the check-in line, exhausted.

Early morning train from Philly to the drop-off location near JFK.

The plane.

The car ride to the hotel.

All the different modes of transportation make the whole eight-hour trip seem endless.

Wyatt pulls at the top button of his white dress shirt, thankful this hotel has good air conditioning, because the cab didn't.

The pretty woman behind the desk greets him. "Can I have your name, sir?" She wears a form-fitted gray suit. Gold bangles hang from her delicate wrist like coil springs. *You like to be noticed, don't you?*

"Wyatt Bishop."

She taps the computer with her painted fingernails. "I'll just need a credit card for incidentals."

Wyatt hands her his personal card. He hates using it for travel expenses, but it's his third start-up tech company in five years, and he's used to the minor inconvenience until the company's systems are all in place. The money will come later, and when it does…

The attendant runs the card, smiles with the slightest wink, and returns it with the room key—350. He slides his card back in his wallet, scoping out the nearby elevator. A water dispenser with fresh fruit floating at the top sits like the holy grail at the center of the lobby. He helps himself to a paper cup, noticing the soapy smell in the recirculated air.

Hotel lobbies are all the same…

His wife wishes he was home more. Rowan didn't complain when he jumped from job number one to job number two, but his third hop brought questions. Too many.

He has a habit of moving onto the next big thing, motivated by the challenge of the work in the start-up phase, bored by the time the actual product launches.

Apex focuses on the remote management of IT services for healthcare systems, making the company's product accessible from anywhere in the world. His purpose for this trip is to integrate a call center in Mexico City to service south of the border.

He pushes the button for the elevator.

"Do you mind if I join you?"

He turns slightly to find a woman in a black pant suit with long dark hair and eyebrows that seem to stretch to her temple, perfectly arched.

The elevator dings and opens. "Please," he says. He extends his arm, ushering her ahead of him.

Once both inside, she pushes the number two button. He taps the three.

"Here on business?" she asks.

"I am. Was it the laptop bag that gave me away? Or the business-casual sneakers?" He grins.

"A little of both," she says. "Although, I'm here on business as well. This hotel is great. Have you seen the rooftop restaurant and bar?"

"No. My first time here."

"You should check out the view. I'm headed there..." she checks her large-faced, diamond-studded Rolex "... in an hour or so."

"Oh." He shouldn't meet this gorgeous woman.

It's a bad idea.

Rowan wouldn't like it at all, but he's not one to stay cooped up in his room. He was planning on searching for food in about an hour anyway, and a rooftop bar sounds nice. "Thanks for the invite. I'm going to check in at home, and if all is well, I may be up." No promises. And he spelled out that he has someone to check in with, so she doesn't get the wrong idea.

"Okay, then. My name is Esme, by the way." The elevator chimes and opens. "See you... well, maybe." She smiles wide, her eyebrows peaking like two spider legs. The doors slide open, and she shimmies out, her breasts jostling a bit in the deep vee of her black suit jacket.

When Wyatt reaches his floor, he finds his room and keys in. He wheels his bag inside and collapses on the bed. The muscles in his body seem to disappear into the burgundy comforter.

It's possible he might not reemerge for dinner and just order room service. If Esme hadn't given him ideas about beautiful views and dinner company for two, he most certainly wouldn't be entertaining the idea of going anywhere right now. He has to be up early tomorrow morning and report to the call center.

He calls Rowan.

"You made it," she says. "I thought I would've heard from you hours ago. I was getting worried."

"Just got to my hotel," he says.

"Your hotel? You were supposed to call me when you landed."

Did I say that? Rowan rambles off requests so often he has a bad habit of agreeing to them without fully listening to what they are. "I was trying to figure out the airport. Different language. I had to find baggage claim. A cab."

"A cab? Apex hired a car service for you. Do you mean the car service, Wyatt?"

Fuck. They did order him a private car and he forgot. His manager is going to be pissed. He'll have to find the number and call the service and let them know he got another ride.

"Right. Sorry. I'm tired. The car service."

She breathes heavily into the phone. He can imagine her leaning over a basket of laundry and folding their clothing into neat little squares. "Detail-oriented. Not one of your strengths."

He stares at the uneven plaster on the ceiling. *But it's yours, isn't it, dear wife.* "It's not like I list it as a skill on my resume, so they shouldn't expect it," he jokes.

She makes a popping noise with her tongue. He hates the sound. "You're lucky you have me. In case I haven't reminded you of that today."

He blanks into the wall above him, too fatigued for this. "Yes, honey, I know."

"Speaking of resumes... you left your browser window open on your iPad and when Landon logged on to play, I saw the job post you were checking out for Information Technology Leader."

"So?" he says.

"Wyatt, you agreed, at least two years with this company. Three, preferably."

He swipes his tongue over his teeth, holding back words better left unsaid. She misses *nothing*. He remembers when she liked his spontaneity. When they met at the Jersey Shore, he coerced her into boogie boarding even though she'd never set foot in the ocean before.

He couldn't even remember the last time they went to the beach.

Not since Landon was born, that's for sure. Rowan somehow convinced him the ocean was too dangerous for children even though it was his favorite place growing up.

"You know I wasn't happy with some of the language in your current contract..." she continues.

"Apex is allowed to ask for a blood draw to test for drugs or whatever else they want."

"Such an invasion of privacy..." Rowan says, HR expert in all-things-benefits.

"Rowan, I'm not going over this again. I was just looking. I'm allowed to look." *Like at the woman in the elevator.* "I check out jobs like you look at houses."

Even though they are somehow managing a million-and-a-half-dollar mortgage for the white, dormered window, colonial home of Rowan's dreams.

"But honey, I don't buy a new house every other year. I really do just look."

"That's what I was doing." He's exhausted and ready for this conversation to be over.

Landon is crying about something in the background. He misses his little boy, but sometimes he doesn't know if he's cut out to be a father—or a husband. Rowan claims they're creating the beautiful life they never had, but sometimes it feels like a future she's designed entirely by herself. Like Rowan could swap him out with any other guy with a decent bankroll and plentiful sperm count and get what she wanted.

"Fine, fine. Just know I worry about you down there. You'll have another child to support soon." She giggles, but their impending bundle doesn't make him feel warm and fuzzy inside.

It only makes him stressed.

THREE
WYATT

Freshly showered, Wyatt dresses in jeans and a polo shirt and makes his way to the lobby.

The hotel attendant from earlier is packing up her purse for the night and waves at him as she punches something into her phone. "Heading to the roof?" she asks.

"Yes," he says.

She points to the left of him. "That way."

"Thanks." He walks along the wall of rounded glass, following the pathway to the stairwell then climbs the terracotta steps lit with white lights strung in between clay and brick pillars. Swishes of white fabric hang wistfully between metal lanterns as they sway in the slight breeze.

When Wyatt sees Esme sitting at the bar, beckoning him with a wave—same black suit, same sultry smile—his body comes alive with curiosity. He's thirsty for conversation that doesn't involve a reminder of his growing responsibilities or a complaint about yet another way he's failed to meet expectations.

Sometimes on these trips he finds himself engaged in friendly banter with strangers. It's like the rush he experiences when he searches for a new career opportunity and finds the perfect fit. It's not so much that he's seeking another woman, it's the formation of a connection, fresh conversation.

He usually looks for the hotel bar to make idle chatter when he travels for work. Being alone in a confined room reminds him of the long stretches he spent in his mother's Wildwood, New Jersey apartment while she worked her waitress shifts at the Shore.

When he approaches Esme, she smiles. "Hello there. I didn't know if you would make it." She's drinking something pink in a margarita glass with jewels on the side, the colors highlighting her slender nose. Her cheekbones form accentuated bulbs when she smiles.

"Yes, I didn't know either. So, what's good here?" he asks.

She pulls her glass away from her mouth and displays the drink for him to see. "You must try one of these. It's called a Pink Elephant."

He smiles. "If you say so, then I must."

Esme laughs and motions to the bartender with her hand, pointing to her drink and signaling another. "Everything okay at home?" she asks.

"Same old stuff."

She traces the rim of her glass. "Sometimes same is good. Sometimes different is better." Esme looks up then, making him squirm in his seat. "I like exploring new places."

"Me too," he says. The bartender sets down the pink cocktail in front of Wyatt. He sips at his drink, greedily. The cranberry, grapefruit, and cotton candy froth leaves him with a sweet and sour aftertaste.

"Married?" she asks with a grin.

He licks his lip at the tartness. "I am."

"Kids?" she asks.

"I have a little boy and a baby on the way."

"Congrats," she says, but her tone's flat, the spider legs resting above her eyes, unenthused.

"Thanks, how about you?" he asks.

"None of those things. I'm not interested in settling down," she answers.

He swallows, taking her response as a come-on. He can see where this is going, and he should turn right around and head in the other direction. "Is that right?"

"Yes," she says, hotly.

He can't place the sharp edge of her accent, and wants to ask her where she's from, but he fears he's just insulted her somehow. "I... apologize."

"No bother." Esme flaps her hand at the air, waving his words away. She's looking out into the skyscape. A red and orange hue has burned itself between a tall building and another metropolitan tower, gleaming metallic and glass. "That's the Torre Reforma."

She points at the taller one, oddly shaped with a three-sided top and one short, flat side. Wyatt can faintly see a herd of cats scampering below in his peripheral vision, the sounds of open-air markets bustling, the bright colors apparent even from above. Wyatt squints into the sun, taking in the building. "It looks like it's twisting in the air."

"It's one of the only three-sided skyscrapers in the world," Esme informs.

He thinks of the Flatiron Building in Manhattan, and the fact that he really does travel a lot. "Very nice."

"Do you like your drink, Wyatt?"

"The drink that's already gone." He holds up his empty glass. He was parched and downed it in a few gulps. In his circle of friends, he would be harassed for ordering a delicate pink drink. He's glad she forced it on him. "Hey, I don't remember telling you my name."

"You drank it already?" Esme gazes at him with concern.

"You did. You told me your name earlier." She smiles wickedly, her eye teeth sharp.

Her response reminds him of the conversation he had with his wife and everything he selectively hears. He probably did mention his name at some point. And he forgot about it, just like the car service he was supposed to take. The night air prickles his neck.

"I have a balcony room where I can show you another view of the city," she says.

"You seem to know a lot about this place for not living here," he teases.

"I travel often," she says.

"Right. I'm actually hungry, though. I'll hang here." If Esme is inviting him to her room, she intends to show him a lot more than a better "view". And as much as he would like to entertain that idea, he can't do that to his wife. He does love her. He just feels a little disconnected from her at the moment. He's needed at home, but Wyatt can see the big difference between need and want in the reflection of this beautiful woman's eyes.

"We can order room service," Esme whispers in his ear. The glow from the lantern casts a pattern across her smooth face, painting tiny stars on her rounded cheeks. "You're a thousand miles away. Enjoy yourself. Forget yourself for a while."

"That sounds nice," he whispers back. He wishes it didn't sound great to his ears, but it does.

"Shall we go? Maybe another drink first?" she asks.

She's saying everything he needs to hear, but another drink won't fix his problem. He's probably just jet-lagged, but his vision juts in and out for a second. He closes his eyes. His body sways to the side, and he grabs the table. When he opens them, Esme's incisors are inches from his skin, her hot breath on his neck.

"Here." She drapes his arm around her shoulder. "You

drank that too fast," she says, but it sounds like she's echoing through a PVC pipe.

"Follow me." His face is suddenly lost in her hair. It smells like honeysuckle and raspberries. His body is lax. He can feel her leading him somewhere through the darkness.

The steps make him trip.

"Oh no," she says. "Stay with me, Wyatt."

Someone lays him down on the bed. His head rests on a pillow. He comes to.

She takes off her suit jacket and reveals a black, lacy push-up bra, overflowing with Esme. She straddles him on top of the bed and begins to kiss him. He lets her, but his senses are foggy. Wyatt tries to work his eyes—open, shut.

Open. Shut.

Wake up.

This is a bad dream.

She unbuckles his pants and pulls them off.

It's the last thing he remembers before he turns to ice.

FOUR

ROWAN

"Hi there." Rowan takes her first sip of morning coffee—lukewarm. *Blah*. It's bad enough that it's decaf. She rubs her lower abdomen. The sacrifices have only begun.

"So, what're we looking at? A civil suit on top of this? Suspension for Klein?" Pierre's sigh has a whine to it.

Rowan places her coffee down and examines her nails, noticing a slight chip in her gel fill. *Tsk*. She does her job well. Is it so hard to ask everyone else to do the same? "I got her to drop the whole thing."

"What?" Pierre squeals in her ear. She can hear him clapping and visualizes him bouncing up and down in his leather swivel chair, the little tassels on his suede loafers jumping with them.

The case involved a recent college grad at their office, Lynsey Hamilton, who bent over in front of the boss, old man Klein. She didn't like the way he looked at her afterward, and then filed a monstrous complaint.

"You are a god!"

"Goddess," she corrects.

"Right! I'm sorry. So not PC of me. Total goddess. How did you do it? Share your secrets, I'm dying over here," he says.

"We just had a heart-to-heart talk about what Lynsey's paragraph of complaints and lack of credible evidence looked like compared to Klein's twenty years here without incident."

What Lynsey needed and did not have in order to file a claim of this sort was a time-stamped, documented paper trail of Klein's offenses, admissible in a court of law. What she had was merely hearsay. Or an unfortunate observation, more like, since the man didn't say a word.

Rowan's more careful about the decisions she makes.

She owns her responsibilities, a no-fail system.

"Oh, for sure," Pierre agrees.

"And I promised a sexual harassment module. We're due anyway. It's part of the fall learning series," Rowan says.

"You're a gem, truly. When HR pans for employees in the stream of job candidates, you're the diamond they hope shakes out."

Rowan smiles. "Oh stop." She could've had Pierre's job if she would've remained in a full-time role, but she knows the sacrifice of prioritizing work over family. Her mother was an overworked nurse. She spent so much time taking care of other people, she had nothing left for her husband when she came home.

So he found someone else.

Rowan believes everything is achievable with a plan—marry the right partner—nurture all the seeds you plant together. Protect the harvest at all costs.

She thinks back to the pistol in her closet...

"So happy this is resolved. Gotta run, though. I have to pick up Bentley from the groomer. The only appointment I could get was at ten o'clock today. He smelled more like a wild boar than a Cavalier King Charles. Dinner party tonight at my place that I can now enjoy, thanks to you," Pierre says.

Rowan chuckles. "Glad I could put your mind at ease. Go on and fetch Bentley."

Pierre is more suited for the position than she is anyway. He has only Bentley and his partner, Trevin, to worry about. Life has spun in a much different direction since Landon arrived, and in six more months she'll have another. Rowan constantly reassures herself that the opportunity to re-up later in her career is always possible.

"I owe you, lady."

"Nah... Mr. K better pad my annual bonus with a little extra something this year, though. And he best keep his eyeballs to himself."

Pierre cackles before he hangs up.

Chloe, the company operator, rings her line. *Busy morning.* Rowan picks up. "Yes, Chloe."

"Hello, Rowan. I've received a call from your husband's company requesting to speak with you. They're on the other line."

Her throat closes in fear. *Oh no.* She makes good decisions. She can't say the same for her husband. "Please, put them through."

Rowan had a horrible feeling about Apex when Wyatt took the job. Funded out of Russia, the lead investor's wife, Irina, is the CEO. Companies that have family members tied to both operations and finances have a rotten stench to them.

"Hello, this is Rowan Bishop."

She can hear someone panting on the line. "Ms. Bishop, It's Irina Orlov." Her tone is severe, which immediately puts Rowan on guard.

"Yes, Irina, hi. Is Wyatt okay?" she asks. Everything in the room begins to sink. She can feel her blood pressure drop, her head suddenly too heavy to hold up.

"He is oh-kay," Irina says.

"Thank God." She exhales, her heart regulating, her blood

pumping back to its rightful arteries. Rowan's forehead finds the edge of her desk, her hand rubbing her pregnant belly.

Breathe. Breathe for the baby.

I won't let you grow up fatherless like I did.

"But he was mugged. I don't know all the details. He did not report to the call center this morning."

Oh my god. "He was... attacked?" She can barely hear the words leave her mouth over the beating of her own heart.

"Yes. I'm afraid so."

Rowan lifts up her head in confusion. "Why... hasn't he called me?" She's struggling to stay vertical, but she must ask questions so she doesn't pass out.

She must keep the words flowing and gather all the information.

"His cell phone was stolen."

"But he called you?" Rowan doesn't mean to accuse Irina of anything, but why would Wyatt call his CEO before her?

"He didn't. The police did. They needed to verify employment. He's fine."

"Where is he now? Is he at the police station?"

"I do not know." She hears a muffled sigh. "One of the conditions of his contract was setting up the technology hub."

"You can't keep him there if his safety is threatened. Why hasn't he contacted me?" Every human resources red-flag-neuron fires off in her brain. And is Irina saying she'll fire Wyatt for not completing the job even though he was attacked? Oh, God... *Wyatt was attacked*, her worst nightmare of him traveling to a foreign country alone.

"I already said. His phone was... stolen. Will be in touch."

No way—wait! There're things she's not telling her. "Irina, what happened to my husband? You need to disclose this information to me. I'm employed in HR. Work-related incidents are my specialty."

She snorts into the phone. "I know your job. We operate on

startup here and your husband delayed our first phase. I don't know all the details."

"What? How do I get in touch with him? Can you please have him call me?"

"I delivered message. I do have to go now. Call for future appointment if you want to speak to me again." The line goes dead.

Rowan stares at her office phone in disbelief. A flurry of frustration hits her hard. It's presumptuous of her to assume they'd make her privy to all the details over the phone if they aren't sure what happened themselves, but there's no way she can just sit there and wait for Wyatt to contact her.

Irina certainly isn't going to help.

Rowan frantically searches for flights to Mexico City on her computer.

She runs her household, dammit.

And something has happened to her husband. If Wyatt's company isn't going to give her answers then she's going to find them herself.

FIVE
ROWAN

The dogwoods in her neighbor's yard are in full bloom, a flurry of pink with white centers. Someday the trees Wyatt recently planted will look the same, and she hopes he's here to see them.

She half-stared at her phone all night waiting for him to call. The rest of the evening she told herself—*you need to sleep for the baby.*

The stress isn't good for anyone involved.

But why hasn't he called me yet?

Landon plays with a block tower on the floor, building it up, then knocking it down again. He's like his father, interested in the creation of his project, and then bored as soon as it's complete.

Landon misses his dad because he asked for Mr. Crackers, his stuffed alligator, two nights in a row, and he only demands him when he's sick or sad. It's an odd name for an alligator, but Landon insisted his spikes looked like crackers, so it stuck. He's probably asking for him because he senses her distress even though Rowan's trying to keep it from him.

Her entire goal as a parent is to shield her children from

emotional harm, but it's time to do more than just sit around and wait by the phone. Why hasn't he called?

Jettisoning off to Mexico City was a dumb idea.

Once she considered the fact that she has no one to take care of her child, and traveling alone, pregnant, in a foreign country with a yellow travel advisory was insane, she stopped searching for flights.

Today, she's off work.

Irina won't take her calls.

Rowan thought about showing up at Wyatt's office since the questions from her conversation with Irina have gone unanswered. She doesn't know any of his colleagues to try to get information that way. Apex is liable for what happened to Wyatt. She searched for his employment contract to try to find his coverage for international travel, but she wasn't able to locate it. Wyatt isn't organized, and he likely didn't print it out. She could break into his personal email, but she's sure what she needs is in his work email, and she doesn't have access to it.

The other option is going to the police station to report Wyatt missing.

Can she really report him missing, though, when someone supposedly knows where he is? Irina told her he was assaulted and the police called her. But Rowan wants to talk to *him*. The police could be lying. Why hasn't he called?

It's driving her nuts, the not speaking to him part.

He was mugged, but what does that mean? Was he injured and couldn't call her, or has he simply been unable to order a new phone and activate it down there? The least he could do was email her, which makes her believe he's really hurt; the dread of not knowing like quicksand in her bones, pulling her down further with each passing minute.

She didn't know how you went about reporting someone missing if it happens in another country. For once, Rowan doesn't know the rules to the game she's playing. How can she make a plan if she doesn't know all the facts?

Coffee cup to her lips, she shields her eyes from the morning sun, slicing through the picture window of their nineteenth-century refurbished farmhouse. The bright beam of light bounces off the partly white siding surrounded by stone, black shutters—the house of her dreams.

It was outside of their price range, but it was meant to be hers.

Rowan had a corkboard from her youth with things she loved about houses and this one checked every box. She told Wyatt that she would cut corners in other ways so they could afford it, and she has.

A thrifty shopper, she accepts all hand-me-downs and only purchases her child's clothing on sale. He grows out of them so fast anyway, it only makes sense. She clips coupons, joins forums for how to find local deals.

Her kids will never have to bunk up in this four-bedroom beauty.

There will be enough room for all their toys so they won't trip over them or be forced to give them away prematurely like Rowan had to as a kid.

She likes that Bryn Mawr is a college town too.

There's charm here and youth and sprawling yards for her children to play, backyard barbeques with neighbors who are sometimes a little stuffy, but mostly okay. Rowan has secret goals of having enough money to be as stuffy as them someday, but she and Wyatt have a long way to go.

One thing her dream is missing at the moment is a fucking husband.

Where is Wyatt?

She watches in dismay as Landon places the very top piece of his tower and fastens it tightly.

It's a lovely pyramid, but she knows it won't last long.

Sure enough, Landon lifts up his plane next. "Hey, buddy, why don't you leave it for Mommy? I like to look at it. So pretty. You don't want to wreck it. You just built it."

Landon stares back at her with an angry face, deep brown eyes *so serious*. His dark hair is mussed and sticks out in two large clumps.

"No, Mom." He takes his mini jetliner and Rowan's heart jumps, because she knows what will happen next. She's not sure why she cares, but when Landon rams the plane into the middle of the tower, and the pieces crash to the floor, she sets her mug down, the coffee rising in her stomach. Then she realizes why it bothers her. Landon reminds her of Wyatt—impulsive.

What danger have you gotten yourself into, Wyatt?

SIX

ROWAN

Her phone rings—*Mom*. "Any news yet, hon?"

"No," Rowan says, breathlessly. "Nothing. Do you know anyone in law enforcement or a lawyer who can help out? Ask questions?"

"Whoa. I know you're worried, but don't you think you're jumping the gun?"

"Mother, it's been two whole days and I haven't heard from my husband."

"But he's in a different country. He had his phone stolen. My guess is he can't figure out a way to make an international call and that he'll contact you the minute he can."

"What about email?" Rowan panics.

"What can he email on, Rowan, if he has no phone?"

"His laptop!"

"Maybe that was stolen too."

"Wouldn't he ask someone to borrow theirs?"

"Who... would he ask? Listen, his company called you to let you know he's okay. Give it one more day. If he doesn't call, we'll figure something out."

Mom knows all about navigating around life's nastiest

hurdles. Her very public, demoralizing divorce taught her how, but even though her advice is sound, it's hard to take at the moment.

Rowan grips her coffee mug harder. "His company won't call me back."

"My guess is they don't know all the facts either. If they release incorrect information, that could get them in trouble. They're probably worried about a civil suit. It's why they aren't being communicative."

Rowan groans. It's exactly the opposite way a human resources department is supposed to act. Although, if they're running on bare-bones infrastructure it doesn't entirely surprise Rowan that they've resorted to ignoring her until they're better informed. "Aren't you worried it's something bad? Something else?"

"Of course I'm worried. But his company would have to disclose if something, you know... really bad happened," Mom says.

"Like you mean we're fairly certain he isn't dead."

Landon throws a block at Rowan's head and she ducks so it doesn't hit her. It crashes into the white brick backsplash on the wall behind her and lands in the deep farmhouse kitchen sink.

"Right," she hears her mother say, although her phone is pulled away from her ear.

"Landon, why did you throw that at Mommy?" Rowan asks.

"Are you talking about Daddy?" He has his furious face on again, but this time Mr. Crackers is pressed to his chest and Rowan feels terrible.

"Come here, buddy. Dad is fine. I'm just having trouble getting in touch with him, that's all. He's going to call soon."

"Hey, Landon." Her mother shouts so he can hear her.

"Grandma says hi."

"Hi," says Landon. He scoots away and returns to his mound of destruction on the living room floor.

"Be careful what you say around him," her mother advises.

Rowan bites her tongue so she doesn't say something she'll regret. Of all people to give that advice... Rowan and her little sister hid in their closet, ears plugged, bodies hunched over one another like a protective, human tent, because their parents used to shout at each other so loudly.

"I know," she gripes. "I'll call you tomorrow, but I make no promises I won't travel into the city and bang down the door to his employer first."

"I don't think that's a reasonable option. They are still paying him, right?"

Rowan sips her coffee. Her mother hadn't wanted her to buy her house and now she's trying to tell her not to piss off Wyatt's employer, because Wyatt makes three times as much as she does.

"Yes, but Wyatt is very employable." She just isn't sure if he's healthy enough to work at the moment, and the uncertainty is driving her over the edge.

"I'd encourage you to wait another day."

Rowan hears noise in the background. Mother is retired from nursing, but she still works various jobs—retail cashier, dogwalker, cleaner. She tells Rowan she likes to keep busy, but Rowan knows her dad left her mother in financial ruin years ago.

"Goodbye, Mom." She ends the call, still feeling salty that her mother had the nerve to insult her parenting skills. Mom had done the best she could with what she married, but she chose her partner poorly, and that's on her. Rowan stretches her arms and glances at her little boy, thinking about what she could do with him today to get their minds off Wyatt.

It doesn't feel right to storm Apex just yet. She fires off another angry email to Irina that she knows she'll regret later.

All she wants is someone to give her a real, detailed update. To hear her husband's voice and be assured he's okay. Rowan wants to feel close to Wyatt, and there's only one person she knows who he might've contacted if he couldn't reach her for some reason. It might be good for Landon to have a little field trip away from home.

"Hey, Bud. You want to go visit Uncle Marco?" she asks.

"Yeah!" he cheers.

Rowan has a love-hate relationship with Marco Lucarelli, Wyatt's best friend from home. Unmarried, a career bartender, he still tries to get Wyatt into trouble from time to time, but he is a sweetheart.

It's almost a two-hour drive from their house to the shore in Wildwood, New Jersey, where Wyatt grew up. Marco still lives there, and she thinks the drive will clear her head. Even though it's only late May, and she hates the idea of adventurous Landon anywhere near the ocean, she quickly packs a swimsuit and a sand bucket.

Rowan offers Landon unlimited screen time on his iPad on the drive there and she doesn't hear a peep the whole way. She knows there's a chance Marco won't be working today, but she has a strong desire to drive somewhere, anywhere, away from the churning anxiety that exists in the confines of her home as she waits.

Maybe Marco will know something. She doesn't want to call him. Rowan wants to read Marco's facial expressions, because if there's one person who would lie for Wyatt if he's in trouble—and to her, specifically—it's Marco. Irina's elusiveness makes Rowan wonder if Wyatt's made a poor decision to cause his predicament.

If anything, she can play with Landon at the beach. He's never stepped foot in the ocean before. Rowan considers the fact that she might be punishing her husband for putting her through this by taking Wyatt to the shore for the first time without him.

Did Wyatt's irresponsibility, his lax alert system, cause this?

Once he let Landon toddle away at the Philadelphia zoo, right by the damn tiger cage, because he was entranced by a swinging monkey.

How did you get yourself robbed, Wy?

He's too damn trusting.

Wyatt will talk to anyone. On the rare occasion they grocery shop together, Rowan can barely get through the checkout line without a stranger telling him their whole life story. *Approachable*, her mother calls him.

Rowan sees Marco's truck parked in the lot of Mulligan's.

She rationalizes why she really wants to see Marco—a man she usually only entertains around the holidays—at a safe distance. And she decides it's because he's the most hot-tempered person she knows. And next to Rowan, there's no one who cares about Wyatt more. She wants Marco to tell her to bust into Wyatt's work and demand answers.

She wants him to insist that she do something.

Anything other than what she's doing right now. *Nothing.*

"Let's go see Uncle Marco, we're here."

"Can we go to the beach, afterward? Please? I want to make a castle," Landon says.

Just so you can wreck it? She hates that she's having these thoughts. He's four. Boys like to smash things. She just wishes the men in her life weren't so reckless.

SEVEN

ROWAN

Landon leaps out of Rowan's late-model Acura. She told him maybe they'd go to the beach, and he thinks all her maybes are yeses, because she's more of a yes-or-no type of mother. Although, everything in the last couple of days has felt like one giant maybe.

Maybe Wyatt is just fine, in recovery at a hospital, eating ice chips, wondering who he can barter with to get a new cell phone.

Or... maybe Wyatt is fighting for his life on a respirator after a hospital-borne infection.

There's no other explanation for his absence. She's tried calling the local hospitals for any record of admittance, but her inquiries have led nowhere.

Rowan lets out an exasperated sigh, a stab in her belly, followed by a heart murmur. This is not good for the baby. If Wyatt somehow caused his own problems, forgiveness will not come swift. "Let's see what Uncle Marco has to say."

It's only two in the afternoon, early for Mulligan's, one of the prime-time night spots on the Jersey Shore that makes up Wildwood. A girl in an off-the-shoulder t-shirt and a neon exposed bra offers them menus. "We'll sit at the bar if that's okay. I want to talk to Marco."

She eyes Rowan, then Landon. "For the last time, he's not paying child support without a DNA test." She withdrawals the menus and Rowan almost laughs in her face.

"What's a Deno test, Mom?" Landon asks.

"No, no. That is not why I'm here. I'm a family friend," Rowan informs.

The waitress does a onceover of Rowan again. "Marco! You know this lady?"

Marco appears from the backroom with a crate of glasses and almost drops them. "Rowan! Lando! What're you doing here?" He raises his chin, his gaze looking past Rowan, his brown-black hair falling in his eyes.

Rowan snatches the menus from the trashy waitress, ignores the exasperated sound she makes, and pulls Landon with her.

Marco sets the glasses down, a question mark on his face. "What's going on, Rowan?"

She holds up her finger, signaling for Marco to wait a second. Then she lifts Landon up on one of the barstools, sets up his iPad for him, and places his headphones over his ears so he can't hear the adult conversation she's about to have.

"Can you get him a chocolate milk or apple juice?" she asks.

"Yeah, sure. I got juice." He quickly pours Landon a plastic cup of amber liquid and sets it in front of him.

"How about for you?" he asks.

"Just a water."

"Right. Feeling okay? Wyatt okay?" Marco sounds nervous. Ice clanks as he scoops it harshly into a glass, then pours a water from the tap and hands it to Rowan. Their fingers brush and his hands are so shaky she wonders if he was drinking the night before. *Probably.* She can't still make him antsy after all these years—the buzzkill to his and Wyatt's lifelong bromance.

"You haven't heard from him, have you, Marco?" she asks. If

Wyatt was in trouble and had to call one person for help, it would be Marco. Wyatt's father had run out on him before he was born and his mother is a drunk. Having grown up together, Marco was the closest thing Wyatt had to real family.

"No... Why? What's going on?" he asks.

Landon takes his headphones off. "Chicken fingers."

"What?" Rowan asks.

He points at a picture on the menu. "I want chicken fingers," Landon says, and then promptly places his headphones back on. Marco nods at him.

"Yes, put him in an order and I'll take the chicken salad. Ranch, please?" she says.

"Got it." Marco enters the order into the register.

Rowan turns to the side to make sure Landon isn't listening. He's smiling and aptly entertained by a *Daniel Tiger* episode.

"Marco, Wyatt went to Mexico City on work and hasn't called me in three days." She can feel the blood drain from her face. "His company said Wyatt was mugged, as reported by the police, but they won't tell me any of the details. His CEO is some brusque Russian lady. She actually hung up on me."

Marco's large eyes widen in surprise. He pours himself a glass of Jameson's. "I don't usually drink this early but this conversation is stressing me out."

The waitress sets their food and silverware down. Landon takes off his headphones and shuts his iPad off because he isn't allowed any devices at the dinner table. She wishes he'd keep them on, but she already said the hard part.

Marco says, "Those fingers look good, Lando!"

Landon smiles. "Thanks. Have you talked to my dad? He calls me when he goes away, but I haven't heard from him in a while."

"Nope. But he's going to call soon, don't you worry!" Marco's voice is like a boomerang heard around the world. His best man speech rivaled any Rowan had ever heard. She knew

Wyatt and he had grown up in the school of hard knocks and they had a special friendship because of it. She only hopes he'll help her find Wyatt now.

Marco places his hand over his mouth to shield his voice. "Listen, he's probably stressing right this minute about why he can't contact you." Marco's expression oozes genuineness and Rowan wants to believe him... but he's sweet-talked her before.

"How can you be so sure?" she asks.

Marco twists his lips sideways, keeping his voice low. He places his hands over Rowan's and holds her attention. "I can't, but if his company told you he's fine, I'd hold onto that instead of worrying about every alternative. He's going to call you just as soon as he can."

She exhales. He tells her what she needs to hear, although it's different advice than what she thought he'd say. His eyes are soft and reassuring, and Rowan can see how he got himself into all the trouble with the ladies... and their pending paternity suits.

Some patrons enter the bar and sit down to order. Marco breaks away to tend to them. She attempts to pick at her salad, but she's not hungry.

Eat... for the baby.

Rowan jabs at the pieces of protein—the chicken, the egg white—and nibbles at the necessary nutrition, leaving the rest. Everything is harder right now. She's pregnant, caring for an active, young son, and she needs Wyatt's support.

When they finish, Marco offers her a hug goodbye. He hangs on a beat, and she lets him. When Landon and Rowan walk outside they can hear the ocean roaring nearby.

Landon's mischievous eyes light up with glee for the first time in days. "Can we go to the beach?"

Rowan decides they can try the beach after all. Landon changes into his swimsuit in the backseat of her car, straps a life jacket to his chest, and she hands him his bucket and shovel.

Could she really just be overreacting, and painting realities that don't exist? Being along the shore reminds her of the one and only time in her marriage she did that before. It's an incident that created a major rift, and one they don't speak of now.

When Wyatt was at his first startup with mostly twentysomething-year-olds, they had a corporate meeting in Atlantic City, of all places. Rowan didn't have a great feeling about the meeting or the tasteless venue where it was being held, a shoddy hotel connected to a casino.

The female employees at the company all friended Wyatt on social media after their initial orientation retreat, and frequently liked his posts. Rowan was used to Wyatt making instant friends, and female fans, but one of his over-filled-in-every-way bleach blonde interns, Tatum, was over the top with her comments.

Is that your house? Omg. You live like a king #YOLO

I LOVE your suit. Is that Versace? #King

And after Wyatt posted a picture of our renovated kitchen, just—KING.

Rowan was annoyed with Tatum before the meeting started, but her posts weren't enough to raise issue. Tatum didn't text Wyatt after hours, respectful of their marriage. Rowan found texts from her during the working day, but they were related to the high-stress projects they were working on in a team setting.

Wyatt insisted Tatum was just friendly, but when Rowan showed Pierre the posts he soundlessly raised his eyebrows at her, which told her all she needed to know. Yes, this young woman was positive and envious of the life she and Wyatt had built together, but there was also nothing stopping her from taking Wyatt for herself. If not permanently, just physically.

Rowan recognized her determined female drive. And it was directed at her husband.

If Rowan said anything outright, it would make her sound like a crazy, jealous wife, so instead she made subtle comments so Wyatt knew she was irked.

"The word king seems strong..."

Wyatt defended Tatum, always. "She calls everyone that."

"I don't think so," Rowan answered.

By the time the meeting in Atlantic City rolled around Rowan was adequately annoyed by the blonde bombshell who revered her husband like royalty.

After what Rowan had endured with her father, the hill they were on was a slippery one.

The second night of the meeting, Rowan called to check in with Wyatt to tell him goodnight. It was early in their marriage, and he always called in the evening when he was away. It was getting late, after nine, and she was tired herself, but she couldn't shake the feeling that something was wrong.

There was noise in the background when she called.

They must've been at a bar or the casino.

A female answered Wyatt's phone, and Rowan didn't have to guess which one.

"This is Rowan Bishop, can you please put my husband on the phone?" she asked.

"Your husband is busy!"

Oh... how Rowan's blood boiled.

"Is this Tatum?" Rowan asked. She wanted the enemy to understand she knew who she was. And that she was going to hunt her down and spear her if she got too close to Wyatt. One of her mother's biggest faults was her tolerance of her husband's activity. Rowan would have none of that, and anyone who got in her way was fair game for a lashing.

Tatum squealed in her ear—*"Yes!"*

"Can you please put him on?" Rowan asked. She would ask one more time before she raged into the machine.

"He can't talk right now. He's eating my—"

The line went dead. Rowan stared at her cell phone for a good three minutes.

Livid. She texted Wyatt that he better text her—*right fucking now!*

Nothing. She waited five minutes—more texts—nothing.

She emailed him at work. She emailed Tatum at work, more —*right fucking now*—messages!

Rowan was so desperate she texted Marco. Marco texted Wyatt and received—no response.

The biggest mistake Rowan made was getting in the car and driving to Atlantic City. She'll never be able to take back her actions that night, how she humiliated her husband in a corporate setting, to the point he used it as an excuse to look for his next job.

If Tatum would've finished her sentence before Wyatt's phone died, Rowan would've heard her say, "He can't talk. He's eating my boss's dessert."

Wyatt had a sweet tooth, and they were at some insane night club with an endless sundae bar, and someone had dared Wyatt to eat one. No one could've convinced her it was something so innocent.

Until Rowan drove all the way there, displayed her driver's license to the hotel attendant, convinced him she was the wife of their guest, secured a room key. Rowan was sure she'd find something life-shattering in that hotel room. Or worse—an empty hotel room, because Wyatt was in Tatum's.

But when she soundlessly keyed into his room, there Wyatt was—passed out asleep—alone.

Rowan was too tired to drive home, so she slept in the other double bed in his room.

Wyatt was surprised to find her in the morning, but she had

to stay and apologize for all the ludicrous messages she sent. Wyatt was irate when he discovered them in his company email, inquiries from Tatum like—*what the hell, Wyatt?*

But when she explained he forgave her. She went to the company breakfast that morning and apologized to Tatum in person. She knows she humiliated Wyatt by the looks she received from his other colleagues.

It's the only time she's acted so rash. Tatum's social media posts were a pain point in their marriage, and Wyatt knew how Rowan had grown up and how it impacted her.

Yes, he forgave her for the incessant messages, the workplace embarrassment, the middle-of-the-night drive-by. She made many mistakes that night, none of which she can take back. It's also the reason she can't storm his office now.

When they reach the beach, Landon runs close to the ocean, but not right to the shoreline, and plops down to fill his bucket. Rowan pops up a chair, lays down a towel for Landon, and applies sunscreen on both of them, taking in the beauty of her wild-haired little son, and the life forming in her belly.

To her surprise, Landon is well behaved. He makes his sandcastle, happily, without destroying it afterward, only venturing to the water's edge with Rowan holding his hand. Rowan realizes she needs to let go of her fears a little.

Just like with the incident in Atlantic City, even though she doesn't have all of the information, and can't locate Wyatt at this very moment, she needs to trust that everything will be just fine.

EIGHT

WYATT

Eyelashes flicker—the wings of a moth laden down with freezing water—blurry vision.

Liquid fills his ears; the drowned-out sound of his own fear. A muffled howl.

Resurface. His lips find the air. He chokes, then gasps.

Water dribbles from his numb mouth in failed spurts.

Bathroom tiles materialize through squinted eyes.

The water is... everywhere. His chest is submerged—in a bathtub. Whose bathroom?

He flails around to find his limbs.

Naked. Ice cubes crest his chin. He can't move his legs.

His heart pounds faster.

He tries to adjust his body. "Ahh." He tremors at the immense pain in his abdomen.

Teeth chatter. Adrenaline spikes as he fights to gain traction over the white lip of porcelain threatening to take him alive.

He dry heaves, then shuts his mouth. His waistline tremors in torment.

He has to get out of this—tub. And call his wife. His wife...

NINE
WYATT

Mexico City

A frenzy of activity: tubes sticking from his arms, workers in scrubs checking his vitals, but he doesn't understand what they're saying.

"Where am I?" Wyatt asks.

"Hospital," someone says.

He blinks. "My wife—"

"Has been informed," a nurse finishes his sentence. "Rest. Do you want the morphine to help?"

He relents at the searing hole burning through his side. "Yes."

"I'll tell them you're awake..." She scurries off.

Memories resurface slowly—flopping out of a bathtub in excruciating pain.

Pain so bad that his eyes rolled back in his head. Squeals reserved for war heroes injured in battle escaped his lips.

Crawling to the hotel phone, using his elbows and feet, dragging himself backward, because he wouldn't dare let any surface touch the wound near his pelvis.

He was sliced with something and sewn back up again.

When Wyatt looked at the red angry flesh of his incision he knew something terrible had happened to him, but he didn't know what. Why would someone cut him open and leave him there like that? Barbaric.

One of the hotel staff members arrived immediately after his call and ordered an ambulance. Then he blacked out again and woke up here.

Another hospital worker tells him, "Someone will be here soon."

He doesn't know what she means. Someone as in a doctor? Someone to take him home? Another human being who can tell him what happened?

His heartrate increases. He can both feel the pitter patters increase and see the red and green lines jump on the hospital monitor. He's having a panic attack. Another one. He thinks he already had one earlier. The dull ache in his side grows more prominent. *Heavy*—hot skin pulling apart. "Ahh."

"Mr. Bishop?"

Wyatt glances up to find a woman with her hair tied up on her head, a clipboard in hand.

"Yes," he says, his voice dry.

"I'm Dr. Marta Santos."

Wyatt can hardly utter a word because the pain has returned, itchy with stabbing fire. He tries to reach it to put out the flame, but his arms are tethered down with wires and plastic.

"Are you suffering? Do you need more medicine?" she asks.

"Yes, please," he utters.

"I'll up your morphine. You rest and I promise I'll come back." Dr. Santos pushes a button and something hits his bloodstream in a warm rush. It both shocks and relaxes him simultaneously. The pinpricks spike at his hairline and race down his back.

He wants the doctor to stay.

Wyatt wants to ask more questions, but his eyes weigh with bricks and he loses consciousness—again.

TEN

WYATT

It's Naomi, leaning over him, giggling, her long brown hair flapping in the wind as she sets down their yoga mats in the Dutch Mountains—Cauberg—449 feet to the top.

"We made it!" she cheers.

Naomi sits with Wyatt atop the plush green carpet of grass. The trees sway all around them. The breeze massages its fingers over their flesh, tender from the spring heat. Wyatt can feel the burn in his lungs from everything they smoked in Amsterdam two days prior.

"This is beautiful," *he says, still catching his breath.*

Naomi doesn't seem to be struggling at all.

She's chosen a spot which overlooks the houses. They look like a scene out of a pastel watercolor painting. The red roofs seem to connect all the buildings in one giant Lincoln log. To their left, Wyatt can see the rock walls they hiked between smeared with dirt from other hikers and cyclists who've blown down the windy roads.

Naomi pulls her hair into a ponytail. "I know you will leave tomorrow, but when you are stressed, I want you to come here... in your mind. With me. And we'll be together again." *She smiles, and her twenty-year-old skin shimmers in the sun as they sit Indian-style on their mats. She tells him to—"close your eyes."*

Without speaking to each other, they outstretch their arms, palms up. Naomi hums lightly. Wyatt remains quiet, his mind releasing into the universe, and the little bit of angst he had for traveling to the next town with Marco disappears into the wind.

Wyatt can hear the wind whistle now, but there's something else making noise too.

He left the Dutch hillsides thirteen years ago, but still comes back to *sit* with Naomi and meditate with her in his mind when he's overwhelmed; but this time he's being interrupted.

There's beeping. So much noise.

Naomi's blue eyes flash open. She turns to Wyatt, fright on her lovely face. "You have to go back now."

"Why?" he asks.

Naomi disappears in a *pouf*. Wyatt's eyes flick open.

Naomi is replaced by men and women in scrubs.

Wyatt's body jerks upward. Healthcare workers all flinch back, unsettled by his spastic movement.

The atrocious throb in his abdomen follows next.

He grabs for the source of torment and wails.

Someone yells, "*Morfina*." Wyatt remembers where he is now.

He's comforted that the name of that familiar drug sounds

the same in every language. Although the uncertain tone in the workers' voices makes him terrified.

"Wait." He pulls the oxygen tubes out of his nose.

The nurse is about to push the plunger to release the medicine into his system, but pauses, and stares at a man in blue scrubs. The doctor? There's some squabbling amongst them. They are unhappy about something and the nurse, distressed, murmurs the word, "*Zo*", a few times, shaking her head until she is shushed by the others.

"I don't want morphine. It knocked me out before," Wyatt proclaims. Everything is fizzling like a cloudy apparition around him. His stomach rumbles with acid and he wonders if he's been fed.

The female doctor who gave him the morphine before, Dr. Santos, comes into focus. "You do not want morphine for your pain?"

"How long have I been under?" he asks, even though he's in tremendous agony.

She flips the chart. "About eighteen hours. You just had a little episode where your heartrate dropped."

"Another whole day?" Wyatt asks. "I need to call my wife." He may have survived the last few days, but when Rowan finds out how he arrived at the hospital, he's dead meat.

ELEVEN
WYATT

The morphine dream ends, and he remembers the woman from the bar and the giant mistake he made. Or did he?

Dr. Santos shines a light in his eyes.

"How long since I've been out, now?" he murmurs. The words are coming out faster in his head than they are through his lips—they sound wonky. Ants dance up and down his skin, a side effect from the drug they've given him, he's sure.

She looks down at her chart. "Eight hours."

If he doesn't talk to Rowan soon, she's going to have his head. He wouldn't be surprised if she hopped on a plane to find him, control freak that she is. But he doesn't want that. It would be dangerous for her and the baby. And he doesn't want her to find out what he's done.

What have I done?

His heart palpitates and he sees the lines rise on the hospital monitor.

"Yes. Try to relax. Stress to your body will prolong your recovery," Dr. Santos says.

"What happened to me?" He still doesn't understand.

The doctor squints at him, taking a deep breath as if deciding how to break the news. "You had your kidney removed. It wasn't done in a hospital setting and your body went into shock. That's why you're in so much pain and why you've been exhausted."

He's still stuck on her first sentence. "My *kidney* was removed? Why?"

The doctor doesn't look at him this time when she speaks. "We're not sure. This kind of thing can happen in areas where healthcare doesn't afford transplants for poor patients. Rare in Mexico City, but not unheard of in this country."

"Someone... stole... my kidney?" Wyatt asks in disbelief.

His hand involuntarily flaps over to the area on his lower torso covered in a tight white bandage. He rubs the spot, mourning the loss of something he didn't even know was missing. He read a horror story about this happening to someone in New Orleans when he was a kid—black magic of some sort—but *this* wasn't *that*.

"We believe so," Dr. Santos confirms.

Wyatt's eyes roll back in his head. He's trying to process this, but his thoughts keep getting caught in a mental net of confusion. "Why... are the police not here? Investigating?"

The doctor turns her head sideways, as if she pities him. "You could file a police report. It'll take a few days for them to respond. Then, you'll have to come back here if they catch the person, but most victims choose not to pursue these cases."

Come back here? I never want to come back here.

"Why don't they pursue the cases?" he asks.

She shrugs. "Are you married, sir?"

"I am." He presses his ring finger and pinky together, relieved his wedding band is still there.

They didn't steal that... just his kidney.

"Most of these cases involve female parties," Santos says,

her face a serious slate. "Were you with a female party before this happened to you?"

"Yes." Wyatt stiffens, his stitches pulling at the incision site. His breath quickens again. Rowan cannot find out he met Esme at the bar. She'll never forgive him, under any circumstances.

"You were very lucky, Mr. Bishop. You're expected to make a full recovery, and should be able to live out a normal life with one kidney. How you choose to share that information with your family and the authorities is up to you." Dr. Santos's beeper goes off.

How he chooses... meaning he could share with Rowan, or he could not.

"One last thing. Does my wife have access to my medical report? And was there a police report filed by the hotel that she could attain? I'm just... trying to prepare myself for when we speak."

"The hotel didn't file a police report. We don't depend on the police to solve all our problems here. Your wife won't be able to see your medical report unless you show her. There's no electronic records at this hospital." Dr. Santos is almost out the door. She turns one more time. "Good luck, Mr. Bishop."

When he slips into his next drug-induced haze, this time Wyatt dreams of his wife, the first time they met.

"What about that one?" Marco asks, of a dark-haired woman with enormous breasts. They're trolling the shore for girls, a spring break tradition in Wildwood. Wyatt was just happy to be home from college to unwind after a tough course load.

"Nah." Wyatt was eyeing the girl next to the brunette, the fit blonde in the polka-dot bikini who looked a little bit bored, instinctively walking away from the waves as soon as they tickled her toes, as if they might bite her.

Marco balks. "She looks like she's applying for a Housewife of Nantucket audition. Those polka dots scream—challenge."

Wyatt smiles. There's something about that statement that he finds fascinating. "I'm going to talk to her."

Marco was due to meet another girl he'd chatted up at the bar. "She's going to shoot you down, but I'm going to talk to the friend." And just like that, Marco was already ditching his first date for the second.

"You know, the water won't hurt you," he says to Rowan.

"What?" she giggles and shoots him a dirty look.

"My friend and I were laughing because every time the water gets near your feet, you jump away."

Rowan looks over her shoulder and her friend is already properly entertained by Marco.

"I've never been here before," she admits, tucking a lock of hair behind her ear.

"To the Jersey Shore."

"Yeah... well, my dad is fair-skinned and burns. He hates the beach. He never took us," she says.

Wyatt's mouth drops open. It was preposterous. Growing up, he spent most days outside of school and work at the beach. "Where're you from? Kansas?"

She shrugs. "Nah, just Philly."

He starts laughing, and she cracks a smile. "That's not that far away!" Next thing he knows, he's grabbing two stray boogie boards, and pulling her into the ocean with him. "Time to face your fears!"

"No, no!" she protests.

Her friend and Marco are screaming, "Go!"

"Come on! I won't let anything happen to you," he promises.

Her face softens and she lets him yank her into the waves.

Later, she admits it was the last part he said to her that made her enter in the water—"I won't let anything happen to you." And that—he made her feel safe.

After they started dating, he promised her he'd always protect her. He'd never do anything to cause her harm or make her worry. And he intended to keep that promise.

TWELVE
FRANCISCO

Francisco takes his long hair, pulls it back into a ponytail.

His South Florida home glimmers like an oasis, the floor-to-ceiling windows, the opulent lighting, the infinity pool.

His phone buzzes.

It's time to meet her. Dangerous, but his last courier quit, and he doesn't trust anyone else to deliver the cash.

Francisco towels off from the pool, slips his jeans and sneakers on, throws a black t-shirt over her head, jumps into his Porsche, heads to Los Olas Avenue.

All of the flashy cars line the Fort Lauderdale street like an elaborate string of Christmas lights—bright red Lambos, robin-egg-blue Ferraris, bright canary-yellow Corvettes. Francisco pulls his black Carrera to the rear of Mama Cita's Mexican restaurant.

Lola is in the back smoking a cigarette when he pulls up. She stamps it out with her foot and the ashes splinter beneath her heel in tiny sparks. He wishes she'd agree to meet at a less public place, but when she isn't running her son, she's waitressing—so that's where he'll meet her—at work. The safer of the two options.

If he closes his eyes, he can rewind time in his mind to eleven years ago when he first met her while attending med school. She was a waitress then too.

He climbs out of the car with the padded envelope.

She has that expression on her face that looms somewhere between anger and pity. At everything they could've been. At what they've become.

He walks to her and hands her the envelope. She holds onto his hand and draws him in with her big brown eyes. The hoops that hang from her earlobes are oversized, her makeup bright. She must've just reapplied it for him, and he can't help but think it's going to rub off on his lips as he draws her in for a kiss.

She accepts his affections, always. No matter if she's with another guy. A relationship. Engaged. Their love is a special kind—born of a time when they had aspirations of a real life together that might have come true if the Network hadn't gotten in the way. He would leave her completely alone, give her the chance to have a decent run with someone else, if it wasn't for Nico.

"How is he?" Francisco asks as he pulls away. He can taste her cheap lipstick. Maybe she'll go to one of the fancy makeup counters she likes and buy the expensive kind with the money he's stashing her way.

"He's good. Quite the baseball player. Kid's got an arm like a canon."

Francisco smiles. Satisfied that if he can't have a good life, at least his son can. As the years have gone by working for the Network, positive updates on Nico are what he lives for.

Sadness sweeps over Lola's beautiful features, and he prays she doesn't cry. "It's been months since I've seen you, Francisco."

"I told you it's better that way. My courier moved to San Juan, and I need to find someone I can trust to deliver you the cash. I'm afraid that when the new courier learns it's money we're transporting, they'll run off, or worse... hurt you, then steal it. But you know it's best I keep my distance."

The money drops to Lola have always been a challenge. He has to transfer her funds in cash so there's no electronic trail. It's for his safety and hers. He can't have the government sniffing out bank transfers over ten grand and wonder how a guy who doesn't file a W-2 has so much dough.

No one can know he's been supporting Lola. The fewer ties to her the better.

He just wants what's best for Nico. Even if he never meets him.

She wipes at her eyes even though no tears have fallen. "He looks just like you."

Francisco allows himself to smile, if only for a moment.

She sniffs. "He already has little girlfriends texting him... chatting him up."

"What? He's only nine!" Francisco knows everything about the kid. Watches all the social media posts. Has an alert in his calendar for birthdays, sends cards, signs them Uncle Z, so there's no trace to his real name.

"They start young these days."

Francisco can't hide his shock, and Lola steals another kiss. "Okay, baby. I have to go. You have someone taking care of you?" he asks.

She shrugs. "Not sure about him yet."

Francisco shoots her a sympathetic grin. He always asks her this question before he leaves. It's not because he wants her to say yes. It's so he knows someone is there to look after her and make her and Nico happy—because he can't.

THIRTEEN
ROWAN

Seven Days Later

Rowan waits at the Philadelphia airport, Landon at her side clutching Mr. Crackers. He hasn't let the stuffed gator go since Wyatt left for Mexico City.

When Rowan finally spoke to Wyatt he was very vague about what happened.

"I don't know. I was knocked out. Stabbed. I had surgery. My hospital room didn't have a phone."

For nearly every question she asked—that was the answer.

"Well, where were you that you were in a position to get knocked out?" she asked.

"The hotel. I don't know... I was at dinner and then... I was passed out and injured."

It's all he offered her, and it wasn't enough. Why didn't Wyatt's company clue her into the fact that he'd been severely hurt and required surgery? She'd nearly lost her mind.

There was more to the story and Rowan would get to the bottom of it. She couldn't badger Wyatt over the phone. He sounded exhausted and sick. That's the only way she could describe his wheezy, dry breath in her ear, his forlorn speech patterns. As if he had the life taken right out of him.

Wyatt called Rowan two days after they got back from the beach.

Her mother and Marco were right; Wyatt was unable to contact her, but she wouldn't really believe it until she saw him for herself.

Until she pressed Wyatt to her body, felt his familiar breath on her neck.

Searched his eyes—which roam when he's lying.

Landon clutches Mr. Crackers when he's worried.

And Rowan embodies her sixth sense when things aren't right.

She always knew her father was cheating again before her mother did. *You're a walking emotion*, her mother used to say. Rowan absorbs the feelings of others around her, even if she is a master of not showing it. She scored extra high for "intuitive" on her personality test at work. It's an innate superpower that helps her weed out disingenuous behavior, professionally, and personally.

If something isn't right where Wyatt is concerned, she'll know.

The whole random attack feels awfully shifty.

How can Wyatt not remember *anything*?

Rowan knows robberies occur everywhere. It's not unusual for Americans to be targeted in foreign countries. Rowan can't imagine Wyatt was a hard one. He once let a homeless person negotiate his donation. Still, her skin crawled like dirty fingers up her spine when Wyatt offered up his lame story about his time in the dark.

"Daddy!" Landon screams.

Landon's little fingers slip through Rowan's grip as he runs through baggage claim toward a ragged-looking Wyatt.

Rowan fights the crowd to keep up, her ever-growing body

making her feel clumsy. "*Shit*, Landon, slow down." She cringes as he cuts off an elderly couple, bee-lining for his father slowly walking toward them.

"I'm so sorry," Rowan apologizes to the couple, their expression one of dismay.

She can barely see Landon now as she makes her way through the crowd, her chest on fire with fear.

Heartburn. Mom-of-a-small-active-child-burn. Pregnant-mother-burn.

"*Landon.*" She can't see him at all now.

Damn it. She hates when he does this. She should've known better. Landon's little palms get sweaty when he's excited, which makes it easy for him to slip away.

Wyatt waves at Rowan, and gives her a thumbs up, signaling for her to slow down. He must be telling her Landon made it to him safely.

And then Rowan sees it—the tip of Mr. Cracker's alligator spike.

Landon is waving it in the air. *Thank God.* Rowan is one head away from Wyatt when she sees his face turn sour. He's picked up a phone call.

Why would you do that when your family has just arrived?

Wyatt is half-hugging Landon when she greets him. Rowan would like a piece of him too, but he's holding his hand up, putting her off.

Rowan imagined a more heartfelt greeting from her husband, the kind where someone was lost at sea and throws themselves into their lover's arms, finally reunited.

Does he know what he's put me through?

Rowan feels her pregnancy hormones surge. She promised she wouldn't become one of those crazy women who flipped out on her husband and blamed it on her rising estrogen levels, but she sure could sense them elevating now. "Get off the phone, Wyatt," she orders.

He bites his lip and looks at her with surprise. She rarely commands him to do anything. His eyes appear sunken, like marbles that've come loose from their setting. Gaunt, his pants hang from his hips; he's certainly lost weight. How can someone lose so much weight in just over a week?

Rowan feels immediate guilt.

"Did you get me a flute? Did you get my flute?" Landon tugs on his jacket.

Wyatt ends his call. "That was just work... checking on me."

Rowan tries to hide her irritation. They make eye contact for a moment. Is he—*scared*? Wyatt smiles grimly before he delivers the blow. "Sorry, buddy, I couldn't get the flute, but we can shop online for one."

"Oh, man!" Landon throws Mr. Crackers on the floor.

"Hi." Rowan goes in for a hug, but Wyatt steers her away from his left side. She notes Landon is on his right.

"Oh, yeah. Okay." Between her baby bump and his recent surgery site, Wyatt manages a half-hug, and it's an incredibly weak one.

"You're growing." He pats her belly, his voice strained.

"Yes. It's only been a week." Only... but so much has happened. "I hope the little one hasn't felt my anxiety." She's not trying to make him feel badly, but she sort of is. "I've been so stressed."

"I bet."

No apology. No apology?!

Okay, now her emotions are flaring. "Where's your luggage?" she asks, sharply.

"Oh, I'm going to need you to get it for me. It's carousel J. I can't lift anything for a while." He points to his side and yawns. Gray shadows hang beneath his eyes like sad window dressings. She remembers the trauma of loss after her house was robbed, and no one was even harmed. She feels for him, but something is really off.

He's still out of it. That's why he's acting like he doesn't care.

"I'll grab it," she says, even though she shouldn't have to carry heavy luggage, pregnant. Isn't that what she married big, strong, six-foot-two Wyatt for? "Are you on any medication?"

"Yes. Percs," he says. "Can we get going? I'm wiped."

He looks about one push away from falling over, and Rowan is searching for her old sympathetic self, the one who would drop everything to put her ailing husband at ease, but she can't be that person right now, because Wyatt is not Wyatt.

Rowan expected a blubbering apology from him. Tears, even, to express how awful his ordeal has been and how sorry he was for putting her through hell. But Wyatt was worse than non-emotive—he's lost. His personality, a shallow casing of whatever it used to be. Forget a warm embrace, his was a half-hollow pat down.

She quickly, angrily, shuffles to the luggage carousel and attempts to retrieve Wyatt's large black bag. She spots it right away and tries to tug it off. Another man sees her struggling and pityingly lifts it with one hand, offering her a tight smile.

"Thanks," she mutters. Rowan searches for Wyatt to see if he witnessed his pregnant wife trying to handle his luggage but he actually has his eyes closed while standing up. He's lucky Landon has calmed down.

Drugs. She needs to get him off those meds as quickly as possible. They've eaten away at him. He never was good on them, even though Marco tries to introduce them on nearly every hometown outing.

She wheels the bag over, about done with this imposter-of-a-husband and he's only been home for exactly forty minutes. "Here we are. Can you wheel it yourself?"

"Ro, I can't." He points at his side and she wonders what the hell they did to him that he can't push something on wheels. At least he's holding Landon's hand this time. "Are you okay with..." He flashes his hands in front of his middle to signify hers.

"I'm fine." She's in very good shape. She still attends Barre and Spin class pregnant. It's not about being physically able to carry the bag; it's the fact that Wyatt is not, and she doesn't fully understand why.

Wyatt nods absently, walking away with Landon.

He'd better tell her what really happened overseas because his glazed-over look and cold demeanor is sure as hell about a lot more than just the drugs.

FOURTEEN
WYATT

She knows.

She knows something is wrong.

She knows I'm lying.

Rowan can sniff out misinformation like a trained German shepherd on a hot blood trail. And once she sinks her teeth in, there's no letting up until she finds the truth. Wyatt can tell she's onto him by the way her tiny nostrils tither in and out, the searching—burning—look in her eyes, even as she merges onto the I-95—even when she should be paying attention to the road.

Wyatt concentrates on Landon so he can avoid Rowan.

How's KinderCare? Have you built any new fortresses?

Mommy said you went to the beach, did you like it?

"Ya, I built a castle!"

"Nice, Buddy." That one stung. Wyatt wanted to be the one to show Landon the ocean.

It was his first love. The place he went to escape when he felt small and alone.

The ocean was never quiet.

When his mother worked long hours, he'd walk there and sit by the crashing waves, watching for new treasures to wash up on shore, treating them like pennies in a wishing well he'd toss back. He and his mother lived on her waitressing wages, but it cost nothing to sit there. Wyatt was just a young boy, but the ocean made him feel big, alive—heard. It's also where he met Rowan, a girl he thought was too good for him.

Not because of where she came from—they'd both grown up low-rent with dysfunctional families—but because she believed so strongly that her life could be different. Better. She thought she could design her own future, a bright one—with him.

There were days she believed enough for the both of them.

This is not one of those days.

She knows something, but, what exactly?

Dr. Santos's words soften his nerves—*How you choose to share that information with your family and the authorities is up to you...* Thank God they took him to a private hospital. They were able to bill his insurance, and he's not sure how much of his stay they'll cover, but Rowan should be none the wiser.

Wyatt's secrets are stashed in a filing cabinet somewhere in a Mexico City hospital, records Rowan couldn't access even if she wanted to because—no electronic medical records.

He has the upper hand here.

"Why was your boss calling you? Irina? You know she refused to answer my calls after that very first one to alert me that you were robbed. This company you're working for doesn't care about their employees. Or their families," she says.

"She wants me to go back and finish the job within two weeks or she says it's grounds for termination of my contract."

"What? She threatened your employment minutes after landing back on US soil? After you were hurt on the job? We can sue for that." Rowan slaps the steering wheel.

"She's right. It is in my contract. I don't think she cares if we sue. The whole company will basically fold if we don't get this call center set up and I'm the only one in a position to do the job."

"Can't they sub the work out? Facilitate it remotely? You can't be the only person in the universe who can build a call center."

Wyatt shakes his head, feeling like a colossal failure. "I'm trained on Apex's software, their systems. They spent a small fortune creating it themselves. It's unique, and it's taken me six months to learn it. They'd have to train someone else. It's not feasible."

Rowan's nostrils do their thing.

"Daddy, I don't want you to go back. You got hurt there," Landon says.

I sure as hell don't want to go back either. But not going back will result in termination with no severance pay. Can they even afford it? He has no idea what his doctor bills will look like from his international hospitalization.

Wyatt can see Landon hugging Mr. Crackers in the rearview mirror. It gnaws at his heartstrings, but he doesn't respond. His father didn't stick around at all for his family, and here Wyatt is just trying to make a living to support his, and he's getting shit for it.

"See what this has done to him?" Rowan asks.

Wyatt tries to laugh, but it comes out a dry cough. He searches the car for a bottle of water, but finds none. "What about what it's done to me?" he asks.

"Well, that's exactly my point, honey. It's why we don't want to risk anything else happening by you going back."

He leans into the headrest and closes his eyes.

Rowan seems to be totally missing the point that he's the victim here. She doesn't know what type of victim, though—the kind that's had a lot more stolen from him than his wallet and a few pints of blood. Not a self-pitier, he's not sure if it's the trauma from the attack or the loss of his vital organ, but he's feeling pretty low since he left the hospital.

It could be the nutrition coaching he received upon discharge—*try to avoid caffeine, alcohol, and limit high-protein foods.*

Only three of his favorite things: coffee, beer, and steak.

Death almost seems preferable.

Worst of all, he can't share any of these worries with his wife, his voice of reason, a woman who has a plan for everything, because she'll leave him. She'll want to know the *why* behind the missing organ.

She still does want to know the *why*, but if he tells her about the missing kidney, it will reveal the rest. It will transform a story of a random tourist attack and robbery into much more, and it will bring questions.

Why were you in that hotel room?

What stranger led you there?

Better to leave it nebulous—*I can't remember...*

And best to keep his answers short. Lying to Rowan is difficult. So far, none of his responses have been untruths. He *doesn't* remember exactly what happened.

But as soon as Rowan finds out a woman was involved, he's gone—no exceptions.

It's one of Rowan's non-negotiable clauses for divorce.

After what she witnessed as a child, if there's even a probability that infidelity is at play, their marriage is over. She's made that quite clear from day one.

He'll be left with nothing. She'll destroy his relationship with Landon, and most likely prevent him from forming any real bond with the new baby. He saw how she ousted her own father from her life. She's never forgiven him for what he did to her mother. Even June encourages Rowan to foster a relationship with her father, but she won't. Rowan's three siblings visit and vacation with Rowan's father. Rowan's always invited, but never attends.

He has to keep his secret about what happened over there. If she won't forgive her father after twenty years, Wyatt doesn't have a prayer. He won't lose everything over one mistake.

It's his organ, anyway.

He should at least have ownership over that, right? Aren't certain things sacred, even within a marriage? And doesn't an individual's body part count as one of those things? Rowan asks him not to pry about how much weight she's gained during her pregnancy visits—*not your concern*, she says—*as long as I'm healthy*.

He was medically cleared. This shouldn't be any different. She has things about her body she doesn't want to disclose and so does he.

It's not like Rowan will need his kidney anytime soon. She's as healthy as they come. Wyatt has no siblings, and given the amount his mother drinks, it's likely she'll require a liver transplant before a kidney. He grimaces at the thought. He texted his mother when he got home and she texted him back letting him know she was happy he had a safe trip.

It's clear she had no idea he was hospitalized in Mexico. Rowan never called his mother.

Rowan drove all the way to Wildwood and didn't think to call her mother-in-law. Forget drop in. Rowan has a way of disregarding people who lead unhealthy lifestyles. She's never admitted it, but Wyatt thinks Rowan holds spite for his mother because of the way she raised him, leaving him alone for long stretches, drinking too much. She did the best she could.

His upbringing made him self-sufficient, but sometimes he wonders what Rowan really thinks of her—or him. If he'll ever feel like he's enough for her. What will she do when she sees his stomach carved up?

You're like the offspring of an Abercrombie and Hollister

model—something she used to say in their twenties that they laugh about now.

Rowan likes things just so.

He hates to think his looks are part of his true appeal, but he knows it's true. What if she sees his incision, then finds out he's missing something inside—will she regard him like his mother, defective?

He sighs at the thought.

It won't always be like this.

I just need to go home, get some rest, ease back into some kind of normal. Maybe someday I'll tell her.

Someday... long after this is over, and the scar has healed. *Oh, yeah, remember when I went away for work and had that attack? They had to remove my kidney. I didn't mention that? I thought I told you...*

It won't work. She'll be pissed. But she'll be less pissed five years from now than five days. It will be so far in the past it won't matter as much as she'll want it to. And the circumstances surrounding it—old news too.

"I made rump roast with potatoes and carrots. Your favorite. It's in the crock pot, onion crunchies on top. Should be ready when we get home." She squeezes his hand. He squeezes back.

His mouth waters and then runs dry. He coughs again and his eyes blow open. "Is there any water in this car?"

"No, I'm sorry. Is something wrong?"

"I'm just... parched." His blood pressure dropped when she said *roast*. The surgeon warned him to limit his protein intake. His mind roved to—*how much protein is in a roast?* He grabs his cell phone and researches it... there's 24–27 grams of protein in a 3 ounce piece of roast beef meat. It's 25 percent of his daily required protein intake, which is probably double for him. 50 percent.

"What're you looking at?" she asks.

"Just checking the weather." He closes his browser window and averts his attention to outside the window.

"Really?" Her question sounds like an accusation. She can hear the deceit in his voice, smell it with her twitchy canine nose. As a lifelong lover of all-things-meat, how's he going to explain if she cooks something that's too high in protein?

"Wyatt?"

Distract her. "It's nothing. I'm a little jealous you took Landon to the beach without me." *There.* A little bit of hard truth. Maybe if he gives her something to nibble on, she'll back off.

"Ah... that's why you're acting so strange," she says, seemingly satisfied. "It wasn't planned. I wanted to talk to Marco to see if he'd heard from you, and I threw a bucket, shovel, and Wyatt's swim trunks in the car."

"Sounds pretty planned to me."

Her face goes rigid and angry. *Why am I pushing her?*

She turns to him, livid. "I didn't know what happened to you. I imagined the worst things, Wyatt! I was hysterical. I *still* don't know what happened to you."

The word—still—hangs in the air. "I'm sorry you had to go through that. What did Marco say?" Wyatt hasn't gotten a chance to catch up with him yet. He must've been surprised to see Rowan. They aren't exactly close.

"He told me not to worry. That you were probably unable to contact me and that's why I hadn't heard from you. My mother gave me the same advice. They're the only reason I didn't file a police report or storm Apex."

"You were going to bust into my work?" *Again?* It didn't work out so great last time Rowan showed up at a company function uninvited. His heart feels like it's going to run out of his chest.

"Yes. That's how worried I was." Rowan peeks in the

rearview mirror, and Wyatt does as well. Landon has his headphones on. "I thought you were dead," she whispers.

"Well, I'm sorry about that, but I think, maybe, you're blowing this a little out of proportion," he says.

"You do? You were hospitalized! In Mexico. But I didn't even know that for days!"

This isn't good. The HR person at Apex may have his records. Rowan is an HR person who knows how to speak to other HR people. They may have already exchanged words.

Does she know everything and she's just waiting for me to crack?

"Did you talk to anyone at Apex? You said you spoke to Irina once, but what about... anyone else?"

Wyatt thinks about this, because he can't recall meeting anyone in HR. Irina did his employee intake, made copies of his license, witnessed him fill out his W-4. Wyatt's chest quivers, and he pushes his head back into the seat headrest again, suddenly exhausted.

"No. That's what I'm telling you. No one would talk to me. The operator said she didn't even work there before routing me to voicemail. Apparently, they use a third party to answer their phones."

"Yeah... typical for a startup. It's cheaper to do that. Temp work."

"Bullshit. That whole company is," she says bitterly.

"I'm going to start looking for something else. I could probably go back to Mexico City to fulfill my contract, and then get another job. Because my signing bonus was contingent on the completion of that project."

Rowan eyes him fearfully as they pull into the driveway. "Will we have to pay it back?"

He rubs his fingers on his jeans, and he knows why she's asking. That money is long gone. They used part of the twenty grand to pay off their credit cards and the other half to pay for their dining set and shutters for the entire house.

"Maybe. I have to look at the contract," he says.

"Shit."

"Don't worry just yet. Let me talk to Irina. See if there's a plan B." Even though he knows there isn't. He was trained on the software and it's his job to roll it out, and there is no good way to do that remotely.

At dinner, Wyatt chews slowly. The meat tastes delicious as the salt and au jus slips down his swollen throat. But he can't properly enjoy it. He imagines the food passing through his digestive system—the stomach acid grinding the meat up into sugars and water, streaming through his blood system in blocks and cylinders like in the biology class textbook he hated to read, and then getting jammed as it attempts to be eliminated from his body.

He can see the substances turning left in his intestines, then right, and becoming gummed up, because there's nothing there to process them.

Nothing to filter them or purify them. He sees the chunk of protein as its thin strings of brown meat turn into toxic waste and build up inside of him until it fills every cavity of his body.

He drops his fork on the plate.

Rowan and Landon jump.

"Are you okay?" Rowan asks, concerned.

He inhales sharply, his eyes darting between his son and his wife. "I'm not feeling well," he says.

I can't do this.

I cannot lie to you.

I can't analyze everything I eat and wonder what it's doing inside of me.

"It's okay. I'll wrap your plate and you can eat it tomorrow. You must be tired." She pats his hand again, like she did in the car. He wants to ask her to join him. He wants to know if they can take a hot shower together and if she'll curl her naked body into his, and if they can just lay there, and if she can just hold him, but he can't.

Because then she'll see what they've done to him.

And she'll know it was more than a single stab and a mugging.

"Thank you," he says graciously. He pushes his chair away from the table, kisses both Rowan and Landon on the cheek, and retreats upstairs. The floorboards creak on the hand-scraped farmhouse-style wide planks as he walks up the stairs.

He is thankful for this life he's built.

Thankful for his wife who was so deliriously worried about him that she drove to see his best friend who she doesn't care for, and threatened to interrogate his company, in person. Beyond lucky that she's a wonderful, strong mother who held down the fort while he was gone, and made sure Landon didn't worry too much even though she was going out of her mind.

Grateful for the meal she cooked, even though he can't explain why he can't eat it.

As he turns on the hot water to the shower, he winces in pain as the spray hits his bandaged wound, gritting his teeth as he soaps his hair.

Why did I go for that stupid drink?

He yanks at it, howling into the showerhead at the mess he's made of his blessed family—and the pain of the secret he has to keep so he doesn't lose them.

FIFTEEN
ROWAN

Wyatt is not the same man who left for Mexico City ten days ago.

All weekend, he stared into open air and pretended to watch his son play, but his mind was somewhere else.

Rowan tried to touch him, hug him, but he shrugged her off citing—*pain*.

For some reason, she senses it's not his injury that's causing it, though.

He wouldn't let her see him naked this morning, quick to wrap a towel around himself when he stepped out of the shower, dressing in his walk-in closet instead of in their bedroom. A beach boy, Wyatt is more comfortable with the sun on his back than fully clothed. He's the mow-the-grass-with-your-shirt-off kind of guy. She knows he's been through a lot, but why won't he let her see him? *What happened to you over there, Wy?*

Their weekend was spent tiptoeing around him.
Daddy can't play, he's hurt.
Don't jump on Daddy, he's ouchie.
Let Daddy sleep, he's tired from his trip.

Rowan doesn't want to think Wyatt is milking it.

He was assaulted, she realizes. Wyatt might have post-traumatic stress. He probably needs counseling, but why won't he talk to *her*? They have a strong relationship, but sometimes he holds back. Wyatt, the only man in his family growing up, had to be strong for his mother. Rowan blames Barb for Wyatt's need to conceal his true feelings, even at his own expense. Wyatt once told Rowan he often lied and told Barb that he already ate when she came home tired from work because he knew there was no food to prepare for dinner. He went hungry so she wouldn't feel guilty.

She's sure Wyatt's doing the same here—lying to protect her feelings. Buy why? Normally she wouldn't be so patient in finding out the truth, but he's injured. Despondent. She wants to give him space to heal, but she also wants to be a part of that process.

Why won't you let me in?

Monday, Wyatt went into the office even though it was a holiday—*to figure things out* about his job and what he can do to maintain it for a little while longer. She hopes given the circumstances they'll let him keep his signing bonus, but she doesn't like to assume.

Rowan was anxious all day thinking about it, but Wyatt didn't say much when he came home. Just—*I'm still working on it.*

It's Wednesday now. Rowan and Landon wait in a long, muggy line to see the historic Liberty Bell. Wyatt was supposed to join them but he said he had things to figure out at work.

Two days after Memorial Day, and it's still a zoo at the visitor center. Landon is shifting his weight impatiently, his light-up shoes going off like firecrackers beneath his feet. He clenches Mr. Crackers to his chest. "And the teacher said every reptile has sails. Snakes have lots of sails. I held a snake yesterday," Landon rambles.

"You mean they had scales, baby."

"Yeah, that's what I said. Scales!" he says angrily.

"No, you said sails."

"I said scales!" he screams. Rowan squeezes his hand.

They're in line at the Independence Visitor Center with a swarm of people and Landon's elevated voice is attracting more than a few sideways glances. Rowan practices deep breaths at his outburst hoping he'll follow suit. "Okay, honey."

Pick your battles, her inner demon flares.

She wouldn't typically agree with him being right when he's wrong. That leads to entitlement. And she sure as hell doesn't let Landon yell at her like that, but public forums aren't the place for learning the hard lessons. Every parenting book she's read preaches consistency and repetition as the keys to implementing good behavior, yet Landon still has a terrible temper, and most often there's someone there to witness it.

She glances over her shoulder, embarrassed, looking for a familiar face, but she sees none, only an elderly couple behind her who appear intolerant to her son's misbehavior.

"Bell!" Landon points at the Liberty Bell which can be seen in the distance through the protective glass panels. He tries to wriggle his sweaty hand free, but she holds him fast. The town square where the visitor center is located is composed of bright red-brick buildings trimmed in white, flowering trees, clean sidewalks full of visitors—and there sure are a lot of them today. Flashbacks of the crowded airport make Rowan uneasy. She grips Landon's fingers tighter.

"That's right. We're going to explore the center first and then make our way to the bell," Rowan explains.

"No! I want to see the bell first." Landon pouts.

Rowan bites the inside of her mouth.

Wyatt didn't want to try for a second baby so soon. But she convinced him by reasoning that he grew up with no siblings, and he didn't want Landon to be lonely like he was. She also reasoned that if they waited too long they might have trouble conceiving, even though they're still in their early thirties. Financially, the timing worked out to offset daycare costs. As soon as Landon enters Kindergarten, the new baby will go into daycare part-time, and it will be a wash.

But she knows deep down that money isn't the reason Wyatt didn't want another one so soon.

Landon is... a lot.

She secretly prays for a little girl. One with golden hair and blue eyes like her who she can team up with when the boys get rowdy. Her mother means so much to her, but she'll be an even better example for her own daughter, should she have one. She'll teach her not to settle like her mother did. She'll empower her to have a career, one where she can balance ambition and take care of her family.

Rowan swallows at the thought of having another boy. Like Landon.

They're one couple from the entrance, and Landon rips his hot hand from Rowan's grip and does a little dance in a circle. She lets him because she doesn't want to hold his hand anymore either. Her head spins at the thought of having two little dancing boys with sweaty palms.

Landon tosses Mr. Crackers on the ground. "When are we getting in?"

"We're next. Pick him up right now. He's going to get dirty."

Landon's grin borders on mischievous. His gaze darts in between the doorway, the stuffed gator, and the back of the line. For just a moment Rowan thinks he's going to bolt. He must read her very urgent display of *don't you fucking dare* on her face because he picks up the stuffed animal instead.

"Next." A lady with chunky red glasses calls to them.

Rowan pulls up the tickets on her phone and grabs Landon's sticky hand once more.

A girl. Please let it be a girl.

Rowan scored the tickets for the visitor center using a Groupon at work and she intends to get her full money's worth. If Wyatt loses his job or has to pay his signing bonus back, this will be the last adventure they have for a while.

She heaves another deep breath at the thought.

Wyatt won't get much severance. Not with less than a year of service. They have six months' salary saved, but they'll blow through it quicker than that, she knows it.

Rowan tries not to focus on the negative.

Everything will be fine.

She and Wyatt will figure this out, just like every other time they'd hit a rough patch. Although, this time feels different. Like her husband left on a business trip and she's still waiting for him to return.

Rowan pulls a reluctant Landon into the dark room showing a movie clip which introduces William Penn, the Liberty Bell, and the unfortunate accident that led to the giant crack that still remains like a historical fault line down the middle of the bell's copper and bronze façade.

She knows Landon isn't absorbing any of the historical facts being rattled off in the video. His eyes are glued in the direction of the actual bell, a few rooms away. Rowan grips Landon's hand tighter as he resists. "Pay attention," she whispers in Landon's ear.

Her phone buzzes in her pocket and Rowan notices that other people are looking over their shoulders at them—the squirmy child and keyed-up mother. Rowan scoots Landon toward the back of the room, out of the way of the apparent serious history buffs. "If you listen, I'll buy you something in the gift shop."

Landon nods, *okay*.

One of the workers leans in. "Madam, if you can please keep it down." She motions to the rest of the crowd.

"Yes, I'm sorry," Rowan whispers back, scowling at Landon.

"Can I get a toy snake in the gift shop if I'm quiet?" Landon asks.

Rowan nods even though she knows very well there's not a reptile of any form in that gift shop. Landon snaps his attention back to the front of the room, a smile on his face. The worker in the ugly pants and polo shirt is still watching them, intently. Her angry eyes smolder through Rowan's. She has a facemask covering everything from the nose down, but Rowan is sure there's a sneer hidden under there.

Geez, you obviously don't have children, lady.

Rowan's phone buzzes again.

She secretly tries to read the screen on her phone in her purse. There's a missed call from Wyatt's office. Rowan programmed the number into her cell when she was anxiously waiting for his boss to return her call.

Wyatt typically uses his cell phone to contact her, not his office phone.

A lurch of warning rises in her throat, the same feeling as this morning, when she tried to look at her husband in the face and he wouldn't engage with her. She couldn't imagine why Wyatt would use his office phone. Unless Apex was phoning her because something happened at the office. Something bad.

Did Irina fire Wyatt?

Did he fly off the handle and do something rash in response? Something to get him arrested?

It wouldn't be like him, but he's been acting so out of sorts. Rowan's imagination is running wild with strange possibilities. She looks over her shoulder and the female worker is gone. Rowan pulls up her phone and quickly texts Wyatt.

Logan is tugging on her hand again, probably bored.

Pennsylvania's founder, William Penn, created a government that allowed citizens to take part in creating laws...

Rowan can hardly blame him. She sighs and lets go of Landon's hand to turn the brightness down on her phone screen, so as not to disturb the audience more, and text her husband. "Don't move," she orders Landon.

Rowan: *Did you call me from your work phone?*

Wyatt: *What? No. I'm at lunch. Why?*

Rowan: *I got a call from your office.*

Wyatt: *It wasn't me.*

Rowan sees bubbles populating the screen. There's more. What is it, Wy? What aren't you telling me? Did you get fired? Do we have six months left until we're scraping bottom to make ends meet?

Fear, like the kind she lived with when she was a child, wraps around her heart and won't let go. Rowan's mother stayed with their father because he made the lion's share of the money.

Wyatt: *Maybe Human Resources wanted to make sure you're squared away. Irina said she wasn't able to return your angry messages, or your threats to sue, because she didn't have answers for you at the time.*

Rowan sighs, disappointed in herself. Her track record of wrongly accusing Wyatt's colleagues of misconduct continues. She did threaten to sue, and that was a mistake, she realizes now. Did Wyatt tell Irina she's pregnant? Rowan hates to use her pregnancy as an excuse, but she knows it's part of her rash behavior.

She rubs her belly and then lets her hand fall to grab Landon's. She felt the weight of his body on her leg while she texted, a small comfort, but when she reaches down in the darkness, flickering images of the founding fathers in the background, she comes up empty.

Rowan glances down and Landon isn't there.

She takes a deep breath, blackness closing in on her from every direction.

A man is standing too close to her, brushing her leg. She mistook his physical contact for her son's.

Rowan pushes him away. He looks at her alarmed. She doesn't care.

She spins in a circle, jutting her neck out in every direction, trying to spot Landon's striped shirt, khaki shorts, small legs, light-up tennis shoes. She'd see them flash away, wouldn't she?

She'll see them flashing now...

Rowan tosses her phone in her purse, spinning and moving through the crowd, frantically. "Excuse me, does anyone see my son? I'm sorry, but he was standing right here, and I can't find him!"

The quiet group of people turn toward her, pityingly, but everyone shakes their head. They were standing near the exit sign and Rowan searches for the woman who scolded her for being loud, but she's nowhere to be found either.

"Landon!" she shouts. "Where're you? Don't hide from Mommy."

People are whispering and pointing now. Rowan grabs her middle as an anchor. She has to leave the dark room.

He isn't here. Her breath quickens. She continues to spin.

He has to be here, somewhere!

He wouldn't go out of the center. He's not brave enough to go outside.

Rowan edges toward the doorway.

An image of the Liberty Bell populates the screen behind her, the reflection flittering on the wall. The rambling of the history of the crack to follow. Rowan's fingers find the railing and she pushes herself in its direction.

The bell.

Landon wanted to see the bell, impatient from the history lesson. Of course, that's where he is.

Rowan sprints out of the movie viewing area and immediately sees a security officer. She waves her hands at him. "Excuse me. I can't find my four-year-old son." Her breath is ragged. "I think he might've gone to the bell." Rowan looks at the line for the bell sitting behind the glass protective wall, but she doesn't see Landon. She stands on her tiptoes. Still no Landon.

The officer makes a motion with his hands for her to calm down. "It's okay. We're going to find him, miss..."

"I'm Rowan Bishop. My son's name is Landon."

The officer radios something into his walkie-talkie, a code Rowan doesn't understand that probably stands for a missing child. But it's *her* missing child and he's not talking fast enough or moving with the proper urgency.

Rowan scans the center again, but doesn't see her son.

"Can you describe him for me?" the officer asks.

"He has a striped shirt, navy and white and tan shorts, tennis shoes that light up blue and red when he steps down."

"Is he a runner?" the officer asks with amusement.

"He is."

The officer chuckles. *Chuckles.*

Rowan glares at him and he stops. "Let's walk, ma'am. We'll find him."

She follows him. "Landon!" she calls. Rowan's head is a swivel, her eyes searching the crowd. She remembers when he slipped away from her at the airport and how he reappeared. She keeps rubbing her fingernails on the underside of her palms, waiting for that blessed moment to happen, for the relief to wash over her like a cool rag.

He was right here. Right at my fingertips.

"He's here somewhere," the officer says.

Then fucking find him!

Another security officer joins them, this one younger, more eager to help. "Ms. Bishop, I'm Officer Liam Jenkins. I've combed the area near the bell and haven't found your son yet, but we will."

"Okay," she squeaks. If Landon isn't at the bell, where is he? Where else would he have gone? It's the only place he wanted to go.

"Officer Osmond," the giggler says, as almost an afterthought.

"Landon!" Rowan shouts again.

Landon is the kind of kid who likes to tempt boundaries, but he never goes too far. He's probably scared right now, looking for her. "Maybe I should go back to the film room. He might've circled back there to find me." Rowan's stomach curdles with fear.

"We have an officer there now in case he comes back," Jenkins reassures. "Let's split up and take a look around. He couldn't have gone far. Is there any other place you suspect he might be?"

Rowan racks her brain. "I mentioned I'd take him to the gift shop if he was good. Are there toys in the gift shop?" she asks.

"Yes," Jenkins says.

"Okay, let's try there," Rowan says, and they're already moving in that direction before she hears Osmond tell her he'll check the rest of the perimeter.

When they reach the gift shop, Rowan butts in front of the other customers, phone in hand and shows the cashier, a college-aged girl with curly hair, a picture of Landon. "I'm sorry, I haven't seen him," she says with a bright smile.

"Come on, lady," a man says, behind her.

Rowan turns around, furious. "My son is missing," she seethes.

The man is about to snap back, glances at her belly, and

then clamps his mouth shut. He better. She can feel her temper flare, the one she left in Delaware County growing up. Her parents paid extra for her to enroll at a private school so she could graduate. There's a woman who most certainly has a fake front tooth today because Rowan knocked it out when she was still attending public high school.

Officer Jenkins lightly tugs on Rowan's arm. "Let's go, this way. He could be hiding in the rack of clothes."

Her nerve endings buzz from her hair follicles to her toes. Landon's not really a hider. He's more of a loud-and-likes-to-be-seen kid, but the hope of finding him in the clothing racks prompts her forward. Rowan waves her hands through the racks. "Landon!"

She can see clearly from one quick glance that he's not in any of them, but still, she calls out. She sweeps her arms over and over again, her temperature rising, her fear ratcheting up and down her body in waves.

Oh my god, where is he?

This is the longest he's ever been out of her sight. Her breath quickens and sputters as she swears under her breath. She searches Officer Jenkins' face for reassurance when he reaches the last rack—empty.

Another male officer arrives, one she hasn't met yet. "Anything?" he asks.

Jenkins shakes his head. Rowan crumbles inside, and slips to the floor. Jenkins catches her before she hits bottom and holds her up by her elbow. "We gotta call it in to Philadelphia PD," Jenkins says.

She can't really see the officers because her vision has turned into a haze of fluorescent lights and tiny Liberty Bell figurines dangling on a souvenir rack beside her. Jenkins speaks into his dispatch, "We've got a missing four-year-old boy at the visitor center. Caucasian, brown hair, brown eyes, striped shirt, khaki pants, light-up shoes."

SIXTEEN
WYATT

Wyatt inspects his deli sandwich like it's the enemy—a turkey club (24 grams of protein, a fourth of his daily allocation). It sits in its wrapper on a white tray, the lettuce green and rubbery, almost unreal, like his situation.

Irina was up in arms when he checked into the office this morning to grab his files off his computer.

"You might as well pack up your whole desk! The investors heard that the call center is delayed, indefinitely. They started pulling their money out."

This is bad.

Really bad.

Wyatt knows the risks of joining a startup company. The last two panned out, but he rolled the dice this third time and the odds are not in his favor now. The facts are imminent.

Ninety percent of startups fail.

Ten percent of those go under within the first year. One of the main reasons they flop is because the company runs out of funds before it turns a profit, and that's exactly what's happening here.

And it's all Wyatt's damn fault.

How can he tell Rowan he's losing his job? She didn't want him to take this position in the first place, too risky, especially with her going part-time, a new baby on the way. He's not sure how they're going to pay the mortgage without his paycheck, or what might come of the hospital bills from his stay in Mexico City from whatever his insurance refuses to cover.

And he's in no condition to interview again. Forget his body, he can tough out the physical pain, it's his head that isn't right.

Why did Apex call Rowan?

His hand hovers over the text message window in his phone, tempted to text his boss and ask that very question, but after the way Irina yelled at him this morning, in her very thick, very scary accent, he can't bring himself to do it.

You had one job to do, now we all suffer!

Irina doesn't have children. This company is all she has. This company is her child, and Wyatt has just killed it.

Wyatt has murdered her child.

He bites his sandwich, chewing slowly.

Irina and her husband sank their personal funds into Apex, and now it's tanked.

Wyatt really fucked up this time, let his guard down, trusted someone he shouldn't have. He never told Irina about the woman at the bar. As far as anyone knows, his attack was completely random. Wyatt wonders if the company could sue him if they found out he compromised their operation by being stupid.

His phone rings—Rowan. *Shit.* It's like she can smell trouble. Sense his failure. He picks up. "Hey."

"Wyatt, Landon is missing! He's gone—"

Wyatt holds the phone away from his ear. A fireball shoots up his hairline, but he immediately takes a deep breath and levels out. Rowan is pregnant, and Landon is likely fine.

"Rowan, just calm down, he's probably—"

She cuts him off. "Independence Center! You need to get here, *now!*"

"*Oh-kay!*" he replies. The line goes dead. He stares at the lettuce for an extra beat, then stands; a rush of blood finds his toes. Wyatt wobbles and pulls at his side, wincing. The secrets he has stitched across his abdomen are fiery and persistent. He walks to the trash with his tray of half-eaten food (*now I can have twice as much protein later*) and dumps it.

Did Landon pull a disappearing act because of me?

Dad isn't acting like Dad, and Normal hasn't found its way back into his marriage yet. He wishes he could snap back to his old self, but it's just not happening.

His breath is ragged as he walks outside, suddenly winded.

Everything is going to be all right.

He keeps coaching himself, motoring along, although he knows he's not fooling anyone.

Rowan caught him glancing at the label on the side of the cereal box today, studying the nutritional information. Her eyes said it all. Wyatt's no calorie-counter. He pushed the box back in the cabinet and disappeared into the laundry room.

He's only happy Rowan didn't follow him, question him.

Landon senses something is wrong too. Wyatt just hopes the tension will melt away like a well-worn blister. Heal. Scab over. Forgotten.

But what damage is he causing in the process? What's he doing to his family? To his son?

This can't be my fault.

Landon likes to explore and doesn't care for activities like museum tours and long movies where he has to sit for extended periods of time. He probably just ran off.

Wyatt told Rowan they should've waited to take Landon to the Liberty Bell until he's older. He suggested the jump park instead, something to keep Landon's legs moving, but Rowan found that damn Groupon and she couldn't pass on a deal if she tried, any opportunity to save a dollar. Although, she often ended up spending twice as much on snacks and merchandise anyway.

He pads his pocket, absent-minded, making sure he didn't leave his keys on the table.

They jangle in his pocket. He pulls them out and hits the button to unlock his Toyota SUV, climbing inside. He starts the vehicle and whips it out into traffic, driving fast, but not as if his son's life depends on it, because he's 99 percent sure Landon is fine. He sighs, pissed off life has thrown him such a curveball right when he's about to have another kid.

Everything bad that has happened since he met that woman for a drink ribs him with guilt and anxiety.

It doesn't matter. What's done is done. But somehow, he thinks maybe it does, because mentally he hasn't been able to move on. If he could tell someone, vent, it would help but he can't.

Just keep swimming... he thinks of a character's saying from one of Landon's favorite Disney movies. His little boy. Where is he?

Panic begins to settle in. Rowan was erratic on the phone. It's so unlike her—even Pregnant Rowan. Wyatt reaches the visitor center and there are cop cars parked everywhere. He tightens his grip on the steering wheel for a moment before getting out.

This looks serious.

He hates that his first instinct is to run away. It's what he did when he was younger.

Eviction notice—*time to move.*

Pocket an apple at the fruit market—caught—*run like hell.* He was hungry, *so what? What's a little apple to that guy?*

When Wyatt is in trouble, he jets away and hides and makes up excuses for why it's okay, but he can't do that right now.

The fact that they apparently haven't found Landon in the time it took Wyatt to drive there is disconcerting. If they had, Rowan would've called him. He lets out a rattled breath, looking at himself in the mirror: thirty-two and scared as hell.

Giant elevens crease the space between his eyebrows, extra deep since he left home over a week ago.

Wyatt exits the vehicle. He walks as quickly as he's able to toward the visitor center. It's been cleared out and several officers are stalking around the area marked with caution tape. One tries to stop him until he explains who he is. It's then that he knows his son is really gone.

It's the way the officer looks at him with such dire pity. *What's happened to my son?*

The officer points to Rowan. He finds her hunched over and panting next to the entrance.

Oh no. The baby.

He sprints to her and wraps his arms around her slouched figure. "Hey, I'm here. How can I help?"

"He's missing, Wyatt. They can't find him," she rasps. Her eyes are bloodshot like she's already cried a mountain of tears.

"Let's go look for him!" He grabs her arm, and she pulls it back.

"We already looked inside, everywhere," she says, exasperated.

"Well, let me try. He'll come to me."

She shakes her head, vigorously, *yes*, but it's clear she's not coming with him, totally spent. Rowan is sometimes jealous, if not resentful, of Wyatt and Landon's father-son relationship. Landon doesn't act up for him the way he does for her.

But she doesn't care about that. Not now.

Wyatt breaks into a light jog, his hands cupped around his mouth, calling his son's name. *"Landon. Lando."*

The cops allow him to enter the visitor center, now, an eerie ghost town. The pearly white floors show his reflection, stretched out and frantic. Wyatt feels it now, the realness of the situation, the depth of the desperation on his wife's face.

He's running through the historic center, howling his son's name, praying to God to deliver him from behind a partition, hidden, and giggling between a piece of greenery, trying to stealthily find a way to tap a bell that no longer rings—but the center is empty.

Wyatt sweats, and his side pulls in agony, but he doesn't care. He'll pop a stitch before he stops looking for his son.

"Landon, please come out for Daddy. I'll get you anything you want. We need to shop for our flute, and we can't do that if you hide from me."

It's not what Wyatt can't see, but what he can feel. He waves his arms around, spins in a circle.

I should've come with them to the center today. Now I've lost my son... and my job.

Wyatt heaves, stops, and places his hands on his knees in a crouched position. "Shit."

His eyes fill up with tears, his heart torn apart. Where is he? Where could he have gone? How can Wyatt return outside and look his wife in the face without Landon? She's pregnant and Landon is a handful. Wyatt should've gone with her today.

He's bad at being a father. Maybe his old man took off because he knew he would make a terrible dad too. Maybe Rowan would be better off without him.

Wyatt's eyes continue to scan the museum, but it's soulless, quiet, no sign of a child.

Landon must've run outside.

The same officer who let Wyatt into the center, a younger guy with kind eyes, approaches him. "Sir, we've pulled the surveillance footage from the visitor center. We think we found something. Can you come with us down to the station? We can give you and your wife a ride."

"Should we leave so soon? Didn't he just go missing? He can't be far."

"We've been looking for over an hour, sir," he says, surprised. "The other officers will continue to comb the area."

"Over an hour? My wife just called me. I was only a few miles away."

The officer shrugs. Rowan waited to call him. Why?

"This way," the officer calls with urgency.

Wyatt can feel his feet moving, although the rest of him is numb. He follows the cop. Rowan is leaning on a bench, her phone pressed to her ear. She startles when she sees him and hangs up quickly. They're escorted to a police car.

Sitting in the back seat of the police cruiser, visibly shaking, Wyatt asks her, "Why did you wait so long to call me after our son went missing?"

Rowan jerks away, eyes wide, as if she's been caught. He's not used to this expression. It's one usually reserved for his fuckups. "I freaked out," she sputters. "Then, I went into full search mode with the cops. You know how Landon is..." Her voice cracks.

"I know, but how couldn't you at least text me and let me know?"

She condemns him with her eyes. "You were supposed to come with us. I bought three tickets. I didn't want you to think this... I did..." She starts to cry.

He places his arm around her and squeezes, realizing how shoddy their marriage is. They're too afraid to tell each other the hard stuff.

If Wyatt had gotten there sooner, he can't help but think he could've spotted Landon.

"We're going to get him back," Wyatt says.

"We're taking you to the station. They found something on the surveillance camera," the officer informs Rowan.

Wyatt's throat closes around his tongue. *Something* could mean lots of things.

SEVENTEEN
WYATT

Wyatt's seated with Rowan in a nondescript questioning room at the police station, a television monitor elevated in the corner. Rowan's breathing is like a skipping record, steady for a bit, then shook, with an ugly hiccup. She continuously wipes her nose on her sleeve.

If Wyatt had a tissue he'd offer it, but he doesn't. He sits stick still. Stiff. His side throbs from running too fast in the visitor center. Spikes of pain radiate through his body.

He grinds his teeth. How have they arrived at this point of no return?

A marriage on the rocks. Secrets between them. A missing son.

Their relationship was contrived, un-messy, like Rowan wrote the story of who they would be before he even met her. Wyatt merely stepped into the role and now he's failing miserably.

The door *clicks*. Wyatt swallows the saliva pooling in his throat. Rowan's breath *skips*.

He wants to find out *the something* the police found on

those surveillance tapes, but he's terrified of what it might be. If that something is Landon's location, they'd have him already, right?

The door swings open.

A male member of the police force they haven't met yet—tall, stalky and pinheaded, walks in with a much shorter, squatter, female counterpart. They're in plainclothes, badges hanging around their necks.

The male speaks first. "Mr. and Mrs. Bishop, I'm Detective Dennis Schrader, and this is my partner, Detective Candice Stone. We're the head of the missing persons unit and center for exploited children in Philadelphia."

Bile rises in Wyatt's throat. *Exploited.* His greatest fear in all of this.

That some monster could take his son, do unspeakable things to him. That even if they got him back, he'd be in pieces, a fraction of the spitfire little kid they know.

"The officer at the center said you found something?" Rowan blurts out. "Where's our son?"

"I understand your urgency. The answer is, we don't know. But we want to show you this." Detective Stone turns on the television and fiddles with the remote. A grainy black and white picture appears on the screen, a movie of the Liberty Bell in the background. "This is the last room you were in with your son, correct?"

Rowan squints her eyes. "Yes."

"Okay, take a look and let us know if you recognize this person," Schrader says.

Person. A person has Landon. Wyatt inhales until his side nags at him. There's no windows in the room. He scratches his neck hard. His fingernails come away with skin and a little blood.

The room on the screen is dark, but Wyatt can make out the

colonial figures of a movie bouncing on the wall. Rowan points at the screen, and Wyatt can see it too.

"Right there." Landon is bobbing and skipping from one foot to the other. Rowan is distracted. She has something in her hand—a phone.

Landon breaks away from Rowan's grasp, but she doesn't seem to notice.

A woman with a mask, polo shirt, and lanyard—a worker—is kneeling near the entrance, beckoning Landon forward. She has something in her hand.

"What is that?" Rowan asks. His wife stands, pressing her nose inches from the screen.

"We're not sure," Stone says.

Detective Stone pauses the footage, taking a closer look herself.

Rowan turns her head sharply toward Stone, but then refocuses on the screen. "What do you mean you don't know? Aren't there specialists for this type of thing?"

Wyatt sees the mottled picture, black and gray, and a long, cylindrical item in the woman's hands. Couldn't be more than a couple inches in diameter. A baton? A... modified stun gun?

"Oh my god." Rowan places both of her hands over her mouth, and falls into her seat so quickly, Wyatt has to push it back so she doesn't bump her stomach. He's worried about his son, and he's also concerned about the toll this is taking on his unborn child.

"What is it?" he asks.

Rowan's eyes have gone cross.

"Landon was going on and on about the snake he saw at his field trip, and I promised I'd take him to the gift shop to find one in there. She must have heard me." Tears are free flowing down her face.

Wyatt shakes his head. "What're the odds she had that on her."

Schrader says, "We can't be sure that's what it was. Although, they were in a museum of sorts."

"But... isn't it odd for a woman to abduct a child?" Wyatt asks. Goosebumps light up his arms. Landon was targeted, and that makes this whole thing so much more horrific than Wyatt running off and falling into the wrong hands. Someone went to that visitor center to take a kid, and they got his.

Schrader sighs, shaking his head. "These days they oftentimes work in teams. Male and female. Children are less suspicious of the female lure. The museum uniform probably made your son more trusting. The abductors remain undetected on our facial recognition software by taking advantage of facemasks these days," Schrader says grimly.

Wyatt's stomach cinches. They always told Landon if he's in trouble, *Look for a mommy*... But he wasn't in trouble.

"Well, who is that woman? Did you ask the visitor center? An employee search? Are they at her house right now looking for Landon?" Rowan's questions are rapid fire. Her voice is shaky, irrational, but Wyatt can gauge from the detectives' faces that these are scenarios they've already considered.

"That's the thing..." Stone deadpans. "There is no one who works at the Independence Visitor Center who meets this woman's description. She's a fraud. But we had to make sure you didn't know her personally. A high percentage of abductions occur by people the child already knows. The child will sometimes go to that person more readily if they're familiar."

"Oh my god. No, we don't know her!" Rowan places her hand over her face in dismay. Wyatt snaps to reality and places his arm around her shoulders. He doesn't understand how this could've happened.

"Who is she?" Rowan wails.

Stone presses play on the video again. The figures move around on the screen, still grainy. Landon takes the snake-like-shaped item from the woman, and then he grips her hand as if he's ready to go somewhere with her. It's hard to make out the specifications of the woman because she's wearing a facemask, but she looks up, almost directly at the camera for a moment, and her eyes glow like an animal's.

EIGHTEEN

ROWAN

Rowan confirms they do not know the lady on the video footage who took Landon, even though Wyatt doesn't say a word, staring listlessly.

An officer rushes out of the room.

Minutes later their phones howl.

Philadelphia Police Department activate AMBER ALERT. Victim is Landon Bishop, age 4. Caucasian, brown hair, brown eyes, striped shirt, khaki pants, light-up shoes. Suspect is a female with long dark hair, brown eyes. Last known location, Independence Visitor Center, 599 Market Street. If observed please call 911.

Rowan stares at the warning message on her cell in disbelief. "No," she mouths at the siren. She tries to silence it, but you can't quiet an amber alert. That's the whole point—you're forced to listen and look.

Detective Stone says, "Now everyone else will be looking for Landon too."

Rowan glances up at her, thinking, *too little too late*. He's been missing for hours.

They're escorted out of the room with the one-way mirror whether they're ready to leave or not.

A police car awaits outside. Stone sits in the driver's seat; the rear driver side door is open. At first Rowan doesn't understand she's to climb inside. "Come on, Ro," Wyatt says, gently, pointing to the car door.

Numb, her lips barely work, but she manages, "What happens now? Shouldn't we stay here in case someone saw them? In case they phone in? At the station?" Her limbs are moving slowly. This is a bad dream. They couldn't really expect her to go home—without her son.

"Schrader will field the calls at the station," the door holder says. It's another officer, different from all the others she's met.

Her heart is beating too quickly. Her thick middle makes her lean to the side like a teapot.

Rowan can't return to her house, with all Landon's things, and just sit around and wait for someone to bring him back.

"The cops said they wanted to look around the house a bit, remember?" Wyatt asks. He's ashen, sickly looking, but he can't be suffering as badly as she is.

He's not the one who lost their son.

He's not the parent who let a stranger take him. "No, I don't remember that."

Wyatt points at the backseat. "Come on." The officer continues to hold the door, grunts, and shuffles his black boots.

Rowan slides into the backseat of the cruiser. What the hell do they think they'll find at the house? That woman at the center saw Rowan, pregnant and alone with a young, active child—a vulnerable target for a kidnapper. That's where they were tailed—at the center. There's nothing at the house.

Looking in the house is a waste of time. "Can we launch a

search team for him? I know my daycare moms would jump in," she says, her voice a whisper.

Officer Jenkins clears his throat. "Search teams are usually deployed when a child goes missing in a wooded or rural area. Places where we can use dogs to sniff for a scent. Because Landon went missing in the city, we're better off with the amber alert and heavily researching the CCTV cameras at all the major intersections and transportation stations."

Rowan's throat closes at this information, and she covers her mouth. The Independence National Historic Park that surrounds the center is a terrible place for a child to go missing. It's crowded, close to busy Old City and Center City, a hop, skip and jump from the train, just over the bridge from Camden, New Jersey, one of the worst crime-ridden, drug-infested areas in the country.

The kidnapper could've come from any direction.

And she could've left from any direction too.

She may have handed Landon off to someone else. Someone not on the camera.

Rowan hugs her sides and shudders. Her insides scream with regret—*I let him go!* She'll never forgive herself.

She clenches her eyes shut in agony, this car the last place she should be.

They should be out there—looking for Landon.

Wyatt sighs loudly. He stares out the window, his jaw set in a straight line, rubbing his fingers over his knuckles so hard she wonders if he's breaking skin. Does he blame her for losing Landon?

She would blame him if the situation were reversed. She would despise him.

When the cops pull into their driveway, she can hardly stand it. Landon's bicycle is outside even though she told him to put it away countless times. A few news trucks are already parked at the curb.

"They'll probably want a statement," Jenkins says. "You don't have to give them one, but sometimes a plea to the public can help."

A plea to the public may be all I have.

Rowan's not one to come apart in front of others, but whatever glue has been holding her together today begins to dissolve beneath the light of the press cameras. Her mouth gapes open like a fish out of water at the bright flashes. And the questions.

She's one of those poor people on the news, the sort she pities. The kind she judges—*How could you let that happen? I would never let that happen. What a terrible mother.*

Her own mother, part-saint, always told her not to be like that. *You never know the other side of the story… or when it'll be you.* Rowan always thought that was a crock of shit, one irresponsible woman making excuses for another.

And now she's the worst of them all.

"And you're pregnant, correct. Mrs. Bishop. How far along are you?" a man in thick glasses asks her. She thinks he already asked her this question. She can't be sure anymore, there're so many reporters.

"Yes, about twenty-three weeks. I don't know if it's a girl or a b-boy yet." Her voice cracks. Wyatt grabs onto her arm.

"That's enough questions," Wyatt says, pulling her away.

"Wait…" She yanks free of her husband. His face is bewildered and uncertain. "Please, if you have my son. If you have Landon, let him go. Let him come home. We'll give you whatever you want. I just need my little—" She wails then. Breaks. The more the tears fall, the harder the cameras clack.

The press close in on her like a swarm of bees. Wyatt hurries her inside the house.

The cops hold back the crowd, barbaric, and hungry for

more now that they've gotten a taste of her maternal anguish. The good stuff. What drives ratings.

She hates to lose it in public, but she'll do anything to save her son.

Wyatt practically carries her to the couch and sits her down, wraps his arms around her. He gives the police free rein of their house, clean, and untouched from the morning. "They'll find him," Wyatt says, but his voice is hollow, unconvincing.

"They always say on those investigation shows that if they're not recovered..." She sniffles.

"Don't think about that. We don't know anything yet." His voice shakes with fear.

"He's gone, Wyatt." She places her head in her hands, practically kissing her baby bump. How can she possibly take care of another one when she lost the first one? Someone should take the next away from her too.

"I'm going to look for him, on the streets, as soon as the officer is done here. Your mother is coming over, right?"

"Yes." She weeps. She doesn't want Wyatt to leave, but she's eager for him to search for Landon. No cop on the beat will look harder for Landon than Wyatt will.

Officer Jenkins approaches them. "Excuse me, sir, were you traveling overseas recently?" He's holding something in his hand.

Wyatt breaks away from their huddle. "Yes, I was in Mexico City for work."

Jenkins says, "We found your passport lying on the floor. Just wanted to make sure."

Wyatt hikes his shoulders as if he's been caught. Does the officer think he was ready to flee? Do they suspect him?

"I put in a load of laundry. It must've come out of my bag."

Jenkins nods and hands Wyatt his passport.

"Jenk. Upstairs," the other officer calls.

"Excuse me."

"What was that all about?" Rowan asks. Then she remembered Wyatt ducked into the laundry room earlier. He was fiddling with a box of food in the pantry and then quickly pushed it back as if he'd been caught with his hand in the cookie jar. What did Rowan care if he was munching on the kid's breakfast cereal? Unless... he was hiding something.

"I have no idea. I guess a passport is an odd thing to find in a laundry room and they wanted to make sure it was supposed to be there." Wyatt looks away. He's been doing that a lot, and before he didn't have a reason, but now he does. If the roles were reversed, Rowan probably couldn't look at him either. The person responsible for losing their child.

"Mr. and Mrs. Bishop, can you come upstairs?"

They both look at each other, fearfully.

What did they find?

Wyatt helps pull Rowan off the couch. Her body aches, her knees cracking, her muscles fatigued from all the time she's spent clenching them. Rowan stares at her husband, desperate. *Help me.* He's still on her side and she doesn't understand why. They stride up the hardwood steps as quickly as possible, meeting the officers in the master bathroom.

"Rowan, are you okay?" Wyatt asks, breathlessly. Those steps took it out of her. She wants to scour the city streets with Wyatt after the cops are done here, but her prenatal body is sabotaging her.

"Yeah," she lies.

"Do you want to tell us why there are bloody bandages in the trashcan?" Jenkins' voice is sharp.

"Oh... I recently had surgery," Wyatt explains. "They're mine." He pulls up his shirt to show the police officers his white gauze dressing.

"Right after you got home from your trip?"

Wyatt fumbles with his words. Rowan's not sure why he

looks so nervous, so she answers for him. "He was attacked during his trip. A robbery. They had to repair his stab wound."

Both of the officers glare at Wyatt. "And you have no idea who stabbed you?"

"N-no," Wyatt stutters.

Rowan can't understand why he answers the question as if he's unsure. She sighs, feeling woozy. He grabs her by the elbow. "I'm going to put my wife to bed. She's exhausted."

"I can't rest, Wyatt."

"You need to lie down. For just a minute. You have to take care of yourself."

He pushes her out of the bathroom, in a hurry to get away from the cops, it seems. He walks her over to their bed and forces her under the covers. She's so tired, she's sick. She could turn her head and vomit all over the floor, but the sheets feel good on her hot skin.

The cops leave the bathroom to check out the rest of the house. Rowan can hear them stomping around in her son's room. *Don't touch his things.*

She closes her eyes for a minute. One, maybe two.

Sleep is impossible.

She can hear the officers talking in Landon's room.

What're they saying?

She imagines words, like, "Such a shame..."

A drawer is opened and shut.

Don't touch his things.

Her eyes pop open.

She can't rest another moment. Forget his toys and clothes. Someone has their hands on her son.

Rowan hears the doorbell. Her mother. Good, now Wyatt can get out there and look for Landon. She swings her legs out of bed. She walks down the stairs just in time to see Wyatt running out of the laundry room.

Why does he keep going in there?

When Rowan sees her mother rolling her suitcase into the house, she hurries down the stairs, clenching her middle so she doesn't fall. Wyatt moves out of the way and Rowan flings herself into her mother's arms—a mess of tears.

"Oh, honey, I'm so sorry. We're going to find him," she says.

Not a single person who's said that has sounded as sure as her mother. Even if it's false hope, she could use some. "Wyatt's going to look for him now."

"We're done here. Detective Stone will give him a ride back to the center to get his car," Jenkins says. "The cops are continuing to patrol and will continue throughout the night. Someone has to have seen this little boy."

"Okay, I want to believe you. I want to come with you Wyatt, but—" she starts.

"You're going to stay here with Detective Schrader." Jenkins gestures to Schrader. Rowan wishes it was Jenkins because he's been with her since the beginning.

"Why?" Rowan asks.

Jenkins and Schrader gape at each other uneasily. "In these situations, if a ransom is the motive, those usually arrive within the first twenty-four to forty-eight hours. Landline calls are harder to trace. We need to make sure someone is here."

Wyatt stares up at the ceiling in agony, silently praying to God, although neither of them go to church.

"Okay," Rowan says.

"We posted the fifty thousand dollars for any solid lead to your son's whereabouts that you asked for, Mrs. Bishop," Jenkins says.

Wyatt bobs his head back down. "You did?"

She knows very well they barely have that much in their savings. But he's guessing the police will help with the funds if an exchange is made. Someone addressed this with her at one point in the flurry of information that's been exchanged, but she can't remember the details, because the value of her son's life means so much more to her than the potential cash required to return him. "Yes."

Wyatt nods in agreement. "All right, let's get moving. Try to get some rest, Rowan." He leans in and kisses her on her forehead. His lips are as cold as a dead fish.

NINETEEN
THE DOCTOR

The doctor strings her hair up in a bun and sits next to a man on an IV drip, but they aren't in the hospital.

A home health unit is set up in a fancy house, intricate design. Spanish influence tickles the wide hallways—stone, brick, colorful tile. The woman is holding the man's hand as he sits with his eyes closed. A monitor beeps nearby, and she stands to check on his stats like the trained medical professional she is. Her cell phone rings, the contact—Zo. She answers. "He seems to be adjusting well so far," she says. "Thankfully."

"Good... Keep a close lookout. Still a lot of chance for rejection. I have to stay in Florida for a bit and check on a few things; can you send my payment there?" Zo asks.

Her face fills with fear. "Too soon, Zo. Your latest... patient is from the US. They'll be all over this if he talks."

He sighs. "Then, why did you pick him?"

"Because this one sat close to home." Framed pictures in the eaves of the house reveal photos of the doctor and the man in the hospital bed. "We were running out of time. And your job is not complete. You know that."

"I told you I don't want the other case. Give it to someone else in the Network."

"I don't trust anyone else to do it," she says.

"I do not want it."

"You knew when you signed on to do this that turning down the organization's assignments was not an option."

"I had no idea what I was signing up for... And you promised after the last case like this one, I'd never have to do another."

"We have the right tools this time. See you soon." She hangs up. On a table beside the phone is a hospital badge that reads, *Dr. Marta Santos.*

Marta walks to a different expansive wing of the house and sits by the bedside of a much smaller patient. Marta pats the IV fastened to the top of his hand. She can't help but think what a curse it is that her husband and grandson's health tumbled downhill at the same time—he's only eight years old.

The disease is taking him faster than the others.

Everything was good for so long...

It's only a shame she couldn't save her own son despite her efforts—legal and otherwise. She's quickly reminded again of why she started her business in the first place. The sorts of healthcare restrictions that condemn the sick, decide who lives and dies, aren't rules she'll follow. Especially when her family is involved.

Although her mindset has shifted. At first it was about just her family.

After her son's death, it became a mission. It wasn't just about her child anymore, but all God's children. Why should people die because of a lack of access to medical necessities—like human organs? Most people only need one kidney to survive; Marta's just forcing the rest of the greedy world to share.

Andre sleeps peacefully as Marta brushes the hair from his

head. There are storybooks piled on a table beside him, mostly old fairytales with worn covers his father enjoyed.

She walks in and checks on her husband. The monitor seems to read out all the right numbers and she smiles in mild contentment.

He made it to fifty-six before he needed his transplant. She winces at the fact that Andre only made it to eight. They're searching for a transplant candidate from their database, but haven't found a match. Marta has of course been tested, and isn't one.

Andre's disease has progressed, and he's now on dialysis.

Marta makes a cup of tea and watches despondently for the pot to whistle. When it finally does, she nearly scalds herself pouring the hot water over loose-leaf tea. She holds the teacup more carefully as she walks down the spiral stone staircase to the basement.

A man in all black sits in front of a giant computer monitor that has a world map and nonstop activity, including dashed lines leading from one country to the next.

"Did you find a liver for customer number sixty-six in Beijing?" Marta asks.

The man nods. "From the prison. The donor was due to be executed anyway." He grimaces as he takes a break and nods at Marta. "Our liaison wants more money."

"No." Marta blows on her tea and then sips it. The red and blue pattern of the Talavera pottery against the white ceramic backdrop is apparent even in the dim lighting. Marta's business is dark. She can't help but buy expensive, beautiful things to dress up her surroundings.

"They're our number one source. If we lose the prison that's forty percent of our donor base," he says.

Marta shrugs. "They can't keep gouging us. Policy will make it inevitable for them to work with us. Soon, The Chinese government will enforce the new law that makes harvesting illegal, and then it will be harder to find a viable market for their business. They need us. Our channel is secure."

The man shrugs, not so sure. "What do you want me to tell him?"

"Nothing. We've extracted the product, Alistair? No?"

"Yes," Alistair says.

"Good. Well, then no renegotiation until the next one."

Marta turns to leave.

"One last thing..."

"What is it?" Exhaustion and irritation hang in her voice. It's been a week... and she's been scrambling to secure every resource she has. She feels pummeled by her family's decline in health, memories of when Damon, her son, passed away, as fresh as the day he was born. He never even got to meet his own son. It's upsetting that underserved countries have to suffer because of inadequate supply, but she won't allow it in her own house. Not again.

"The hospital in Mexico City is getting inquiries about the American," Alistair says.

"From who?" she asks.

"The board. It's the second illegal organ transfer victim in eighteen months. No more for a while, okay?"

She glares at him. Who does Alistair think he is? She calls the shots. Marta can't imagine him talking to her husband that way before he got sick. She didn't ask to be running the show, but she won't be patronized for it now.

"You just stick to what you're good at, and I'll worry about my specialties."

He nods. "I have a bad feeling about your latest patient."

"Yeah, well, you can keep your feelings to yourself. I don't pay you to have feelings," she says with spite. "You know this one was special."

TWENTY

WYATT

Detective Stone drives to Society Hill and Wyatt stares straight ahead. "I'm only giving you a ride to pick up your car. You can grab Mrs. Bishop's tomorrow. I can't tell you what to do, but I do think you should go home and be with your wife now."

Wyatt doesn't respond. He can't make any promises about what he will or will not do. The surrounding areas like Old City have gone to shit. His son could be holed up somewhere around there while the police knock down doors. He could troll the streets asking the vagrants and other people in the area if anyone has seen his son.

He could go home, comfort his wife, wait by the phone.

Or... he can come clean right now to Detective Stone—about everything. Doing so would result in him losing what he has left of his family—Rowan and the new baby.

"It's hard to go home and do nothing," he admits.

Stone nods. "I get that, but the police are doing everything they can, patrolling the streets. We don't want to get into a situation where you become a liability poking your nose in the wrong place. Violence is up in the city since the pandemic.

Someone will see Landon. And when they do, the best place you can be is with your wife."

"Right," he says. He bites on his lip. Wyatt clenches his jaw. This isn't what he signed up for.

He's played the part for Rowan, did the whole happy family act that was not part of his childhood. It's not in his DNA. Having a family didn't need to be part of his future. Now, it's his downfall.

He was never meant to fulfill this role.

Someone else should step in, step up, marry Rowan, raise their baby.

"Mr. Bishop?"

Wyatt snaps to attention.

Stone is parked beside his car. "Get home now. We'll be in touch as soon as we hear something."

Wyatt nods, but doesn't answer her. He's become very good at lying to women. Not because he wants to, but because he has to. Stone's red taillights turn into hazy pinpricks in the night.

TWENTY-ONE
ROWAN

The day Rowan learned she was capable of murder was a Tuesday during her sophomore year of high school; a blustery day that made it hard to breathe. When she did, puffs of white air escaped her lungs like billows of smoke from one of the nearby factories.

Colleen McVay's father worked in one of those mills. Rowan always assumed Colleen messed with her because Colleen's father picked on her first. It wasn't anything known, just something Rowan gathered from their community where a lot of the men drank way too much whiskey and came home swinging. Rowan's mother tried to convince her that they were lucky their father didn't drink like that, even though it hardly made up for every other way he misbehaved.

It was the wrong day for Colleen to antagonize Rowan.

The night before, Mom had caught Dad cheating again.

A mystery earring in his car this time. He claimed it was one of theirs or had come with the used vehicle years prior and *must've just made its way up through the upholstery.*

Mom placed the dangly, slutty-looking lightning bolt in the

center of the counter, and both Rowan and her younger sister, Riley, said it was not theirs.

You probably don't remember. It looks like one of those plastic pieces you got out of the junk vending machines you threw your quarters away in when you were little.

Rowan shook her head, fury rising, his lies fueling her anger. The way he cast the blame back on her struck the match. His words lit her arms on fire until they were moving toward him.

She took the plastic neon-green lightning bolt and swatted at her father with it, aiming for his gray-blue eyes, the same ones she shared with him. She narrowly missed his eye, but she got his face good.

"Ow." He ducked away, blood streaming down his cheek.

"It's one of your whores, you fucking liar!" Rowan screamed it, over and over again, so fed up with his inability to tell the truth.

Smacking and swatting away with her hands, ripping at pieces of his graying, thinning brown hair. There'd been years of this bullshit and she always remained quiet, but that day she couldn't hold back anymore. Rowan hit him for herself and her siblings, but most of all she beat him for her mother who didn't have the strength to do it herself.

Her father didn't fight back.

It was her eleven-year-old younger brother, Gavin, built like a tank even in middle school, who yanked her away.

Her father was left with a mess of scratches and bruises, a bloody lip. Her mother, a face full of tears that never fell below her bottom lids. Hell, maybe she was a little happy someone finally gave it to him.

"You might listen to his bullshit, but I'm done." Rowan turned from her mother to her father. "You should get the fuck out if you can't respect this family." He held up his hands, red-faced, and ashamed.

And then he did leave.

Dad packed his bags and left that night—and he never came back.

The rest of Rowan's family blamed her for his departure, even though they didn't say it outright.

"At least you get to leave in a couple of years. The rest of us will have to struggle with Mom," Gavin said. The youngest, Brennan, was spared both the fight and their father's leaving. He cried often about missing him, though, and Rowan did feel bad about that, but life was better without Dad. If there's a reason she doesn't have a relationship with her brothers now, she can pinpoint it to that evening.

No one said much about it afterward—until Colleen taunted Rowan a few days later.

Still simmering, still wondering if she'd really done the right thing for her family, Rowan was lost in her thoughts, walking briskly home from the bus stop when Colleen cornered her.

Rowan can still remember the way the chilled brick felt as it ground into her back. Petite and small-boned, Rowan appeared the perfect candidate for a good bullying, but Colleen didn't realize Rowan was carrying an extra gallon of spite in her veins that day.

She'd never received an acknowledgment from her father or a breath of an apology. It's what burned her most.

When Colleen pushed her and said the words, "Heard your daddy finally had enough of you and your mom and left..." she made a grave mistake. Rowan sucked in a deep breath.

Colleen, a gum chewer, chomped in her face.

Funny how when you hit someone for the first time, the second isn't as bad. Rowan pushed Colleen away. "Fuck you." Rowan's small, balled fist connected with Colleen's horse mouth next—and then again—and then once more.

It's not strength or size that always wins out.

Sometimes it's the madness of the person behind the punches.

Colleen's long and limber body slipped backward, a spray of red contrasting with the snow so brilliantly, the only thing Rowan could do was make more red. More and more...

Rowan's daddy taught her how to punch. *Thumbs out. Thumbs in and you'll break 'em.* She thought about her father's face as she decimated Colleen's. And then the imaginary face of the whore and her dangly earring.

A nearby shop owner was the one to pull Rowan off the girl who'd tried to curl into a protective ball, a little centipede. But Rowan had squashed her.

When the ambulance came, Rowan lied and said Colleen jumped her—threw the first punch. Self-defense.

She got out of it without a criminal record.

Colleen left the fight with a missing front tooth.

June sent her to private school after that, afraid of what would happen if Rowan saw Colleen in school. Her siblings grew more resentful, because tuition for private school took money out of their budget, and Rowan had already cost them their high-earning father who hadn't paid a cent of child support since he left. Provisions for their family of five were tight to say the least.

The financial trouble wasn't the thing that bothered Rowan most, though. It was the fact that she could've kept going.

That if the shop owner, a large butcher with a leather apron, hadn't held her back, she would've kept hitting Colleen until she was blind.

Until she was dead.

Rowan was possessed with that kind of rage right now. Some people don't have it in them to hurt someone like that. Rowan knows she does.

TWENTY-TWO

ROWAN

As Rowan awakes, she thinks of Colleen.

The shock and fright of yesterday has turned into something ugly and feral overnight.

She thinks of the shockingly satisfying feeling of striking Colleen after she said those awful words to her, watching her life leak from her body. Disfiguring her face. The yellowed tooth, stained from smoking, lying next to the bright-white snow, the sparkling ground turned ruby red.

Rowan pulls her bedsheets to her chin and imagines gallons more blood pouring from the person who took her son.

Their insides torn out, hanging like spaghetti from their body. She'll do it.

I'll do it.

Rowan bites her bedsheets, her teeth digging in.

I'll do it.

She's so angry, she could scream. She should get up. Check in with the police. She can hear Wyatt talking to them downstairs.

She took some Tylenol and somehow dozed off last night.

Life is a nightmare. And she's just a numb animal moving through time and space. She doesn't know when Wyatt came to bed. Or if he did at all. She only knows what she thought when she laid down.

They never called.

The police were stationed at her house last night, waiting by the phone. Rowan slept with her phone clenched in her hand.

But the kidnappers never contacted her.

The best-case scenario is that there would be a ransom.

That the people who had Landon would contact her and offer to return him for a set amount of money. It's possible someone called Wyatt, but Rowan can tell by his depleted tone downstairs that they haven't.

Which means they must want Landon for something other than money.

Rowan's stomach turns. She kicks off the covers, drenched in sweat.

She imagines Colleen's smashed-up face in the snow. If Rowan finds the person responsible for this, they will die. She will kill them.

She's already decided.

She doesn't have a criminal record. It will be her first offense. They'll show her mercy. She knows how to work the system. Like she'll know how to work the blade over every inch of the motherfucker who took her son.

She'll never stop looking.

It may have taken sixteen years of built up resentment to lash out at her dad, but she'll be quicker this time.

Rowan holds on to the dresser—*balance*.

She stares at herself in the mirror, her eyes, bags of sadness. Evil lives there too. Why do *they* turn her into this person when she just wants to do good? It's all she's ever wanted. Even after her last dust-up with Wyatt when she mistakenly thought he was cheating. A simple mix-up, but when his colleague answered his phone at their meeting in Jersey, she lost it.

"I will kill you," she whispers at the mirror.

She slicks back her hair and walks downstairs.

Her mother and Wyatt appear freshly showered and are standing around the kitchen table with Detective Stone.

"Rowan, did you sleep, honey?" her mother asks.

How she feels isn't important. Whether she slept doesn't matter either. She doesn't answer. Rowan grabs a cup of coffee instead. Wyatt says nothing.

Has it sunk in for him yet? What she's done?

That she's responsible for losing their son? That she probably shouldn't be responsible for raising another child?

She should be drinking decaf, but fuck it all. She takes a sip.

"Did any calls come in?" Her voice croaks, dry and parched from silently screaming into her pillow half the night. Her voice box is stretched from crying into the void. Her head pulses with unrest. Loss is its own torture device.

"None have. There's been a GoFundMe started from someone at your work to aid with necessities," Stone says.

Pierre.

"I don't need money. I need my son!"

Detective Stone eyes her seriously. "We're doing everything we can."

"What about the CCTV cameras? You said that they'd likely pick something up."

"That's only if they used mass transit and made Landon visible."

"What does that mean?" she asks, exasperated. "Made him visible?"

"If he was in the back of a van, the CCTV cameras would just display the van. We're checking the cameras around the center," Detective Stone says, solemnly.

Rowan picks up her nearly full coffee cup and fires it at the sink. Everyone in the room jumps. Dark-brown liquid sloshes up the white tiles, all over the deep farmhouse sink. Shards of ceramic litter the sink like jagged snowflakes. "This isn't good enough! Let's up the reward. To $100,000. Give the kidnapper a bigger payday over whatever someone is buying him for."

"Oh God," her mother whispers. Rowan looks over at her and just notices she's crying.

"What? You don't think I know what they're going to do to my son! I know. I'm not stupid. Fucking monsters. Do you know what I'm going to do to the person responsible for this?" Her teeth chatter in pure anger.

Wyatt approaches her to try to calm her down, but Rowan pushes him away. She points at her mother. "You know. *You know what I'll do.*"

June puts her hand up. "Stop talking like that. You're still a child of God. Two wrongs don't make a right."

"You made me go to Catholic school, but you know I don't believe in that shit, right, Ma?"

My Philly comes out in an instant when I'm pissed. I've practiced good manners and appropriate dialect, but I'll return to my roots in a second if cornered.

Detective Stone. "May I interrupt?"

"Please," Wyatt says.

Rowan glances at the other two, embarrassed, as if she forgot they were there.

"If you want to bump up the reward, we should do that sooner rather than later. Also, your appearance had an effect on the public. Your GoFundMe me is up to ten thousand already. There's outrage. Strangers stick their neck out and try harder for people they feel for. Do you want to do another press conference?"

Rowan shakes her head. "Wyatt can do it." She'd played the part of the crying mother on TV, but she's so fired up today, there's no way she'll prove to be a reliable actress.

He looks at her surprised. Scared.

But she's a different person than she was yesterday. Maybe he can see that too. She's not the sappy, broken mother still hopeful for her son's return.

She's a woman out for blood.

TWENTY-THREE

ROWAN

Stone left to arrange the new reward for Landon's return. Rowan wonders if it will matter. How much will be enough to return him?

Is her little boy lost forever?

The hole in her heart is vast and growing. Her health has declined so much in the last twenty-four hours she imagines her unborn child gasping for air inside of her womb. Rowan has held her breath so many times trying to survive the moment. The only time she can consciously allow herself to breathe is when she thinks of the baby.

Stone's arranging a press conference for Wyatt.

No one argued with Rowan when she said she couldn't face the media again. Not after how she abused her morning coffee.

Screw the press and their hungry cameras vying for her tears. They want to increase their ratings with her heartache, but she doesn't have anything left for them.

The cops have given her the one thing she doesn't want—time.

She doesn't want minutes to wait for someone else to find

her son. She doesn't have that luxury. Every second that passes, Rowan imagines Landon traveling further away from her.

Into the arms of someone who will do him great harm.

The laundry room is a safe haven from her mother's watchful eyes. She's frightened of her after her morning demonstration, she can tell, but what does she expect?

How can anyone sit still?

She's probably hoping Rowan doesn't transform back into the troubled girl who was sent away to private school to save her soul.

What really gets Rowan is that Wyatt hasn't blamed her yet—even once.

If the situation were reversed, Rowan wouldn't be as supportive.

It's more of a testament to his character than hers, but why hasn't he said the words she's been waiting to hear even one time—*how could you have let him go?*

She wants Wyatt to barrage her with that poisonous question, because she deserves it.

She walks back to the kitchen, her mother forlorn in a chair. Rowan pours Clorox into the sink. She's scrubbed it multiple times, sure to get every last piece of ceramic, so she can have a clean house for her family. What's left of it...

It's such a role reversal for her and Wyatt, neither one of them knows what to do. Usually, Wyatt is the negligent one.

Rowan returns to the laundry room, rifles through the clothes, searching for something clean to wear.

She peels off her sweat-stained clothes and throws them in a pile. She finds pajama pants and a sweatshirt and slips them on. She sees Wyatt's black travel bag still sitting there, unzipped, clothes inside. She thought he would've washed them by now, but she's not surprised he hasn't, moping around the last week like a zombie.

She grabs his neatly folded dress clothes that she can tell he hasn't worn. Of course, he hasn't. He was jumped the first night of his trip, no chance for any kind of business. She throws the clean clothes in a laundry basket to carry upstairs and put away.

There's no sign of any blood-soaked shirt in there, but Rowan assumes the hospital threw it away. Maybe they even had to cut it off him. When she reaches the bottom of the bag, she sees a folded white paper and an unopened prescription.

Unopened.

Wyatt, what medicine didn't you take?

Maybe that's why he's so out of it.

Rowan lifts up the pills and shakes them. The seal hasn't been broken. She reads the label—Codeina. *Codeine?*

Rowan picks up the paper and unfolds it. It's written entirely in Spanish. There's a section on dietary restrictions. Rowan can tell from the pictures which foods are acceptable and which are not by the Xs marked through them, but she can't understand what it says.

She takes her phone from the top of the washing machine and pulls up the translation app.

Cuidado de la extraccion de orgranos.

Translation: care for organ extraction.

What?

Rowan's blood throbs in her ear. She closes her eyes and grips the washer. She must not be understanding this right. Maybe she fat-fingered the letters into the translator?

But... it all makes sense.

Her hair tingles hot and cold. She places her hand over her mouth, her other one still clenching the paper and the pills. She gets it now.

The way Wyatt's been acting. How he won't let her see him naked—because he doesn't want her to notice the extent of his wound. Why he was acting so weird when she caught him in the pantry. Why he's been checking the nutrition information on the side of the damn cereal box.

Rowan's eyes flash open.

He's been lying about his injury.

What else is he lying about?

She pushes her body off the washer. *God give me strength.*

She nimbly creeps out of the laundry room and finds her mother whispering to Wyatt.

"I hope I'm not interrupting anything," Rowan says.

Her mother jumps. Wyatt takes a step back. *What're they talking about? More secrets?*

"Hi, honey," her mother says.

"Mom, I'm going to need you to leave. I have to talk to Wyatt about something alone." She grips the white paper and bottle of pills so hard they rattle.

The sound attracts Wyatt's attention.

He glances down at what she's holding, and then looks away. *Liar.*

He doesn't say anything. Not a fucking word. He stares out the window instead.

"What's wrong?" June asks.

"Go, Mom. Go, now!"

"Should I get my stuff?" she asks, confused.

"You can come back, just go for a long drive."

June looks between the two of them and then grabs her purse and leaves. Rowan waits until the door slams shut.

She holds up the medication and paper and waves it in Wyatt's face. "Tell me what this is. Tell me what happened to you over there. Right... fucking... now!"

TWENTY-FOUR
WYATT

There are variations of lies in all shades and colors. The person who created the white lie only did so to hide the black ones—the kind a person can deliver while looking someone dead in the eye—the soul crushers. Today, Wyatt chooses a shade of gray for Rowan—truth with some lies spread around the edges, just the right mix. It's not for him; it's for her.

Telling Rowan the whole truth, right now, would destroy her and their unborn child.

He can see their marriage coming apart right before his eyes. But more importantly, he can tell Rowan is hanging on by a thread.

Guilt eating her from the inside out.

One step away from a mental breakdown.

She'll never forgive herself for losing Landon, and she'll never forgive him for what he's about to tell her, but if he divulges the whole truth, no one else will forgive him either. He might as well preserve as much of his life as he can.

He twitches in the hallway as he faces her. His facial muscles move beneath his skin without his permission. His nerve endings were burnt from unrest, long before his son was stolen away. Landon's absence hangs between them, an impossible void. How do couples survive this type of loss?

They don't, he hears a voice whisper. He holds his breath.

Wyatt searches for the right words. Since Landon was taken, until this very moment, he hasn't thought about what he's missing on the inside of his body even once.

Only his missing son.

One horror replaced another. He and Rowan must remain a united front if they have a shot at finding Landon. Having the press on their side is pivotal. The media will broadcast their message far and wide, put Landon's face in front of every viewer willing to take in their sorrow. But a cheating husband will lose the public's support.

"Well?" she asks, impatiently.

"Let me explain." Wyatt places his hands in the air. His cheeks sizzle. He's caught. He hates the feeling. He wanted to deliver this information in his own time.

"Waiting for that." Rowan stands in the hall in between the laundry room and the kitchen. The one thing he hates about this old house is the low ceilings. They're framed in old barnwood, the white walls a nice contrast. But right now, his petite wife looks like she's about to tear through the ceiling.

"I was attacked in Mexico City. And I don't remember what happened. That part's true. But I didn't tell you what they did to me because I had a hard time dealing with it myself."

Her eyes flicker at the words—*I didn't tell you*. "Tell me now."

"I didn't want to stress you out with the baby," he defends.

"Wyatt..." Her voice is low, controlled—cold. "You know what keeping things from me does." Her nostrils flare.

Wyatt tries to take a step forward. Rowan shuffles back into the hollow of the hallway. Her hand clamps around the pill bottle like she's prepared to launch it at him like a grenade.

"Please, just let me finish," he says.

"Go on, but don't you dare take a step closer to me." Her voice is almost a whisper. It's hoarse and gravelly. She *hates* him right now. It's why he chooses his words like he does. Why he dances in the gray. The truth won't set her free. It will drive her insane.

"Whoever hurt me slipped something in my drink at the bar to make me pass out. Drugs. I remember being led down a dark hallway. Male voices." *Lie. Charcoal lie.* "I was in a trance. I woke up in a bath of ice. I had an incision in my side."

Rowan's mouth drops open. Wyatt searches for sympathy in her bloodshot eyes but can't find any. It makes him wish he'd come forward sooner.

"Why?" she rasps.

"My wallet, laptop, and phone were gone, but I don't think that's what they were really after. They wanted something else from me." He glances down. "They took me to a hotel room and set up a makeshift... operating table. And removed... my... kidney." He coughs. It hurts. "Shit." He grabs at his side.

He remembers from when he got his appendix out that *a cough is one of the human body's most violent actions...*

Rowan drops the pills on the ground. Wyatt startles at the sound. Her eyes oscillate in horror from Wyatt's stomach to the ceiling to the floor. "What the fuck, Wyatt?"

"I don't know." Wyatt tries to take a step forward. Rowan takes another step back.

She's almost at the entrance of the laundry room. "Stay away from me. I don't know you."

"I was the victim here!" he shouts.

"Were you? Then why didn't you tell me? Why did you lie? What is this really about?"

"Ro, I thought my company must've told you what happened to me and then when it was clear that they didn't, I wasn't sure how to tell you. I know how you like things..."

She turns her head sideways, then back at him. "What's that supposed to mean?"

"You like things just so... And having me gone for so long was one thing. But then I was afraid you would blame me for going out to the bar. But it wasn't my fault—"

"I do blame you! For lying to me. About so much. Let me see it!" Rowan still won't move toward him.

The space between them is not one she wishes to fill. Old feelings of abandonment rush in like a tidal wave. "What do you want to see?" Wyatt places his hand over his side, protective.

"Lift up your shirt," she demands.

Does she really want to see his wound? Or is she just reestablishing her dominance? "It doesn't matter, Rowan. It's healing. I'm okay. I can live a perfectly healthy life. The incision is still hard to look at."

"Let me see it," she commands. "Now."

It's an awful feeling, being forced to show someone such a vulnerability. He takes his t-shirt by the fingertips and slowly lifts it up. A bandage covers his injury.

"Undo the bandage." She moves forward now, eager.

Anything to get her closer to him. Wyatt tentatively peels back one side of the white medical tape. It pulls at the tender flesh beneath it, and he bites his lip.

Rowan gasps. "Oh my god. Why is it zigzagged like that?"

Wyatt feels heat creep up his neck again, self-conscious. This is one of the reasons why he didn't want to show her the damages. He tries to find his wife's eyes as she scrutinizes him like a broken toy. "I don't think the guy who did this was interested in making sure they sewed me up nice and pretty. They stole my damn organ, Rowan! I'm lucky to be alive."

Rowan clamps her other hand over her mouth. She looks like she's trying to asphyxiate herself.

Wyatt tamps down his bandage and drops his shirt. "Is it

really important at this point? I'm here. I'm okay. Our son is not. I don't want to argue with you about this. I can't change it now."

Rowan wipes a tear from her face. She's leaning on the wall now. "Get out!"

"What?" he asks.

"I don't believe a damn word you're telling me. I can't trust a thing that comes out of your mouth."

"You can't kick me out. Not now." Wyatt points outside. The news cameras are lined up, ready for fresh blood.

Rowan follows his gaze, seemingly unaware.

"The media. It will affect how much people back us if they see us fighting. We won't be the couple who lost their son. We'll be the couple falling apart *because* they lost their son." Wyatt takes a chance and steps forward. He places his palms on Rowan's shoulder. She stares at his hands like they've grown legs with stingers on the ends. "Let's not let that happen to us, Rowan. We have to remain strong for Landon."

She smacks his hands off her shoulders. "Don't you dare use him. Just grab your things, and leave. I don't care where you go. You don't have to tell the press either. Put your clothes in your gym bag if you're so worried."

"The press are already here, Rowan. I can't leave." He runs his fingers through his hair. "I'll sleep in the other room until we get past this. Think about what's best for Landon."

Her eyes are waspy, red daggers. "Fine. But I know you're lying to me about more than the kidney."

Rowan pushes past him. The hump of her belly rubs against his incision site. He yelps, but she doesn't seem to notice. And she's right.

He is lying about more than his missing kidney, but their missing son is much more important, so he'll dance in the gray as long as he has to.

TWENTY-FIVE
WYATT

The press will be ready for him in one hour.

Wyatt has one hour before he pleads to the press for his son's life. What will he say? What's enough of an offer to the hateful soul who took Landon to give him back? What's the right amount? What can he offer? He's never had much.

It isn't until Wyatt stands in Landon's empty room that the grief settles on his chest like a freight train barreling down, and he really thinks about where his son is at that moment. Who he's with. What they've done to him.

He's pinned beneath the rails, being around all Landon's things—his stuffed animals, a dinosaur, a teddy bear from Rowan's mother that Landon hates, but uses to bash against the dinosaur.

Ugh. Wyatt can envision Landon in there making crashing noises, his sweet, energized little boy.

Wyatt cries for the first time since it all happened.

His emotions were suspended.

He's been like that since a kid, his thoughts always present —who's watching? His mother? Rowan? He doesn't like to make people worry over him.

He's fighting for air now.

He and Rowan will get over what happened in Mexico City, but without Landon, there's not much left holding them together for the long haul.

It's so quiet in Landon's room, and it never is when he's there, and the silence is deafening. That's what got him into trouble in the first place. The quiet. Once he had a family he was never supposed to be alone again.

"Shit." He leans over his son's painted dresser, the one he stained himself before he was born, when Wyatt had so many questions of uncertainty.

How will I be a father when I never had one? What advice will I give my son so he ends up better than me?

Wyatt takes a good look in the mirror. He's not a good parent and he knows it. And the media will know it too.

He breathes in and out sporadically. He thinks about calling for Rowan. Worried he's having a panic attack, but then he remembers she hates him.

He needs to get into a better headspace so he can help his son.

Wyatt picks up a piece of Landon's laundry and presses it to his nose. "No..." He cries harder. The smell evokes Landon's scent, his Johnson and Johnson No More Tears shampoo they still use because he's incapable of staying still in the bath when they wash his hair.

"I hope you're giving them hell." Wyatt wipes his eyes. "If you're still alive," he squeaks. It's inevitable Landon's not. It's been too long. But if he is... "I need to get into a better place for you, Landon. To bring you home."

His father left him. But Wyatt's still here. And he'll remain there until he sees this through. No running this time.

Wyatt sucks in a deep breath, trying to level out. There's only one thing he can think of that might clear his head.

Wyatt drops down to Landon's ABC rug, crosses his legs, and retreats to his hillside.

It's windy on the mountaintop. At first, he can't see much. The sky isn't bright blue. The houses aren't decked with red roofs. It's too blurry, the cloud cover... or smog... makes it hard to see anything.

"Naomi!" he calls for her.

He needs to see her smiling face.

He likes to remember what it was like to be loved, for him.

Not for something somebody wanted him to be. When he was younger, he didn't need to produce a six-figure income to prove his worth. He was enough for the people around him, just being him.

Wyatt realizes now he hasn't felt truly loved since he left that mountainside. It's why he returns. It's imagined, but it's what his soul needs.

He's not used to it being cloudy here.

He doesn't understand why it's murky. His last time there ended dark and dreary too.

Finally, he sees her thin form appear out of the wispy clouds. Like an angel, her hair hangs long down her back in a glowing streak. Her skin is as clear as a doll's, smooth as a still body of water.

He waves his own hands in front of him, younger, less worn. She sits next to him and places her head on his shoulder. She doesn't say a word. He doesn't have any words for her either.

Finally, she whispers, the same words she typed to him via email earlier that year. "Sorry."

"Why?" he asks. These are the good times. They're supposed to be happy here.

"I can feel your pain. I'm sorry for it. I think everything will

be okay. It might take a little time. Give it time, Wyatt. Everything will be clearer soon." She waves her hand into the smog.

The sky splits open with lightning.

He's losing his place there. Losing her. He can't stay on this mountaintop for even a moment. His mind is trying to trick him, and there is no peace here either.

Thunder tears through the valley. A sound like broken glass shatters in his ear. Naomi stares at him, frightfully, then stands. "Remember what I said."

He opens his eyes, and the sharp sound is his wife. He jumps up on the carpet, stumbling around like a dog that's lost its footing.

"What're you doing, Wyatt?" Her expression is bewildered.

Wyatt shrinks away to the corner of the room. His heart hammers from the interruption, the intrusion on his one moment of peace. She's never caught him visiting the mountainside before, and now he feels exposed twice today. Rowan glares at him like he's been doing something vile, as if she caught him masturbating in the closet, and it's more than he can handle. "Meditating, all right. Sometimes when I'm really stressed, I do."

"Since when? Who are you?" She asked the same question earlier, and he's not sure anymore.

He used to be exactly who she told him he was for a long time. Wyatt Bishop, IT executive, proud father of Landon Bishop, adoring husband of Rowan Bishop of Bryn Mawr. But who is he now? "I'm just trying to hold it together, Rowan. Just like you."

"Well, you better wake up, because the press are ready for you!" She points at the window. He peeks through the blinds and sees all the cameras lined up. His heart pumps in his chest as he leans on the windowsill. He looks for his wife, to ask for encouragement, but when he turns his head back in her direction—she's gone.

She despises him for everything he hasn't revealed about his attack, but she'd be even more unmoored to learn that the place he goes to escape is an imaginary land on top of a mountaintop with another woman who he loved more than her.

TWENTY-SIX
ROWAN

She watches her husband take the podium, the press like a pack of wolves on the front lawn, ready to pounce. She only hopes one of them broadcasts something worthwhile, leading them to her son.

How much time do they have before the smugglers move Landon to his next destination? Rowan imagines her little boy in the back of a white van somewhere... right this minute.

Her vision goes hazy with rage.

Someone can still spot him.

Wyatt's right. *We need the press.*

We need them to like us.

She digs her fingernails into her forearm and pushes down the thought of being trapped with a man because she needs something from him. The same way her mother was bound to her father for so long. There's no way for her to be sure Wyatt hasn't lied to her about other things if he's not told her all the facts here. She just can't live like this... always wondering if her husband is telling her the truth.

Rowan leans into the windowsill, the drawn blinds nicking her cheek.

She wishes she could hear what he's saying.

She can see his mouth moving.

"Do you want me to open the window?" her mother asks. She returned an hour or so ago with groceries, but Rowan can barely look at her.

"No," Rowan says. She doesn't want the media to see her. What she's become.

It's not enough that the kidnapper returns Landon. Rowan wants to cause them physical harm too. Rip them limb from limb. Every missing-person show she's watched has the parent pleading, *just please return my child...*

And that's all that really matters, but Rowan's out for blood if they've touched a hair on Landon's head. Vengeance isn't an emotion she's all that familiar with, but it's consuming her now.

She's afraid the press will see it too.

Rowan holds onto her belly.

"Eat something. For the baby. Here." Her mother shoves a yogurt cup and spoon in her face. Rowan takes it and peels off the foil top. She wants to focus all her energy on Landon, but she can't neglect her other child. Rowan ladles some of the strawberry yogurt onto her spoon, barely tasting it as she plunges a dollop into her dry mouth.

Her belly growls in response.

Stress has destroyed her appetite, but she must remember to eat. She reminds herself she's blessed with another chance at being a mother if Landon is lost forever, but she doesn't know that she deserves one.

Her mother sets a sandwich down beside her on the kitchen table. June doesn't say a word. She knows better. She knows that Rowan's anger is directed at herself. For literally letting her child slip from her hands.

Rowan reluctantly picks up the sandwich, reminding herself that she can't punish her unborn baby for her mistakes. Even though she wants to.

She wishes she could starve herself and push her fingernails into her flesh until it bleeds, drink alcohol until she can't see straight, just so she can make the pain go away for a few minutes, but she can't.

How is she supposed to go on like this? Just waiting? This isn't living. It's waiting for someone to find her son's body so she can die too. Maybe they can keep her on life support until the baby is born, but there's no way she'll be able to go on knowing she's the one responsible for losing her child.

Rowan sees Wyatt retreating into the house, his forehead sweaty, his polo shirt wet. He hurriedly walks through the door and slams it behind him. Wyatt sees the two of them sitting at the table and he walks around to the side where Rowan is and pulls her into his arms. She lets him hug her, but she doesn't indulge in squeezing back. Only someone with a fully functioning heart could do that.

"What did you say?" she asks.

"I increased the reward. I begged. What else is there?"

She glances up at her husband—his eyes watery, his face pained, but she can't give him the comfort he needs. She doesn't trust him anymore. She doesn't trust herself either. "What questions did they ask?"

"They asked if there were any leads. I said, no."

"They're going to think they've won." Something inside her flames hot and angry.

Wyatt stares down at her long and hard and the only unspoken words she can read in his eyes are—*they have.*

Stone enters the house and Rowan tries to read her blank face. She's never seen the woman smile. "Mr. and Mrs. Bishop. We've had a couple of calls come in since you raised the reward, but they weren't credible leads, and I want you to be on guard that this could happen to you too."

Rowan sways to the side. Wyatt catches her. "What do you mean they weren't credible? What did they say?" he says.

"They claimed they saw Landon, and if we gave them the money, they'd tell us just where he was. Then, when we explained it doesn't work that way, they hung up. We tried to dangle money for a location, but they were obviously scammers."

"What about the horrible people who did take our son?" Rowan asks.

"We've got our team on it. It's a top priority," Stone assures.

"And? Anything?" Rowan asks.

Stone looks down at her worn black boots. "Not yet."

Panic races through Rowan's body. She feels the baby move. "Do you really have your team on it? How many people? What're they doing right this minute to find Landon? Be honest, have they given up? Has it slowed down?"

"Rowan—" Wyatt tries to temper her.

"No, Wyatt! We need to know these things! These are pivotal hours. Everyone lies!" she flips. June shoots her a worried look.

"We have a team of six to twelve. They're monitoring every form of mass transportation and facial recognition software available. Who's lied to you, Mrs. Bishop?"

Rowan pulls away from Wyatt. She looks between Wyatt and Stone and June, suddenly dizzy.

"Do you need to lie down, honey?" June grabs onto her shoulder.

"Answer the question, Mrs. Bishop. Who's lied to you?" Stone asks again.

"Wyatt!" She points at her husband. "He wasn't just attacked in Mexico City. They took his kidney." Her lips tremble as she says the words, so impossibly unbelievable.

Stone squints at Wyatt. "Is this true?"

Wyatt looks around, uncomfortable. "Yes. I don't see what difference it makes. Our focus should be on Landon. I'll be fine."

"And you don't know who did this to you?" Stone asks.

"It was a random attack," he says.

The tone of his voice is uncertain. He holds the same expression as when they found his passport and bloody bandages in the garbage can. For the first time Rowan wonders —was it an isolated incident?

Everything shifts in the entire room when Stone receives a call. Stone's face lights up and then flattens back to her normal grim expression. "I see. Thanks."

"What is it?" Rowan asks.

"We received a call from our tip line, but it was false. As I said before about the scammers, now that you upped the reward you may have people call you directly or try to contact you who just want the money. *Never* ever meet someone who claims they have your son. If you get a tip, you come straight to us."

TWENTY-SEVEN
THE DOCTOR

Marta watches the little boy play in her yard now.

He hauls a load of dirt with the toy front loader and then lets it fall out, rock by rock. Her sons used to love digging in the dirt too. Her boys gravitated toward it, the base of their soul, part earth.

Marta remembers when her sons were younger; simpler times. She was always busy with her work schedule. They lived in a smaller home in a busy, affluent neighborhood with tons of kids who bounced from house to house. Marta swears she fed the whole neighborhood as they scampered in and out, laughing and playing.

Back in the day, she let her boys run in the summertime—*be home before the street lights come on!*

It's hard to believe her biggest worry was what might've happened to them alone, at night, on the streets.

Now, one is dead, and the other is absent from her life. If her younger one could be free of her for good, she's sure he'd make that choice.

Her mother warned her this would happen.

When you marry a man who's not like us, it will poison the bloodline.

Her mother portended a much worse fate than Marta could've imagined.

Walker was on a business trip when Marta treated him in the hospital for an injury after a minor automobile accident. When he was being discharged, he asked her out to dinner, and she accepted, immediately taken with his confidence and charm —and the fact that he didn't share the machismo attitude of the other men she'd dated.

Marta's draw to her profession was the healer aspect. She loved being able to scan a chart and rule out ailments, qualify others. Each medical chart was a puzzle, each patient a new case for her to solve —to heal. It fascinated her much more than the fact that she was also a wealth generator. But all the men in her neighborhood saw were the dollar signs she was raking in, more abundant than their own.

Walker loved the fact she was a self-made, independent woman. His business took him to Mexico City frequently, and soon he decided to make it his home—with her.

Walker was never accepted by Marta's family, even when she decided to keep her maiden name, because her doctor's license was attached to it.

Her parents didn't attend the wedding, and when her first son, Damon, was born, they denied him their affection. Luckily, Walker's parents were more welcoming, but they lived far away in Austin, Texas.

Marta lives on a private estate now—a compound, really. No one will find her tucked up on the Bosque de Las Lomas hillside. Her home is barricaded by walls and gates, a security guard always on staff.

All the money and security in the world couldn't save her from the worst curse her mother bestowed upon her, though— the poison.

The men in her family—the exception being her youngest who somehow bypassed the awful fate—carried a terrible genetic disorder.

Her mother told her Walker would poison her bloodline. After his diagnosis and then Damon's, she sometimes wondered if her mother was right. If the genetic plague that had fallen over their family was somehow her fault.

And when Damon stopped running through the safe streets of their neighborhood and frequented the streets of Tepito instead, picking up a lot more than a bargain at the open-air market, she really questioned her decisions.

They kicked him out after Marta and Walker found the needles.

He didn't return until he was in kidney failure, but the hospital wouldn't put him on an urgent transplant list because of his drug use.

Other candidates who didn't abuse their bodies were bumped ahead of him, despite Marta's connections. She knows she did everything she could for him. They all did. It wasn't enough.

She continues to watch the curious little boy in his surroundings.

Children amaze her, always have. Their innocence is intoxicating, a fresh slate to mold and teach. The boy has built up the rocks into a grand pile, a carefully orchestrated wigwam with sticks in the grooves to hold it together.

He lifts the toy truck in the air.

She walks closer. "Why don't you leave it? You've worked so hard on it," Marta says.

He looks her right in the eye as he thrashes the truck into the center, the pieces crashing to the ground. "You sound just like my mom. When am I going to see her? This tour is lasting... days," he says, confused. "That lady had the painted flute

Dad picked out, and I went with her, and I haven't seen Mom since."

"I have a story to tell you, and then maybe you'll understand," Marta says, sadly. She wonders how long she can lie to him before he begins to act out. Alistair is at the market now buying him a few outfits, a toothbrush, a night light he requested. Alistair asked if they needed all these things for his short stay. She told him he asks too many questions.

Marta pats the space beside her on the wooden bench.

The boy wipes his hands on his legs and sits next to Marta beneath an old weeping fig tree, its trunk a conglomerate of thick branches that wind together until they reach the top. Its plume is like a springy floret of broccoli that shields the unforgiving sun. It's the type of tree made for telling stories.

Marta's thought long and hard about this one. "This fairytale is one of my favorites, called 'The Bear Prince'," she says. Although, hers will have a bit of a twisted version she hopes he understands.

"Okay." She has his full attention now. Landon squints up at her, his cheeks streaked pink. She'll need to remember sunscreen next time.

"Once upon a time, there was a very poor woodcutter who had three beautiful daughters. Of the three daughters, the youngest was the least well behaved." Marta smirks, because in the real tale the youngest was the most beautiful, but she's telling her own version here. The one that will make the most sense to Landon.

"A woodcutter..." Landon follows.

"That's right. He chops wood for a living, and doesn't make a lot of money."

"My parents always fight about money," he says.

"Right. Like the woodcutter. One day a bear sneaks up on him and is upset he's cutting wood in his forest. He says he's been stealing his wood and now he must pay the price. The bear would like one of the woodcutter's daughters."

Landon's face pinches in fear.

"And you know which one he offered, right?" Marta asks.

"The bad one."

"That's right. You're a smart boy," Marta says.

She watches as Landon processes her fairytale. He seems wise beyond his years, which is helpful in this scenario, but may cause challenges later.

"So, where is Mom?"

"Your mom needed money too. Like you said, she was always arguing with your father. You were acting up at the museum, ran off, really..."

Landon looks down at his tennis shoes. "So, she traded me for money because I was bad?"

"That's right. But we're not so bad here, are we? Certainly better than the bear."

Landon turns his head left to right, his eyes bouncing over the acres of land, the trees, the mountains in the distance, and then back at Marta. "How does the story end? Does the daughter ever go back to her family?"

"We'll finish the story another day. It's important that you follow the rules here. Why don't you go inside and wash up for dinner?"

Landon nods, fearfully, hops off the bench, and runs inside. Marta doesn't know what to tell him about the ending of the story, because she's not sure how this one will wrap up either.

TWENTY-EIGHT

WYATT

On his way to the office, Wyatt receives a curt email from Irina to his personal email letting him know the company has decided to cut its losses and fold. He won't be receiving his final paycheck or refund check for his trip to Mexico. It won't come close to covering his signing bonus, but she said she won't sue for the rest, being that he's in breach of contract and all.

Thanks a lot.

She says nothing about his son.

Landon's picture is all over the news. The police have released an additional video that shows the woman leaving the facility with Landon, but then it cuts off and they're lost around the corner. It's inconclusive, but the video bothers Wyatt for some reason, and he can't put his finger on it.

Since he has no job to return to, he pulls over and replays the video. It's hard to see his son vanish around a corner, lost forever. But something catches his attention. The woman looks at the camera, mask still on her face.

It's her eyes that grab Wyatt—and the arched eyebrows that rest above them. *Esme?*

Post-panic mode, and Wyatt still doesn't know what to believe.

Are his eyes playing tricks on him? Did he see that woman from the bar because he wanted to? Or is it someone who closely resembles her? What would Esme be doing all the way over here, anyway?

He pushes his hand over his face. This doesn't make sense. He should tell Stone, but he can't be sure that it's Esme. He plays the video again, and he's not certain. His memory of Esme is fuzzy.

If he tells Stone about his hunch, it'll most likely be false lead—one that will steer them further away from finding Landon, and brand him as the cheating husband whose psychotic one-night stand kidnapped his child. His wife will divorce him, and the public will hate him. And what about the new baby?

He scrolls through his contact list looking for an answer.

Everyone he's ever met has sent him a message on social media or to his personal phone with notes of sympathy and encouragement. His mother asked if he needed her to come over, but he informed her that June is there, and they're okay for now. His mother replied that she'll pray for them and to let her know how she can help.

She was never one to deal with the heavy stuff.

Yes, Mom, I'll be fine home by myself a few more hours. Don't worry about dinner. Make your money.

Even though strange men hung on the outside railings of their apartment drinking bottles out of brown paper bags, their silhouettes vertical shadows on the living room wall like a silent movie.

There was one—a man wearing a top hat who skittered up and down the wall, jangly, like he was being manipulated by a marionette. Death metal blared from a radio matching the rhythm of his flailing arms.

His limbs swiped around like he was painting Wyatt's apartment with his fingers, long and sharp like knives. Wyatt pulled the blinds closed tighter, shabby and thin, but it didn't keep them out—the shadows or the fear.

It was better his mother didn't know the truth. That way, she could work instead of worry. Just like it was better Rowan didn't know everything either. The only problem now was that he wasn't sure if the shadows he saw on the police station's video screen were real or imagined.

The cool leather of the car seats creak as Wyatt leans back. How can he go back to his wife and tell her he just lost his job? He sits there for a minute, marinating in silence. He can practically feel the bills piling up on his lap, weighing him down. He's tempted to call his insurance company and ask about what uninsured costs he should anticipate from them, but he's too afraid to find out.

Pretending everything is okay... for one sacred moment.

He had so much quiet when he was younger. Too much.

He'd turn on the TV just so he didn't have to hear the refrigerator buzz, and when the television couldn't drown out the sound or his loneliness, he'd sneak out to the water's edge.

Sometimes he'd jump in, even though it was dangerous. Even though he promised his mother he'd never swim in the ocean alone, and especially at night. She made promises she didn't keep, too, though.

On those nights Wyatt played in the water, he let the black swells lap over his head, push him upside down, carry him too far out to sea. Sometimes the ocean would have its way with him, but he always made it back to shore, the white foam spitting him out at the end of the night like he was too much to carry.

He'd leave his night swim feeling sated and victorious as

though he'd conquered the world. It was a secret no one knew, but even if they'd found out, he wasn't sure who'd care.

His mother was his only family, but every year he lost her a little more. He was most afraid she'd die before he made it through high school, and then what? His friend, Marco, cared too, but he had a real family who didn't let him swim in the ocean at night; the kind who would send a search party out if he did.

If Wyatt could fight the waves and win, even if he swallowed a belly full of saltwater, even if he scraped his feet with coral and other unidentified sea shrapnel, those shady figures hanging off the motel railing were no match for him.

And nothing else was, either.

Wyatt would strut right past the men on his way back, drinking, smoking—and sometimes they'd say shitty things about the kid, soaking wet, prowling around way past his bedtime, and sometimes they wouldn't. But after Wyatt returned to his apartment, he wasn't afraid anymore—of anything... the men, or how his mother would pay rent that month, or when they'd eat their next meal, because in that moment he was capable of facing whatever was thrown at him.

Wyatt wishes *this* was like *that*.

He's looking for somewhere he can go to make his world clearer. He can't be sure the person he saw on that monitor was the same woman or a ghost he imagined. When he reviewed the video again, he made eye contact with the woman, and he could've sworn it was *her*.

His stomach filled with cement. His blood sunk with extra gravity as it plummeted to his toes, so sick he almost threw up.

How could Wyatt possibly tell Rowan about his suspicions? *I know the woman who took our child.* Rowan's health has already suffered since Landon went missing. Telling her about Esme will instigate a rapid decline, and he needs to think about the baby.

It's obscene. He can't know the kidnapper. But that woman looked right at the camera like she wanted him to see her. Like she was taunting Wyatt.

The facemask made it impossible for the facial recognition software to detect her, and she probably knew that. It's the precise reason she likely wore it in the first place. Then again, the image is so grainy, how could he possibly think he recognizes her?

He must be going mad.

The thought makes him want to dive into the ocean and never come out.

Because what type of human could be so awful?

The more minutes that pass, the more Wyatt is sure that he imagined the woman was Esme. What're the chances, really?

Wyatt's foot is pressed firmly to the brake to start his Highlander, but still, he does not turn on the ignition. Where is he going? Where is he to look for Landon?

He exhales and pushes his head into the back of the seat.

His cell rings.

Rowan?

He bolts up, alert, but it's not Rowan.

"Hey, Marco," Wyatt says.

"Jesus, man. Is it true? Is Landon missing?" Marco sounds out of breath, like he just ran up a flight of stairs.

"It is. I'm looking for him now," Wyatt lies. The fact that he doesn't know where to go or what to do is one of the hardest things about this whole situation.

"Oh my god. Do they have any leads?" Marco asks.

"A woman took him from the Independence Visitor Center. Right under Rowan's nose. They caught it on camera, but the woman was wearing a mask, and the facial recognition software can't detect her. The police think she was working in a team. Handed him off to someone else."

Marco is silent for a beat which makes Wyatt clench and

squirm because the only time Marco is quiet is when he's sleeping. "I'm so sorry, Wyatt. What can I do?"

Wyatt's skin erupts with chills when his best friend says "sorry" because people only say that when someone has died, and Wyatt knows that's what he's thinking.

His little boy is dead.

"I may eventually need a place to stay." Wyatt's mind is spinning, because if they find Landon dead, Wyatt will have to tell Rowan about Esme. It will destroy him if he doesn't. And then he will no longer be able to stay in the beautiful, renovated farmhouse he bought just for her.

When Rowan told him she wanted to buy the house and fill it with family, Wyatt agreed. She knew how to sell him on the property. And now it seemed, once again, he'll end up all by himself.

"Of course, but—why?"

"I don't think Rowan and me will make it through this one if they don't find him in one piece." Wyatt's voice finally breaks. Panic sets in like a serrated knife slicing his chest. He pats his throbbing heart.

He should tell Marco what happened in Mexico City.

He wouldn't judge him. Marco would keep his secrets.

But Wyatt doesn't understand how his attack and Landon's kidnapping could be connected.

Esme already took a piece of him. Why would she come back to take what was left?

"Don't say that, man. You'll get through this. Do you want me to drive up? I'll bag my shift. We'll walk the streets all night, looking for him."

"No, don't do that. It's chaos right now. The press are camped on my lawn." Wyatt looks around helplessly, at all the city streets he hasn't walked. He's such a liar. He doesn't deserve the things he has. Maybe that's why they've been taken from him. "The cops said all mass transit is on high alert. If it's an organized crime group, he'll be kept alive, for a while." Wyatt coughs. "Landon can't go undetected. Someone has to have seen him. We're depending on strangers for help. We put out a reward, and lots are motivated to find him."

Wyatt can't put his best friend up right now, not with Rowan in an awful state, and June and the press there. And he knows Marco can't afford a hotel.

"All right. Well, if you need me, you call me, you hear? I won't be sleeping anyway until they find him. Lando..." His voice breaks too. "Ugh. I can't imagine what this must be like for you."

Wyatt hears someone hollering for Marco in the background. Life would've been so much easier if he'd just stayed at the shore with his friend. Lived carefree.

But he decided to try college. And then he attempted to date a girl seriously. And before he knew it, he was in it—the whole shebang. Marriage and diapers and responsibilities. As much as he misses his son, he wonders now if he would've made different choices if he had to do it all again.

"I'll let you know, brother. Thanks," Wyatt says.

He ends the call and slips the phone into his pocket.

Exhaling, he opens the car door. The air is dewy and thick. The street lights cast a light fog over the city—still he looks out, hoping to spot a ghost.

Then, he receives a message from Stone.

Stone: *There's been a potential break in the case. Can you come home?*

TWENTY-NINE

WYATT

Wyatt was excited to receive an invitation to return home, but when he got there and saw Stone and Schrader's disgruntled expressions, he knew something was horribly wrong.

"What is it?" he asks.

He takes a seat beside his wife, who looks absolutely haggard.

She avoids eye contact, still angry with him. June's lips form a straight line of disapproval, and he wonders what he's done now.

"Have you been making it to your doctor's appointments?" he asks Rowan. It would be an unparalleled tragedy if they lost the baby too.

Rowan nods affirmatively, but won't engage him.

"Mr. Bishop, the hospital where you were treated in Mexico City is under investigation. After you told me about your attack, I made some phone calls, and your incident is linked to a case the CIA has been investigating for some time."

"What does that mean, exactly?" Wyatt asks.

"Tell them more about what was said to you. Before you were drugged. At the hotel bar," Rowan says.

"I don't remember." He already gave that statement and he needs to stick to it.

"Who did you talk to before you... blacked out?" Stone asks.

Without thinking, he says, "No one."

"Mr. Bishop, we pulled the receipts from your credit card."

The bill I'll have to pay out of pocket.

"Okay..." he says.

"How many drinks did you have before you woke up in that hotel room?"

"One," he says.

"We pulled the receipt. There are two drinks on your bill."

Uh oh. Wyatt shifts in his seat. He knows where they're going with this now and he doesn't like it. But how much do they really know? "Maybe I had two."

Rowan throws him a death stare. She knows what two drinks mean. Hell, she drove over an hour to Atlantic City when he'd once merely shared someone's dessert. What would she do when she heard he had cocktails with an attractive woman?

"Mr. Bishop, we're going to be frank. These cases have occurred all over the world where a vital organ was taken after an encounter: most of the victims were male, and almost all were seduced by a female lure."

Oh Christ. It's over. That word—*seduced*.

Rowan will leave me based on that word alone.

There's also no point lying anymore. His medical record at the hospital may be in a sealed cabinet, but he couldn't have predicted they'd look at his credit card receipt.

"Tell the truth, Wyatt! They think it might have something to do with Landon. You piece of shit," Rowan says, voice defeated.

Stone flinches at her response.

"I don't understand," Wyatt says, but that's not true. He

does think he understands after reviewing that video footage, and he hopes he's wrong.

"Can you answer the question about the female party, Wyatt, so we know if the dots are connected? If your case is linked with the others?" Schrader asks.

"Yes... okay."

"I knew it!" Rowan yells. "You asshole. You cheated on me with this woman?"

"I—I don't think so. I woke up and I was bleeding."

"You don't think so!" Rowan stands above him, screaming at the top of her lungs.

"Don't upset yourself, dear. Think of the baby. Calm down." June tries to grab Rowan's arm, but she pushes her away. "Oh you, probably love this!" she says to her mother.

June looks horrified. "What? How can you say that?"

Rowan doesn't answer, just clenches her fists and shakes, like a little volcano ready to erupt. "Tell us the rest of the story, Wyatt. Every second you wait delays our chances of finding our son."

"Um... she befriended me at the elevator and told me she was going to the rooftop bar."

"You met her at the hotel?" Stone says as she writes in her notepad.

"Yes."

"And nothing strange happened before that? No one followed you? Greeted you oddly?"

"No. She definitely spotted me by the elevator."

"Can you describe the woman? What did she look like?"

Wyatt feels like he's under fire. He chooses his words carefully with Rowan still observing him from a standing position while he withers beneath her searing gaze. "She was average height, long, dark hair. Dark eyes."

"Did she tell you her name?" Schrader asks.

"Yes. Esme."

Stone sighs. "They're all named Esme."

"Do the other Esmes sleep with their victims?" Rowan asks.

The answer doesn't matter. Rowan's already assumed that Wyatt has cheated on her, and that will be her truth.

"We don't know," Schrader says.

"Try to think of anything she said that might be helpful," Stone says.

"She just said she was there on business. She had no kids or family. She told me we could see a better view from her room—"

Rowan makes her clucking noise. "You're such an idiot. Some loser beachboy from Wildwood. Should've never married you."

"*Rowan*. Not helping," June says.

"I—I told her I didn't want to go to her room. That I was hungry. And then I got woozy and she said I drank my drink too fast." Reliving the moment is excruciating but admitting it out loud is freeing too.

"She said you drank it too fast?" Stone clarifies. "So, the drugs probably hit faster than intended."

"Yes, I could barely walk. She had to help me." He glances at Rowan. "Nothing could have happened between us."

Rowan won't look at him.

The words hang in the air.

Schrader says, "These organs are brokered on the dark web. The CIA may have a link to this case that will help them crack this awful organization. It's great they're getting involved. We'll have more people looking for Landon that way."

"What're you talking about? Dark web?" Wyatt asks. He tries to ignore Rowan. He's accepted that their marriage is over at this point. He did everything he could to save it, withheld what he could, as long as he could. He already feels the deadly quiet of his childhood enveloping him once more.

"The organ harvesting organization posts their buyers' request on the dark web. The Network, that's what it's called.

The buyer is usually desperate for an organ by the time they've found the Network, and they're able to negotiate a hefty price, and transfer."

"Organ... trafficking?" Wyatt asks.

"That's right. We're sometimes able to break the code for the dark net and see the requests, but they constantly change it and it's been impossible to trace. There was a post for a patient with a rare disease in need of a kidney a few months ago. This patient likely would have a difficult time finding a match the traditional way, depending on the disease. They may have to do additional testing beyond a blood test to find a proper candidate. What's odd is that we had a request more recently for the same thing—but it was for a child."

"And? What does this have to do with Landon?" Rowan asks. "He's perfectly healthy."

Stone answers, "We think, but are not sure, that the afflicted parties may have a genetic disease and are related. A father and son, maybe. And that, if the donor successfully accepted Wyatt's kidney, they may have come to the United Stated to secure a kidney for the child in need."

"Oh my god." Rowan gasps out loud, holding onto the counter for support. Wyatt's fairly sure it's the only thing keeping her on her feet. "Are you saying... it was planned? That not only was the kidnapping planned, but they specifically targeted Landon? Because he's Wyatt's son?" Rowan asks.

"We think, but are not sure," Stone says.

Rowan launches herself across the room at Wyatt. She swats wildly at him with her fists. He places his hands up, but it doesn't stop her. She smacks his head, his ears, pulls at his hair.

"You piece of shit! I thought this was my fault. I thought it was my fault he was taken. It was you. You did this!" She cries.

Schrader and Stone are on their feet now, holding Rowan back.

"You should leave, Wyatt," June says harshly. She stands, trying to calm her unhinged daughter.

"I had no idea..." Wyatt tries to defend himself.

"You need to leave!" June shouts. The cops nod at him to do as his mother-in-law asks. He takes off for the door, devastated, because Rowan is right. This truly is all his fault.

THIRTY

FRANCISCO

He shouldn't stay in Florida.

Francisco gave up on the prospect of having true human connections of substance with anyone, but he'd never forgive himself if something happened to Lola or Nico.

He's hurt a lot of people.

He's helped a lot, too, he tries to tell himself. The recipients of his labors have survived whereas they might've lived miserably on dialysis, or died on some endless donor list somewhere if he hadn't intervened.

It's hard to believe the two people he loves most have been spared.

The easiest way to destroy Francisco would be if the Network went after Lola or Nico. That's why he's never told anyone about them. All he has to do is walk the line—take his assignments and his money—keep quiet.

But Francisco's not able to take the next job offered, and he knows his own safety is threatened now. If he's to be killed, is it so awful to ask for a few uninterrupted minutes to watch his son play ball?

Francisco parks his vehicle outside the fence that circles the baseball diamond. He can watch the game from his car. He texted Lola for Nico's baseball schedule this week, and when she asked him if he was coming, he said he wasn't sure.

Lola sits in the bleachers with a man in a muscle shirt, hat backwards, bad tattoos, a complete douchebag. Francisco hopes he at least has some money.

She must see him parked, but she knows the rules. She can't approach him in public.

He has the air conditioning cranked on in his Porsche, and he sips water as he watches the little leaguers take the field. His son is a third baseman, and Francisco has a good view of him as he takes position.

Tall, like Francisco, even for a kid, Nico crouches with his glove—in it to win it. Francisco smiles sadly. He's clearly competitive. Good, that trait will serve him well.

Francisco's heart swells at the lost life in his front view. He could be the one sitting next to Lola in the stands. Instead, there's some dude in work boots and a nasty shirt that exposes his armpits, grabbing her knee.

There's no reason Francisco should be at the baseball field, putting them all in danger, but his latest assigned case has him thinking more about the child he left behind—and the one he killed.

2019

Francisco reaches the assigned location and is distraught to find a little boy on the makeshift operating table. He's been drugged or gassed like the others.

"What is this?" he asks his team, which consists of an anesthesiologist and a nurse.

"This is our mark," the female doctor says.

"Why didn't anyone inform me it was a child? I don't do children. I've never operated on one before. There're different risks involved. Protocols I'm not familiar with..."

The nurse is already placing gloves on his hands. "You know we only have so much time, Dr. Zo. Let's go. It's an order from the Network."

Francisco shakes his head, but there're IVs being placed in the child's arm at record speed. He's handed a scalpel.

There's no way out.

There never has been since the day he signed up for this job. It's not just himself he worries about. It's his mother and father too. The Network will go after them if he doesn't complete his assignment.

But not before they've killed him first.

Francisco makes the incision in the boy's left side, just below his ribs.

Immediately, he notes a problem. He has to clamp the renal artery, but the clamp provided is too large. They sent an adult clamp for a pediatric procedure. "The clamp is too big," Francisco says.

The other doctor hands him a rubber band. "Use this to help. You don't need to clamp it for long, just until we can get the organ out."

He gapes at her in a state of panic. Francisco's worked with Heidi before. She's no nonsense and ruthless, and in this case, impractical.

"I don't feel comfortable with that. They should've disclosed this patient's age."

"We are on the clock," Heidi says, making him fully aware this procedure needs to be completed before the boy wakes up.

With an open patient on the table, Francisco does as Heidi suggests.

He carefully extracts the kidney, but the clamp must've come loose, because the boy begins to hemorrhage.

Francisco will never forget how the monitor screamed, and never stopped.

They tried to stop the bleeding, but with few supplies, the boy bled out right on the table. And Francisco couldn't do anything to stop it. He let it happen once.

He won't let it happen again.

THIRTY-ONE

ROWAN

Rowan rocks in place on her couch. Her little sister has appeared.

She's never gotten along with Riley, much too passive for Rowan's liking. They're polar opposites, really.

Her brothers both sent text messages and left voicemails, but they live too far away for Rowan to return them—or care. They basically disowned her when she was a teenager, anyway.

"Amir works for a cyber security company. Maybe I can have him hack this dark web," Riley says. She's a contractor for the government. Rowan doesn't know which agency this time, Riley changes jobs so often. She lives in DC with her boyfriend, Amir, who she has no intention of marrying.

Rowan's upbringing made Riley long for what she never had, whereas Riley's made her steer completely away from the nuclear family.

"Don't you think the government will frown on Amir using his clearances that way?"

"I don't know, Rowan. I'm just trying to help."

"It sounds like they're trying to track these people using the donor database—those in need. Find the sick patient or patients, find Landon," June says.

"They've probably already taken what they need from him." Rowan's voice quivers, aghast at all the dangers children face in this world.

She could never have imagined this was one of them. "I can't believe Wyatt could've been so stupid. I mean, he's always been clueless, but this is..."

"A tragedy," Riley finishes.

"Let's not forget he's a victim too." June rises to rinse empty cups and plates and places them in the dishwasher.

"You can't say that, Mom. I know how you like to stick up for cheating men, but you cannot this time. At least Dad's girlfriends never got any of us killed."

She wants to annihilate Wyatt. Murder. All her thoughts of bludgeoning the kidnapper have been transposed to him. She couldn't despise him more.

"It's awful that this has happened to your family," June says. "We know Wyatt would do anything to change his course of action."

"And now he has to live with what he's done," Riley says. "A fate worse than death."

"Who knows if he even slept with that woman, Rowan? The types of drugs they gave him make it difficult for men to perform." Mother always has to pull out her nursing card, but it doesn't help in this case.

"It's not whether he did or did not, the intent was clear," Rowan says. "It doesn't matter... now. My son is gone. All because my husband can't stay at a job long enough to let the ink dry on his contract. He's so impulsive. It's our downfall."

"It's what made you fall in love with him." Riley is on her feet now, eyes out the window.

"What?" Rowan says. "No, it's not."

"You're so careful. You've had to be," June says. "And Wyatt is adventurous. I wouldn't condemn him for the same things that made you fall in love with him. I'm sure he didn't mean to follow that woman back to her room. It sounds like he was coerced."

Rowan can feel an old familiar anger light her up inside. "Mother, maybe it's time you go home. I understand you forgave your cheating husband time and time again, but when you ask me to do the same it makes me want to rip out your hair."

Riley exchanges a terrified look with her mother. "Fine! I won't mention it. Let's get you to the doctor to check out the baby, no?"

"My appointment is tomorrow."

"Can I come?" June asks. "I'm concerned about the effect all this has had on your health."

"No, I'm fine." Rowan just felt the baby move this morning, but she couldn't enjoy it. The child is going to be born into a broken home with a depressed grieving mother and an absent father. Wyatt will never lay a hand on this baby, cause it harm like the first. It's the only thing keeping her going at this point.

Riley receives a text message. "Amir says that the CIA is most likely trying to track the sick patients through a database called IRODaT. The International Registry on Organ Donation and Transplantation. Most of the patients try to attain an organ legally first. If there's a son and a father with the same genetic defect, they'll be trying to track them that way."

Rowan shakes her head. "It's been days... They left Wyatt in a bath of ice. Where did they leave Landon? We're running out of time!"

"Amir's trying to research it. Can you find out what kind of genetic mutation or specific disease they're looking for? Ask the police to disclose the information. You have a right to know."

"He's just a child..." Rowan mumbles. She still feels so guilty. If Landon was targeted, it would be hard to avoid the abductor, but her job was to keep him safe from outside predators.

"The saving grace is that they let Wyatt live. They don't kill their victims," June says.

"Ah!" Rowan shouts. "This is so sick. Wait until the press gets hold of this information."

"Don't tell them this part. They'll sensationalize it," Riley says.

"I understand that. But they're going to find out," Rowan says.

"Could it help your cause? Maybe someone knows something about this network," June says.

"I don't think that's a good idea," Rowan says.

"Me either," says Riley. "Has anyone called the tip line?"

"All false leads and people just looking to get the reward money. One man said he could tell me what he knows, but I have to meet him in a dark alley in Kensington." Rowan clucks. "I didn't think the world could get anymore terrible."

"Speaking of reward money... Dad wanted to know if..."

"No. No solid leads. He won't have to give up his money yet," Rowan says. Although she was led to believe the precinct or the government would front some, if not all, if it ever came down to it.

June appears taken aback that she's spoken to her father. It wasn't a decision she came to lightly.

"He'll do anything to get on speaking terms with you again. He feels awful about Landon. He said he didn't even get to meet him," Riley says.

"Well, tell him thanks for offering the money, and I'm sorry he won't get to meet him either." Rowan's pained she had to ask him to front the other half of the reward money, if needed.

She places her face in her hands thinking about all the men in in her life who've paid dearly for their mistakes and the ones who haven't paid nearly enough.

THIRTY-TWO
WYATT

Marco's couch is sticky, and Wyatt doesn't want to ask why, but his apartment is a safe haven, so that's where he'll stay.

"I know a PI in Jersey City. He might be able to crack this thing," Marco says.

One certainty Wyatt can count on where Marco is concerned—he's half full of shit. He probably knows a PI, but not one that has connections to finding his son. His PI is probably one of his regulars who drinks too much and solves very few of the cases he takes.

"The CIA are on it, Marco. But thanks."

They're having beers in Marco's two-bedroom apartment, the one Marco's had in Wildwood since his twenties. Everything about Wyatt's return home seems like one giant step backward, but there's relief in his failure.

He no longer has to try to be something he's not.

He's lost his family and returned home with his tail between his legs, a fear he worried might become a reality when Rowan figured out he wasn't cut out to the play the lead in her fantasy life.

"The government doesn't always want you to know what they know, man."

Wyatt wants to tell him to cut the shit, but he's short on allies right now. "Landon is a handful. Temper..."

"Where does he get it from?" Marco asks, and Wyatt knows he's just distracting him by asking the question. Anything but talking about the grim reality that traffickers have his son.

"His mother has a terrible temper. Violent. She knocked a girl's tooth out in high school," Wyatt says.

Marco bites his fist. "Damn."

"She always tries to blame Landon's demeanor on the fact he's a boy, but I think he runs hot because of her. He's like Rowan, plus testosterone." Wyatt smiles and then lets it slip right off his face. He talks about these players in his life like they're still here.

"They're going to find him, Wyatt. His picture is all over the news. Someone will see it."

Wyatt sulks. "It's just... the way I was attacked and left in that bathtub of ice. If they leave Landon somewhere to find his way back..."

"Hey, don't talk like that. I did some studying up on this black market and most of the people receiving donations are from third world countries who can't source the organs themselves. That's why there's a market for it in the first place. So, the recipient is likely not in the US. Which means they're probably transporting Landon overseas."

Wyatt shakes his head at this information. "What does that mean?"

Marco answers. "There's still time to find him. It's probably hard getting him out of the country unseen and they'll need him healthy at the time of surgery."

Wyatt puzzles on this information. Marco is equal parts genius and bullshit, and Wyatt's become an expert at sifting through the garbage for the pearls. "Why couldn't they just perform the operation here and transport the organ. On ice, or whatever?"

That's the scenario Wyatt painted for himself when he processed the devastating information Detective Stone shared, and after he came to the horrible revelation that all his recent nightmares were connected.

He's tried to take the emotion out of it for Landon's sake. To keep a clear head, but it's been hard. If only he would've revealed what really happened sooner in Mexico City, the police could've gotten a jump on the investigation. It's a mistake that will haunt him for the rest of his life.

Marco shakes his head. "A kidney can only survive twenty-four to thirty-six hours on ice. If the patient was international, that would take too long, with prep and everything. They wouldn't risk a delay of any sort, and the patient has to be ready on the receiving end too."

Marco's wrong. These guys weren't performing regulation surgeries. They're human chop shops. If they cut his little boy two days ago and flew it overseas, say an eight-hour flight, it would be all said and done by now. And would they really fly him to a foreign country? If that's true, then any hope of ever finding Landon seems to evaporate. Wyatt just assumed he was still in the United States. If anything, this information crushes him with devastation, not relief.

"Where're these surgeries taking place? Someone has to have seen something," Wyatt says desperately. But as the words tumble out of his mouth and his friend humors him with an expression of sympathy, they both know international trafficking of all kinds exists, and just how sick and depraved the outcome can be.

"Organ harvesting wasn't even illegal in China until this year," Marco says. "They just changed the policy recently."

"How can that be?"

Marco shrugs. "It's a problem. They take prisoners' organs

against their will. The country is overpopulated. A lot of people in need, not enough supply."

Wyatt shakes his head at this information. "Landon is a difficult child. I can't see them..." He can't speak the rest out loud. There's no reason they'd keep him alive or bring him home if he gave them a hard time. They'd take what they wanted and get rid of him.

"I don't think that's the goal. Don't go there, man. You need to stay up, for him. We need to regroup, figure out a strategy."

"I don't know what else to do."

"It sounds like the CIA has a good lead. They've got to be able to track down this father and son combo with the same genetic disease. There's probably a database."

"Why do they even want mine? And his? I don't understand any of this," he says.

"These people do not want to kill your son. That will prompt an investigation. Make their organization more visible."

Wyatt stares long and hard at his friend, a fast talker, a professional wordsmith as a career bartender. But now, more than at any other time in his entire life, he prays Marco is telling the truth.

THIRTY-THREE
ROWAN

Rowan leaves her doctor's appointment with a set of health orders. She's dehydrated and her blood pressure is a little high—Ha. They should've tested her yesterday when she found out someone stole her child with the intention of extracting his organ. Rowan's surprised she even made it to her appointment today. The new baby is the only thing keeping her going.

Something as simple as taking a prenatal vitamin. Drinking a glass of water. These small tasks are keeping her alive, because she must stay healthy for her other child—the one growing inside of her.

If she makes it through this, it will be the baby that gave her strength.

She needs to double her fluid intake, but other than that, she and the baby are fine. *Fine.*

The doctor told her to make sure to get some rest.

Rowan gave the female physician a death stare—because what pregnant woman can sleep with her other child missing? The doctor looked back to the patient chart and said, "Right... I hope they find your son, Rowan."

The doctor leaves swiftly, because no one wants to breathe

in the torment of a woman with a missing child. The unknown overcomes the atmosphere, suffocating anyone in its presence. To be near it is to embody it, feel the inevitable loss of what hasn't been made official yet.

No one understands what to say to comfort her. It's not like they can tell her *time will heal all wounds*, because this one is still fresh—open—with no prospect of closure.

Rowan walks alone, realizing this is her new reality—just her and her unborn child. What did she do to deserve this? All she wanted was a normal family. A good life.

She'll never come to grips with losing Landon, but now that she knows what they plan to do with him, she can't imagine they'll spare his life.

Why would they?

He's a child who can't fend for himself. If they leave him alone in a medically compromised state, he won't survive. And even worse, he'll suffer first. Rowan lets out a sharp squeak, trying to maintain her sanity.

She holds onto the hallway railing of the hospital.

Even though his kidnapping isn't her fault, she still can't believe she unleashed Landon into the claws of such evil. She imagines it, the way her fingers uncoiled from his so she could pick up the phone call. He slipped right out of her grasp. Landon may have been targeted, but she let it happen. The guilt still gnaws at her.

The anger comes next, the two emotions oscillating inside of her in a tumultuous dance.

It's hard to direct her anger anywhere other than her husband.

She hasn't had time to think about life alone, as a single mother with two small children. It's too much dealing with a marriage split and a missing child at the same time. Even she knows that. Rowan secretly hopes Wyatt will hang on until after the baby is born, but she'd never tell him that.

She worries she'll find a lead and won't be physically capable enough to chase down the kidnappers—and murder them.

Because God help her, if she finds them, there will be no mercy.

Her mission this morning wasn't entirely devoted to her prenatal appointment. Her next visit is with a different kind of specialist, and she only hopes that he'll be kind to her. The police and CIA aren't moving fast enough.

It's impossible to sit around and wait for information knowing her little boy is out there, possibly injured. And he needs her.

She enters the nephrology office and is greeted by the receptionist.

"Appointment for Rowan Bishop," she says. Maybe the woman won't recognize her from the news. It's something she has to worry about now. A customer at the local pharmacy broke down and started crying when she identified her. Rowan didn't have the energy to comfort her. She strode quickly away with her medication, leaving the woman in tatters.

It doesn't matter anyway. The whole world can cry a river of tears, but it won't bring her son back.

After gathering her information, the receptionist asks Rowan to have a seat, and all she can do is think about what she's going to say to this man. A patient appointment was the quickest way to talk to a professional about kidney health and this physician had an opening. She'd called everyone in town for a next-day appointment and Dr. Wilks had a cancellation.

"Mrs. Bishop," a nurse calls from an open door.

Rowan hoists herself up and walks to the examination room.

She sits on a table draped with white paper.

The police wouldn't release the genetic anomaly shared by the purchasers on the dark net. They don't want her conducting her own investigation. The people she's dealing with are *very dangerous*, they advised.

No kidding, she wanted to scream at them. It's the precise reason she's doing this. The police have more cases than just Landon's. They don't have time to spend every waking moment of their lives looking for him.

She does. Rowan took a two-week leave of absence from work for mental health reasons. It's the most she could request with her pending maternity leave. Her work will stack up, but she's hoping Pierre will cover for her. She's convinced if they don't find Landon in that time, they never will. They'll have taken what they wanted from him and disposed of the rest.

The kidney disease element of this has thrown a whole new level of worry into the mix. Now she's afraid Landon has some sort of genetic disorder too. Is he sick and she didn't notice? Is Wyatt? It doesn't make sense.

Dr. Wilks walks in, white coat, stethoscope. He glances at her, amused, as she holds her small belly with one hand. "Hello, Ms. Bishop. I see you brought a guest."

She chuckles at his joke. "Yes, although I'm actually not here for myself."

"Oh, I don't do neonatal, I'm afraid. I could offer a referral."

"No, that's not it either." She shakes her head and gives him what she decides is a clinical brief on her situation. Her missing son. The fact that they attacked her husband. And then came back and took her son—for his kidney. Rowan begs him not to release that part to the press, because so far it hasn't been leaked.

Poor old Dr. Wilks turns an extra shade of white. "Oh my. I'm sorry for your troubles. And you want to know..."

"What type of disease could this be? One that affects father and son? Maybe I can narrow it down somehow on this dark web."

"And both victims are male?"

"Yes."

"There's a few. But my first guess, since a child is presenting with these symptoms, is a disease called X-linked Alport syndrome. The males develop more rapidly, although most of the time Alport syndrome is treatable and patients don't decline until they're in their forties or fifties."

"What is it, exactly? And why would my son be a match for it?"

"It's a genetic disease that affects collagen production and connective tissue. Kidney matches are determined with blood tests, blood type, tissue type, and a testing called crossmatch. There's no way to know for sure if your son would be a match. My guess is your husband's recipient accepted his kidney, and they're banking on the little boy's recipient doing the same. Hoping he has the same genetic makeup as his father..."

Rowan stares up at the office lights and blinks back tears. At least Landon isn't the sick one. Unfortunately, he was picked because he may be the compatible one, though.

"I don't understand all the tests. What would a match mean, exactly?"

"There are three tests they use to determine a match. Blood type, crossmatch—to make sure the recipient won't reject the donor—and HLA testing, or tissue testing. It's presumptuous to think that just because Wyatt was a match that your little boy will be too, because he's part you, but my guess is that's what they were hoping for."

"Ah." Rowan covers her mouth. "This is all too much."

"I'm very sorry. If there's anything else I can do..." Dr. Wilks hands her his card.

"Thanks for the talk. Have you heard of this happening to anyone before?" she asks. One of the hardest parts of learning why Landon was taken is truly feeling like she's on Horror Island all alone with no escape. This situation is so bizarre.

There are no online forums, chat groups, or anyone she can commiserate with to share her pain.

She feels like a freak even telling the story, like she's the crazy one.

Rowan has no support system, only Riley and her mother, who she can barely look at.

She blamed her mother for staying with her father for so long, tolerating him. There was a little bit of judgment on how she could've chosen him in the first place. Her mother told her you can't always pick the perfect partner. Up until a few days ago, Rowan thought she knew better.

"I've only heard of this happening once before. In New York City somewhere. A man..." Dr. Wilks trails off, as if the memory is a struggle.

"Please continue... I just want to know what's happened to my son." She wipes at her eyes. She thinks she knows the ending to this story, but she needs to hear it with her own ears.

"The father of the missing little boy's name is Wesley Baxter. It was a number of years ago. When they found his son..." Dr. Wilks looks away. "Well... I'm afraid... they were too late."

THIRTY-FOUR
THE DOCTOR

"We're waiting for you, Zo." Marta hangs on the phone, hoping he'll come through for her. Praying she doesn't have to call the other guy on the Network's list. He's a good surgeon, but he's also a savage, and Marta doesn't want to welcome him into her home. Introduce him to her family. Because the surgery will be performed there.

"It's dangerous to conduct the procedure on the compound," he says. "Too close to homebase. On homebase."

"We did the last one in the area."

"And there are red flags now. I spoke with Alistair. Mexico City isn't what it once was. Tourism is up. They do not want the negative press. They're fighting to keep what happened at the hospital out of the news. They're saying the attack could even drive down GDP."

Marta laughs. "That's foolish. And that man didn't file a report. I talked him out of it."

"Yes, but the hospital did. People are still talking. What you're doing is foolish. And putting us all at risk."

"If the last one hadn't made it to the hospital there would be less chance of a report being made." Wyatt Bishop's transport didn't go as planned. When she found out, she didn't request for the man to be killed, but she did mention it wouldn't be the worst thing if he didn't make it.

"I'm glad he did. I'm no murderer."

"You're right. You're not. I have every medical tool you could ask for here, Zo. A full operating room setup. It's for Andre. He's done nothing wrong, but for some reason his disease has progressed rapidly. He needs a transplant."

"I know. I just told you I would never operate on a child again. I was very firm. Did you make sure he's even a match?"

"Not yet... His father was."

"Well, I still don't want the job."

"It could be Andre's only chance." Marta watches Landon amble around outside on the grounds. He's chasing the chickens beneath the blazing sun. If Marta closes her eyes, she can envision her sons some twenty-odd years ago, doing the same thing. Why did this disease have to destroy it all? Their lives could've been so beautiful.

"I don't like anything about this." Francisco sighs into the phone.

"This isn't about you. It's about Andre. And your brother. We did everything we could for him, and it wasn't enough. We can save his son."

Francisco hangs up the phone and stares at his infinity pool before he jumps in. He spreads out his arms and lets the cool water lap over his body, wondering how long he can go on like this.

Flying from city to city; taking things from people that don't belong to him and giving them to others. His mother used to tell him what they did wasn't all bad.

As the years pass, he struggles to find the good in it

anymore. It feels like he's on a ticking clock. What is this cursed life if he can never get out? He's considered suicide, leaving all the money he's amassed to Lola and Nico. But then, the Network would likely search them out, and kill them. Even in death, they weren't safe if he broke his allegiance to the Network.

There didn't seem to be an exit. His best utility was to provide organs for people who couldn't source them on their own and gift his son the profit from his endeavors.

And now his mother puts his nephew's life in his hands.

He resents her for getting him into this more than she can ever imagine. He's fantasized about burning her entire estate down with her and his father inside.

His father let this happen.

Before he got sick, he was the one who called the shots, but she's worse. She's the one who discovered the Network. Got them all tied up so tightly in its nasty web that they couldn't wiggle away now if they tried.

He knows this all started from a place of desperation for her.

That's how she excuses herself. That's how she makes it right and is able to look at herself in the mirror. But Francisco's never been able to do the same.

She was only trying to save Damon. But Damon was dead to Francisco long before his disease took him down. Drugs killed what used to be his bigger-than-life older brother. When Francisco left for medical school in Miami, Damon was living on the streets somewhere, and that's where Francisco thought he would die.

He'd chosen a damned life, and Francisco had picked a different path, and he was saddened by it, but had made peace with it all.

His parents were so proud of him—their shining star.

Following Mom's footsteps to become a doctor, in America. Not just a doctor—a surgeon.

During class, he received the phone call that would change his life. Damon had returned to his parents' doorstep. He was dope sick, but he was also a different kind of ill. He had tested positive for a rare kidney disease and was already in end-stage renal failure.

They learned their father was also a carrier of the disease. Even though he'd always been hard of hearing, his father was otherwise asymptomatic at the time.

His mother was livid that they wouldn't give Damon an accelerated spot on the transplant list. The fact that he was a drug addict and had relapsed multiple times pushed him to the bottom of the list.

She searched high and low to give her boy a chance. He promised he'd be better this time. He *always* promised.

Over the years, Damon had made many promises and had repeatedly broken their hearts. None worse than their mother's. She always wanted to believe him when he spouted his lies about kicking his addiction.

She somehow found the Network based overseas. They told her for the right price they could supply her with a compatible kidney, but it would take too long to secure a surgeon for the transplant. Andre would be dead by that point.

That's okay, his mom said, *I have a surgeon.*

Francisco never felt like he had a choice. He either flew home from his final leg of his surgery fellowship and performed the operation, or his brother died. He chose to save his brother.

Unfortunately, Andre's weakened body rejected the organ the Network had procured for him, and he still died.

Little did Francisco know that his mother signed his life away. There was a contract involved that anyone who performed the surgery with the provided organ would continue to work for the Network for an indefinite period of time.

It's been almost nine years. And they still haven't released him.

THIRTY-FIVE
WYATT

Marco reported for work and left Wyatt to his own devices.

He offered Wyatt a job as a barback if he needed a distraction, but he declined. Especially after all the insightful information Marco shared with him. The fact that Landon could be mid-air right now changes everything.

There's still time...

Wyatt's over the initial shock that his son has been kidnapped. Every minute that stretches forward now is a lost opportunity to find him.

Yet time keeps marching on. He wishes he could pause it, or slow it down, so he can figure a few things out.

There're many possibilities if they indeed smuggled Landon out of the country.

An immediate amber alert was issued, which would've made commercial air travel difficult. Although, if they came specifically for Landon, Wyatt has to believe they'd create a passport for him. They could have a private plane. His boy would fight them tooth and nail, though. There's no way he'd go willingly with a stranger.

He barely obliged his own parents.

Although Wyatt has to remember *they* got him too. He was tricked—drugged.

Landon is only four. He may be obstinate at times, but his fear would overcome his feistiness in this case.

"Ah, God." The thoughts of what his little boy is going through are stifling. He shouldn't be doing this alone. If Rowan's as determined to find Landon as he is they should be working together.

No one knows him better.

Wyatt texts Rowan.

Wyatt: *Call me. I have information to share.*

He feels so utterly disconnected, a state away, even though the detectives promised they'd keep him informed. If they're assuming anything they tell Rowan will be communicated to him, they're sadly mistaken. He understands her rage to an extent, but they don't have time to be mad at each other right now. Let Rowan fume after they've put their heads together to recover their son.

Rowan calls him. "What is it?" She sounds tired.

"Hi, it's good to hear your voice."

"Don't do that. Tell me what you have."

"Okay. Marco did some research while we were—"

"Marco? Stop there. He once tried to convince me you guys hadn't been smoking weed by rubbing a copper ring on his cheek. He told me it would turn green if you'd been exposed to cannabis."

"Do you even want to find him?"

"What?" She clucks. That annoying sound... "How dare you?"

"I just told you I might have a lead."

"Okay. What did Marco say?" she snaps.

"The market for organ harvesting is entirely overseas."

"What does that mean?"

"It means they likely had to transport Landon alive. He needs to be healthy at the time of his surgery. And if his recipient is located internationally, we may have more time than we think."

"It's been four days, Wyatt."

"Think about it. Don't lump this into other child abduction cases. Our son has to be alive to get what they need from him."

"Wouldn't they have already taken it by now?"

"Do you think it would be easy to transport a little boy out of the country? One everyone is looking for? Flying commercially would be impossible."

"Okay... I see what you're saying. I have something too."

He knew it. She's holding out on him. To punish him. And it's so fucking cruel. "I went to see a kidney specialist today. I know the detectives wouldn't give us details on the dark net to try to keep us away from it, but the specialist seemed to think a father and son genetic disorder that presented in childhood would most likely be something called X-linked Alport syndrome. It affects males only."

"We might be able to search somehow—"

"It's extremely rare for children to be severe enough to need a transplant. I have Amir looking for me. For any posts about children with this disease."

"Did the doctor say the genetic disorder could be anything else?"

"He did. But this is most likely it."

"We should be working together on this, Ro. I know you're mad at me—"

"Mad..." Her voice is so even, it's chilling. "Mad isn't even the word for what I feel for you. You've always been careless, Wyatt. Irresponsible. But this mistake... is unforgivable."

He closes his eyes. He knows everything she's saying is true. "I understand. And I'll leave you alone after this is all over. I'm just asking you to work with me here. Together we're stronger to bring Landon home."

Wyatt's line clicks like someone is calling Rowan. "It's Detective Stone," she tells him.

She puts him on hold. He huffs, frustrated she didn't answer him about working together. He just wants to come home. And work with his wife to help find his son.

Rowan clicks back over. "Well, you got your wish. They need us both to come down to the station. They want to do blood-typing, and I have a call into the pediatrician for Landon's. They're on the same page as us, trying to track the recipient, and they confirmed your suspicion that Landon may not be in the United States."

Rowan's voice cracks. "They also said it makes it harder once a child crosses the border because they don't have international jurisdiction, and the other country may not be as speedy or cooperative as we'd like."

THIRTY-SIX
THE DOCTOR

Walker is up and about now, pacing the hall with a rolling bag of fluid attached to his arm. Marta knows he won't be happy about how she's handled Andre's donor... who nearly trips on Walker's IV pole as he runs around him down the hallway.

"Chase!" Landon screams.

"Not right now, Landon," Marta says. They played chase last night—all through the long hallways. She remembers running after her own boys when her house was much smaller, her hallways a lot shorter, her knees more flexible.

Walker guts Marta with his eyes. "You brought him to our home?"

"Francisco's been reluctant to do the surgery. We're delayed. He's just a boy. Where did you want me to take him?"

"Then get Corazon," he rasps.

Marta hates the idea of the other surgeon on deck so much that she closes her eyes at his name which means "heart". "You know I won't."

Even though the requests are rare, Francisco won't perform heart extractions. Because it kills the patient. Corazon conducts them and then leaves the bodies on the table like he's carving up an animal to be served for dinner. No remorse—he's just doing his job, he says.

Marta's son has a heart, which is why he can't willingly take someone else's. She tells Francisco he's doing the Lord's work, extracting organs for the poor, unfortunate souls who might die waiting on a donor list for one if he doesn't. He's like a dark angel, she told him once. She knows he doesn't agree.

Marta's proud of her son even though he resents her for clipping those angel wings.

She knows what would've happened to him if he'd continued his schooling in Miami. He would be living what's perceived to be the American dream with that floozy waitress he was dating. She'd drain his bank account, cheat on him, and then take him for half. That's the part of the American dream he never saw coming. On top of that, Marta would never see him again.

He was a naïve boy when he left her home, and now he's a smart man. They're tied together forever through their collaboration at the Network.

He can't leave her now. Like the first one.

"This isn't healthy, Marta, and it isn't going to end well. Have you tested him yet? To see if he's a match?"

"I haven't gotten him to sit still long enough. I considered doing it in his sleep last night, but I didn't want to scare him."

Walker looks at her as if she's lost her mind, his face sunken from the trauma of his surgery, his cheeks stubbly. "He's going to be cut open, one of his organs removed, and you're afraid of extracting a blood sample in his sleep? The connection you're forming to this boy is dangerous. He needs to stay somewhere else while we get the details sorted. This is taking too long."

She waves him off. She had to take the reins when Walker became sick, and everyone but him will admit to the fact that operations have gone smoother with her in charge. "If he trusts me, it will be easier to convince him we're not trying to hurt him."

"We are trying to hurt him! You're lying to him. And you're lying to yourself. You're becoming attached to this boy."

Marta shakes her head at her dense husband. They're bonded through so many life events—marriage, being ousted from Marta's family, the births of their children, the death of one. And most of all, their connection to the Network.

They're business partners in a worldwide organization to secure organs for the needy. Walker has a LinkedIn profile as a contractor for the nuclear energy job he held for a number of years and Marta still works part-time at the hospital, but no one would believe that's what pays for their fourteen-acre, private hillside estate, and gated mansion.

That's why they rarely have friends over. Marta reasoned that if this was to become their life, where they were bound to their home, involved in illegal activity, sworn to secrecy, they could at least do it from a nice venue.

Alistair has a room in the basement, and an apartment in the city, but no family or steady girlfriend. A loner and computer whiz, he's the best employee anyone could ask for. But lately he's been questioning her more than she'd like. She wonders if he might be working for someone on the outside, but then dismisses it when she realizes he'd only be outing himself.

With no visitors, Marta doesn't see how having Landon as their guest could pose a problem. It's not like his little legs can scale a sixteen-foot wall. "I've introduced him to Andre."

"What? Why would you do that? You know if he's able to go back he's going to remember all these people he's met? They'll be able to trace us. What're you thinking?"

Marta hates the word "able." Of course, he'll be able. Marta's going to let him recover here too. Not that she'll mention it to Walker, but surely he can't expect them to leave this little boy to wake up by himself like the others?

"He calls him Andy. There's a million Andys in the world. He doesn't know where he is. He thinks he's still in the historical center in Philly and that he walked through a magical door and here he is." Marta laughs, and she is protective of this little boy. But she wouldn't say she's "attached." That's severe.

"But there aren't many Andys with a congenital kidney disease under the age of ten," Walker says.

Marta replies, "He met Andre, because when he has his extraction, I want to tell him before it happens why we're doing it. He'll feel better if he knows he's donating something to Andy."

Walker shakes his head. "This will be our undoing. You haven't even checked him to make sure he's a match. What if he's not?"

"We'll have to find a way to release him then, but hopefully he is."

"If he's not... I don't think we'll be able to just... release him."

Walker can be callous when his lucrative kingdom is being threatened. He once confessed that he feels like it's all he has left since Damon died. Marta doesn't disagree. Their sole purpose is to source organs for the less fortunate and they make an incredible sum of money doing it. They have to put everything they have behind their business, or die on the hill they built it on. There's no other choice.

"I will not let you harm that boy," Marta says.

"Like always, we can't always predict what happens to them once they're on the table," Walker says.

Although true, Marta doesn't like the tone in Walker's voice. Is he saying that because they've only had one other extraction on a child and it didn't go well? Or because he truly believes Landon is a threat—and he will ensure he doesn't make it home?

"It should be a more predictable positive outcome with the

setup I have in the basement. Proper tools and such." Marta will have to oversee the procedure. If Francisco does it, he'll take extra measures to make sure the boy is okay. If Corazon is the surgeon, all bets are off.

"You're still not in a pediatric wing of the hospital if something goes wrong." Walker sits down beside the monitor. New requests are coming in for kidneys and livers, as others are being fielded. A billion-dollar industry, some organs go for as much as $100,000 a pop. The brokers, like them, take 50 percent, because they put up the most risk, securing the money transfers, arranging the sites, and the lures. The surgeon's fee is 25 percent, and the Network gets the rest. Marta only knows that the Network is located in Eastern Europe, and her main contact's name is Enid.

She wishes she would've asked Enid more questions when they initially made contact years ago, because she's refused requests for calls ever since.

Marta's family is locked in, that's for sure.

The day Francisco refused a heart extraction, a man with a drawn gun showed up at their door. "He will perform the surgery," the man said, insistent. He was tall with a European accent of some sort.

Francisco would not compromise on the extraction to the point he was willing to trade his life and that of his own mother's for the unknown patient. It was his firm line in the sand. Francisco was so angry at her for putting him in that position in the first place—mad enough to stake her life on it too.

Marta stretched her arms out at the man like a mother bear protecting its young. "Shoot me, then." Walker watched in horror from the hallway but didn't interfere. Marta wouldn't put it past him if he ran when gunfire broke out.

In that moment, Marta was ready to meet her maker. She'd buried her son the year before, and she just wanted to see his face again. Her other son wished her dead. What was the point in carrying on?

But instead of shooting her, the man withdrew his gun, and cracked his neck with his non-gun-bearing hand. He received a phone call, nodded at Marta, and said, "Fine. No hearts for Zo. But there will be no more exceptions."

After that terrifying house call, the Network hired Corazon. In a way, the two men competed. In another, Marta thinks Francisco is happy not to work at all. Performing surgery on a child, this child, would be his second exception, although Marta is the buyer.

The organ is for her grandson. She has the upper hand here.

The Network has already received their money. Her money.

If this surgery never happened, they wouldn't even know it.

And if Landon never returned to his parents, they would assume he was as good as dead. Walker and Francisco are right, though. She needs to extract blood and complete all of the necessary testing right away. There are no more excuses. She's had her fun.

Landon runs toward her, all dirty, his face rosy from the sun. She needs to remember to apply the sunscreen before he sneaks out on her again.

"Hey, little man. I need to take a sample of your blood," she tells him.

"Why?" he asks, drawing his arms behind his back. He knows what blood means. *Needles.*

"You know how Andre is sick?" she asks.

"Yeah..."

"I need to see if you have the magic blood to make him better. Like a test."

"Ooh. Will it hurt?" Landon asks.

"No, just a pinch."

"Okay."

"Sit in this chair."

Marta returns with her syringe and a Band-Aid. "Just... a pinch," she says, before she extracts a tube of Landon's blood. And then another. And then one more...

He's still shutting his eyes even though she's all done. She applies the bandage. "All done. You can go back to playing."

He opens his eyes and sprints off the chair.

She goes right to work with a blood sample kit first. Next, will be the human leukocyte antigen test, and the crossmatch test to determine if Andre has antibodies that would attack Landon's donor cells, but out of all the surprises that've come with her job, the one before her is one of the most unexpected.

THIRTY-SEVEN
ROWAN

Rowan sits beside her husband at the police station, but she won't look at him. She can barely stomach having him in her presence, knowing that while she was at home caring for their son, making plans for their future family, he was meeting a woman at a bar in a different country. Probably thought he'd never get caught.

Perfect opportunity.

It's impossible to be near Wyatt, smell his intoxicating cologne, and not picture him sitting in a tropical location, entertaining his guest, a sweet smile on his face. Rowan's mother warned her about guys from Jersey. She should've listened.

"Hey, Ro. How're you feeling?" he asks.

She doesn't answer him. The quicker they can get these blood tests done the better. Although Rowan's not sure why they can't just pull medical charts and get what they need.

Detective Stone and Detective Schrader enter the room. A woman with gloves, cotton balls, and a plastic sample kit sits down at the table with them.

"Is this necessary? Can't you just look up our blood type off our medical charts?" Rowan asks, because she's been poked and prodded enough with syringes today.

"As you know, we're moving as quickly as possible to try to find Landon before an extraction occurs. We want to eliminate any chance of human error," Schrader says.

Wyatt is already rolling up his sleeves. He's such a hero.

The woman wearing the gloves says, "You don't have to roll up your sleeve. I just need to prick your finger. I'm the forensic pathologist, Dr. Anya Reyes. I work for the county."

Rowan rolls her sleeves back down, but as she does so, she reveals a taped cotton ball on the underside of her arm from where she was jabbed earlier. "From my doctor's appointment."

"We don't want to exhaust you," Stone says.

"I'm fine. It has to be done." She agrees now that she's heard the logic. She doesn't want to leave any stones unturned either. So far they've found *nothing*. "But isn't there more to organ matching than a blood draw?"

"There is. Tissue matching and a crossmatch test to start, but this black-market operation doesn't follow all the rules. They likely don't have time to do all the tests, but at the very least I'm sure they'd do a quick blood test so as not to waste the organ."

Rowan shudders at the desperation of the situation, and all the people paying for something that has a decent probability of not even working. Every time someone says the word "organ" or "extraction" she has a visceral reaction, like someone is pulling a string attached to the rib cage surrounding her heart. Of all the dangers she could've thought of protecting Landon from, this wasn't one of them. She read last night that 10 percent of the world's organ transplants are suspected to be illegal, and the thought sickens her.

They've already taken Wyatt's blood and Dr. Reyes is using a dropper to place it in a plastic tray which has three idented plastic wells—A, B, and Rh.

What about O? Rowan wonders. She thinks that's what blood type Wyatt is, and there's no slot for it.

Minutes later, they've got the two trays lined up on the table. One each for her and Wyatt, Rowan assumes.

"How long will this take?" Wyatt asks. "And how does it help us?"

"Six minutes," Dr. Reyes says. She's pricked their fingers and is sitting there mixing the blood with a small stick of some sort. Rowan is starting to get nauseous. She doesn't know if it's the blood or what they plan to do with it. They're beyond the point of finding Landon on the city streets where he was taken. He's probably in some makeshift hospital somewhere awaiting to be cut open—or worse. It's more than she can handle. She's losing hope.

"On the dark web, they list the blood type with the donor. It will have something miscellaneous to start, like, Geo72 K, AB. That stands for the user's name, which is only traceable by the broker, the organ, K is for kidney, and the blood type. The blood type is always listed."

"Why can't they trace the broker? Wouldn't that bust them all?" Wyatt asks.

"The network protects the broker's information at all costs. You'd likely be able to find the Network's location before the broker's. They're constantly changing the dark web's algorithm so it's hard to crack, and once an order has been filled the request vanishes, but we have screenshots and if we know Landon's blood type and Wyatt's we can maybe start to narrow it down."

"Okay, what do we have?" Wyatt asks.

Rowan looks over and notices that Wyatt has a timer on his smartwatch. Tech nerd. She does miss him, but not enough to ever forgive him.

"Hold on here." Dr. Reyes keeps mixing the results with a confused expression. There's a paper file with Landon's medical chart in front of her. He's had regular checkups since he was born, but only had his blood type recorded at birth, in the hospital, that Rowan can recall.

"What's wrong?" Rowan asks.

She can also see that two of the plastic wells that hold her blood sample are clumping—the B and the Rh. None are clumping in Wyatt's. She doesn't know what that means, but the doctor is looking at it as if it's bad. Maybe Wyatt does have a genetic blood disorder.

The doctor, a clean-cut woman in her thirties with a shiny ponytail, clears her voice and glances between them all. "According to Landon's chart from his pediatrician, his blood type is AB+. Wyatt's blood type is O-. Rowan's blood type is... B+."

They all stare at Dr. Reyes as if this means absolutely nothing.

"Blood type O and B do not make AB blood. It's impossible. They reject each other," Dr. Reyes says.

Nothing seems to be registering for the detectives or Wyatt, but Rowan thinks she knows what the doctor is about to say, and she stands to excuse herself, because she can't be in the room for this.

"Sit down, Mrs. Bishop," Schrader says, with a commanding voice Rowan hasn't heard before. It's so startling she drops right down in her seat with force. The blood samples jiggle on the table. Her breath heaves in her chest. *No, no, no.* This can't be right.

"I don't understand," Wyatt says.

"Mr. Bishop, according to these results, Landon is not your biological son. It's scientifically impossible."

"What?" Wyatt turns his head toward Rowan, but she can't look at him. "Rowan... this can't be right?"

"I'm not feeling well," she says. "You told me to tell you if I was unwell. I am—"

"What type of blood type would the father have?" Stone asks.

"A," Dr. Reyes responds, solemnly. "A child with AB blood that has a mother with B blood, would have a father with A blood."

Wyatt looks like he's going to cry. "Who is it? I can't..."

She can't either. She can't imagine this scenario is actually happening. Rowan closes her eyes. She thinks she's going to pass out, when the worst of the information is released next.

"What does this mean for Landon? And the transplant?" Schrader asks.

"It's not good. Wyatt has a rare blood type. Only 8 percent of the population has O negative blood—although Rh factor doesn't matter for donation compatibility. At all. However, they could've tested Wyatt for other genetic markers with a crossmatch or an HLA test, depending on how long they had him before they operated. If they were targeting this little boy in the hopes he'd have the same blood type and genetic composition as his father, they'll find out real quickly that's not the case. Blood type AB can only donate to blood type AB."

Rowan sprints out of the room without talking to another soul. This time... no one stops her.

THIRTY-EIGHT
WYATT

Wyatt leaves the police station in a state of complete and utter shock. He did not speak to his wife before he left. She seemed just as stunned to learn Landon's paternity as he did.

Wyatt *has* to believe that she was surprised to learn he wasn't the father either.

The evidence that Landon didn't belong to him was under his nose all along in the medical charts.

Rowan couldn't have known Landon wasn't his. If she did, why would she agree to the blood test? Although she did complain about it.

He rubs his hand over his face.

Who is the other guy? Maybe they've been looking at this all wrong, maybe he's the one... who took Landon?

It's not that Wyatt's furious or overly jealous—he just can't fathom Rowan having an affair. She's not promiscuous by any means. To Wyatt's knowledge, Rowan's only slept with two men beside him in her life. A boyfriend in high school and one in college.

Well, apparently three guys now...

Wyatt shakes his head in disbelief. His wife is the most

measured human he's ever met. Everything she did was with their family in mind.

Or at least that's what she led him to believe.

He's seen inklings of her irrational behavior when she's pushed too far. As she playfully called it when they were dating —*You don't want me to break out my Delco.*

She's referring to Delaware County where she grew up.

Rowan has a simmering anger that rarely comes to a full boil, but when it does...

He's still missing a chunk of hair from when she attacked him.

Marco said—*that's not normal, Man...* And that no matter how angry she was, she shouldn't have put her hands on him. Abuse goes two ways, he reminded Wyatt.

Wyatt didn't disagree, but now he wonders what "that's not normal" really means.

It all seems like a ruse now, his entire marriage.

His wife is not the person he believed her to be, and his son is truly not his son.

Landon is not mine.

My God, it's unfathomable.

It doesn't make him any less determined to find Landon. He's still his boy, and Wyatt's the only father he's ever known. A blood test doesn't change that.

His wife cheated on him and he doesn't understand why. Or, when? It had to be early on in their marriage, when things were good between them. Before the stress of children and their hefty mortgage payment.

There's always been something inauthentic about Rowan that Wyatt didn't want to admit to himself. It's silly to compare a carefree fling to a marriage, but when he was with Naomi that glorious summer abroad he never wondered if she was really into him or not.

The way she looked at him as if he was the only other

person in the world... how she's told him as much, virtually, in fits of nostalgia.

Even though their communication is sporadic, she's made remarks about how smart he is, and how she knew he was going to do great things with his life. She was also the only girl who liked Marco first, and then moved onto him. It was usually the other way around.

He thinks about Naomi now, searching for validation that he's someone worth being loved after all he's just learned.

Naomi told him she liked the way his mind worked, and that his heart was beautiful.

Rowan never said things like that to him. It wasn't her love language to express herself verbally. Rowan would sneak up behind him, kiss him softly behind his ear instead. Make him a meal she knew he liked, care for him in different ways.

He didn't realize he longed for her to say the words "I love you" to him until right now. Until he wasn't sure if she ever did.

It's like she couldn't give herself entirely to him, because she relinquished control that way. She wanted the upper hand—always. Emotionally. Financially.

Or maybe it's because her heart belonged to somebody else.

It's all so dysfunctional. What a joke, to think he could've grown up like he did and just move into a fairytale life in suburbia.

Wyatt drives back to the beach.

All he wanted to do when he left Jersey was go back home, but it's truly over now—the life he built in Bryn Mawr, the beautiful house he bought for his wife; his family. They're not even really his.

What about the second child, the one Rowan is carrying

now? Is that one his? Does Rowan have a separate life with another man?

Wyatt sits on the shore alone, not another soul in sight. It's the same stretch he'd find himself on when he was a boy. He's pretty sure it's a private beach, but no one's ever bothered him. He picks up a rock, throws it in. It's swallowed in a wave like it never even existed.

His whole life seems to have vanished just as quickly.

Rowan doesn't even have male friends, or a single person Wyatt might suspect as her secret lover. Her best friend at work is a gay male, and all of her other colleagues are what she describes as old, boring white men. Wyatt has met them—she's not wrong.

Her exes live far away, one in California and one in Japan.

Wyatt never got the impression she loved either one of them with the typical heartbreak that comes with that first true love.

For her high school ex-boyfriend—she refers to him as *the boy who was around, and he had a car...*

For her college ex-boyfriend—*he was just part of our friend group, easy...*

Rowan's not linked with either of these men on social media and never so much as mentions them in passing.

This leads Wyatt to the scary realization that the man who fathered Landon is someone completely different. Someone Wyatt has never heard of. If this is true, then Rowan *must* be living a double life. Maybe she still is, and Landon's biological father has him right now.

This thought offers him comfort—and not.

Comfort that the biological father wouldn't likely harm his own son.

Wyatt takes his flask out of his shorts pocket. Marco gave it to him as a wedding present. Back then, they had talks about whether Rowan was the right woman for him. Marco thought she was high maintenance from the jump. From the moment she ran away from the waves on the beach as if they were affronting her toes. After she pulled her stunt in Atlantic City, Marco made a quick comment that there was still time to get out.

They hadn't started a family yet. The warning signs were there.

Somehow Wyatt excused her behavior, but now looking back he recognizes the red flags.

A true loving connection with him was never Rowan's goal.

She just wanted a man to give her the house of her dreams, the family she never had, a joint bank account she could draw from. One she could monitor.

She never really loved *him*. In fact, she loves someone else.

Wyatt did.

Love her.

He loved Rowan. As much as he doubted himself, he was committed to the life he created with her. And now he's lost it all—his wife, his child, his money. The impending hospital bills and job loss will do him in before he can figure this all out, he's sure of it.

It's what he thinks as he leaves his empty flask on the sand and steps into the water.

The waves caress his legs, an old friend.

He walks further. He wants the ocean to engulf him whole like it did when he was a boy. He wants to feel weightless, and lost in the current. He wades deeper into the sea.

The wicked waves toss him up and around.

He closes his eyes and tumbles back and forth beneath the water.

His incision site on his side burns and screams as the saltwater rakes at it.

He doesn't care about the pain. Not anymore. He just wants it to end.

He allows the sea to enter his mouth, fill his lungs, turn everything black...

THIRTY-NINE
THE DOCTOR

"He's not a match," Marta says hopelessly.

Marta and Walker watch from the hallway of Andre's room. It's bad enough the kid lost both his parents to drugs, but he's been fighting this disease for years. His hearing is compromised, but Landon has already learned that. They're playing Connect 4 again, a game that doesn't require sound, as Andre rests in his bed.

"What're we going to do now?" Walker asks. "And how could we let this happen?"

"There was always a risk that it could happen. A type O and a type B could make an O or a B. The fact that the boy is an AB, well, that was never considered. He can only be a donor for other AB blood types."

"Are you saying Wyatt Bishop isn't the father of this boy?" Walker asks.

"That's correct," Marta says.

Walker shakes his head. "You shouldn't let him befriend Andre. The more he learns about our family, the more he risks giving us up. You're really being careless here. I don't understand..."

"He's good company for Andre. He's so lonely since he's not in school. I can't bring Landon back right now anyway. The authorities are everywhere looking for him. We have to wait until things cool down. We really put a lot more at risk trying to get him back to the States at this time. We're all safer with him here."

Landon erupts into giggles as he slides the bottom of the catch on the game letting all the red and blue chips fly out onto Andre's comforter. They look over to see he has beat Andre at Connect 4 again. "I win!"

Andre offers Marta and Walker a wink beneath his glasses. The Alport syndrome has affected his eyes as well, and his vision is horrible. But one thing is clear: he's letting Landon win. Walker smirks at him, unhappily, and Marta knows why. Damon used to let Francisco win when they were younger. He was a sweet boy and a great big brother at one time.

"I see what's happening here. We've got to keep the boy somewhere else, Marta."

"What're you talking about? Like where?"

"They're four years apart, just like Damon and Francisco."

"So?" she asks. She had to space the birth of her children out because she was juggling a lot with med school. It was the hardest time of her life. Until Damon died.

"These boys aren't replacements. You can't keep this boy here. I'm going to talk to Alistair about seeing if he can stay with him in the city and work remotely until we get him back to the States."

"People will see him in the city, Walker. He's secure here. What about Andre? His health is declining and Landon keeps his spirits up."

"He may be secure, but you're not..."

It's not true that she's unstable. She's had to sacrifice a lot for their lifestyle. Their bloodline dies with Francisco and Andre. Francisco said he'll never have a family of his own as long as he's in the Network. There doesn't seem to be an out there. She's thought about finding a replacement for him, but there's no one in the world who would want to take his place.

As far as Landon goes, she could keep him here if she wanted to. The fee to the Network has been paid. The Network never cares what happens to the donors after the transplants are made. The Network finds the donors. Most of the time they've managed preliminary medical testing one way or another before an attack occurs, and the rest of the operation—the where, the how—is centered around the patient. Some of the donors make it and some of them don't. Marta always alerts the Network if there's a death, but she's not sure they even keep track.

There's no one actively looking for this boy in Mexico.

He's darker complected, umber hair. A few more years, and he'll be unrecognizable as the boy he once was. Marta could lie and say he's a cousin's child whose parents perished in an accident. She could send him to private school. Maybe they can change his name.

But not right now... right now they have to figure out how they're going to save Andre. And they have to wait until Landon's missing person file is deemed a "cold case."

By then, Walker will have come around.

He'll see that there's another way forward other than carting the boy back to Philadelphia in a shipping container or cargo train, or however he expects to get him across the border. Marta saw few good options here.

She logs onto her database, and once again puts in a request for: Delta5, PED, K, O.

FORTY
ROWAN

Rowan heads to New York to pay a stranger a visit. She'd like to go home first, pack her gun, but she can't return and tell her mother the reason Landon is missing and likely dead, her family destroyed, is because she repeated the actions of her father.

Her mother would be disappointed to the point of despair. Rowan's so sick with regret she can't stand herself. The problem she's created is too big to face, and too devastating to explain to those who love her.

She doesn't hope to get anything from the man she's seeking out.

But she needs a place to run and hide from what she's done.

She's been meaning to reach out to him. He's the only one who knows what she's going through. Well, her, and Wyatt, but she certainly can't look to her husband for support right now.

She can't forgive him for what he did in Mexico City, and he'll never be able to forgive her for what she did. They're justified in their cancellation of each other. They've both made horrible errors in their relationship, and the only path forward is one where they aren't together. She's tried so hard to do things the right way, but it turns out her sister had it right all along.

Buck the system.

Refuse marital norms. They aren't realistic or sustainable. Someone is bound to screw up and create irreparable harm. Rowan truly never thought her blip all those years ago would be discovered.

She cannot believe Landon is not Wyatt's.

Wyatt must be so heartbroken. She tears up imagining him coming to grips with the fact that the boy he's raised for the last four years is not his own.

Given the time of Landon's birth, the thought crossed her mind that Landon might not be Wyatt's, but not so much that she thought to do anything about it. What's done was done, and Wyatt was so happy to become a dad.

He really embraced the whole fatherhood thing, striving to do better than his own father who he's never met. Rowan had the same aspirations, but they both failed.

And the ugly cycle continues...

Marriage. Infidelity. Divorce. Damaged children.

Maybe the baby in her womb will be spared because their marriage will be long dissolved before it's born. There won't be discord and unhappiness for the child to witness at every turn, merely a normal existence comprised of two parents who live separately, but are at peace.

She hopes Wyatt will grant her that.

Although, she doubts it, once Wyatt learns all the details of how Landon was conceived.

It's been hours and Rowan's bladder is feeling the pressure of both the baby and the liquid she's ingested to make the tenuous trip. She parks her car between two others in the Bed-Stuy neighborhood in Brooklyn. A man argues with another outside as a child kicks a ball into the street. Rowan pauses and picks up the ball for the little boy. He grabs it and darts away.

She stands there and watches him, thinking of her own active child, and is overcome with grief.

If Landon is not a match for the child who needed his organ, they wouldn't keep him around. If they haven't received a ransom to return him, they've likely killed him by now. The fact that Wyatt is not the father has never meant more.

In the end, Rowan is the villain, and she can't live with that.

She won't survive with that as the ending. She needs to figure out what happened. For her little boy. For the new baby, because she can't rest with this outcome.

The brownstones line the street, and are nearly identical with their brown brick, large doors, long windows and black steel frames. The man Rowan is looking for rents a unit in one of them.

She doesn't know if the address she has for him is accurate or if he's even home.

He's the only one who can answer her questions. Eventually, a man appears at the doorway who matches the pictures Rowan pulled from the news, although he's a much older and worn version.

She knows the look he carries—one of lost hope.

He appears as though he's just woken up, his shirt rumpled, his graying hair standing on end. "Yes?"

"I'm sorry I didn't call first. If I could've found a number for you, I would have. My name is Rowan Bishop. Do you recognize me from the news?"

He looks at her sideways. "No. And if you're a reporter I can't help you." He starts to shut his door and Rowan sticks her foot in the doorway.

"Please, Mr. Baxter."

"Excuse me."

"I'm not a reporter. I'm Rowan Bishop. They took my son. The same people who took yours."

He looks at her then with a combination of misery and pity. "Then no one can help you, I'm afraid."

"Please, can I come in? I really have to pee." She's holding her belly and he looks down in shock. She can tell he didn't realize she was pregnant until that moment, and if she has to use her pregnancy for leverage, she will.

He sighs and opens his door wide. She nearly trips on a pile of shoes as she makes her way inside. "First door on the right. Don't mind the mess."

She meanders around piles of boxes with files and books inside. At first, she thinks he might be moving, but as she makes her way down the hall, she notices the same thing. An untidy apartment with piles of junk everywhere.

She makes her way into the dirty bathroom, crusty hand towels, a faucet that hangs at a slow dribble. This guy's water bill must be insane. Rowan hardly thinks he cares. She washes her hands, thankful there's hand soap, and finds Wesley Baxter at his kitchen table looking like he'd rather be anywhere else. He's scrolling on his phone.

"Thank you for letting me use your restroom."

He nods. "When I looked up your name it doesn't say anything about organ trafficking on these websites."

"They haven't released that information to the public yet."

"That's wise. Don't let them know you're onto them." He sighs, and Rowan can only guess it's because he didn't have that same luxury where his son was concerned.

There's a cluttered shelf in the corner with dying plants and pictures displayed. Rowan picks up one of a happy family —Wesley, a wife, and his little boy, Owen. She read about him before he arrived, a smart boy who was involved in cub scouts.

"He's beautiful."

"Yes, that's my boy. It says yours was taken at a museum..."

"The visitor center. That houses the Liberty Bell. I drove up from Philly." Rowan takes a seat, suddenly exhausted.

He makes a face that says—*make yourself comfortable*. "Guess we're doing this... Would you like a flavored water? The only other thing I have that's non-alcoholic is coffee or tap water. I have a whole lot of whiskey. I won't judge."

Rowan thinks of the drippy bathroom sink with the brown water ring and the dehydrated plants. "A flavored water would be great."

He pulls a cherry water out of his fridge, hands it to her, and then proceeds to pour himself a whiskey. "I'm sorry for what you're going through, ma'am, but please excuse me if I lack the emotion to show it. It's hard for me to relive any part of this."

"I understand my being here is triggering. I just need some answers." Rowan can feel herself coming apart. She drove to Wesley Baxter's house on a complete whim. She didn't actually expect him to open his door to her, although she did sort of force her way in.

"First, tell me how you're sure the people who have your son are the same who had mine?"

"I guess I'm not. But they're called the Network. Does that sound familiar?"

The way Wesley's face twists in pain tells her all she needs to know. "I'm so sorry," he whispers. "Rowan, is it?"

"Yes. Please just tell me what I need to know."

"They're barbarians. Run entirely internationally somewhere. No one can say quite where. People post their requests on a site and the Network goes to work seeing who they can victimize to obtain the desired compatible organs for a set price."

"My husband... was a victim. He survived and returned home to me. They let him live."

Wesley looks up, shocked. "That's great. He must've had the other surgeon."

"What does that mean?"

Wesley slugs some whiskey and lets it slide down his throat before he answers. "My son had all of his organs extracted. I don't even think it was the order. He was sent to a man they call

Corazon, because he does the hearts. He's a killer. I hear there's a more merciful one. The dark net calls him Zo."

"Zo?" Rowan repeats.

"That's right."

"So, that must be who let Wyatt, my husband, go?"

"I don't know. Why did they take both your husband and your son? Were they together and the boy just got wrapped up in it?"

"No..." Rowan has a hard time with the second part. "My husband had some kind of genetic marker, they think, and an O blood type. And the recipient had another family member that needed the same thing, but it turns out, after some testing, we discovered my son doesn't have the same blood type as my husband. He has... mine."

Wesley winces at this information. "These were two separate attacks, then?"

"Yes."

"You poor woman," he says.

She nods, although she's moved far beyond the pity stage. "How do I find him? Show me how you accessed the dark net, Wesley."

"Call me Wes," he says. "And that is not a door you want to open. I spent hours trying to crack that thing. Looking for codes. I cleaned out my savings on..." he motions around him "on private investigators and people who claimed they were hackers only to be scammed time and time again."

"I don't care," she rasps. "Show me."

"If the cops are working on it, let them. Please let them. For your own sake. I lost everything because of my obsession with that dark net. My job. My wife. I have nothing left."

The way he says those last words crushes her, because she believes him. "I lost my husband already. All I have is this baby. But you see, I know I won't make it through the pregnancy if I can't figure out what happened to my boy. I just won't. I'll go mad." She crushes the empty aluminum can with her hand. He must see her despair.

They sit in silence for a while as Wes mulls over what she's said—two people placed in terrible situations. One in a position to help.

Wesley grabs his laptop from a drawer and refills his whiskey. "Okay... I warned you. Slide over, miss."

FORTY-ONE
WYATT

Wyatt spews the sea from somewhere deep inside of his body—the cavernous pit of his stomach, his lungs—the water expels from his nose, echoes in his ears. It shoots from every orifice as men in navy blue uniforms pump on his chest and draw water out his mouth with theirs. He coughs and fights to breathe, starved for air.

A mask is placed over his face.

Oxygen. He gulps to retrieve it but throws up more water. They tip him on his side. He's on a stretcher being lifted into the back of an ambulance.

The last thing he sees before the doors close is his best friend, soaked head to toe.

His mother is at his side when he wakes. Her eyes and skin have a yellow tinge and she's let her hair go completely gray. He knows it's a trend from the younger women at work who've gone silver, but it makes her look twenty years older.

"Hi, Mother."

"Wyatt..." She grabs his hand. Hers shake. "Why didn't you tell me all the trouble you've been having? Marco says you've been staying at his place. You could've come home."

Home? Where's that? Wyatt is not even sure of the address of his mother's current apartment complex. He thought about calling her when he was displaced, but it seemed absurd to contact his own mother to find her address. He went to the more stable place—Marco's. "Thanks, I may take you up on that."

"Why would you go swimming by yourself? You know how dangerous that is," she says.

He closes his eyes. He used to swim by himself all the time as a kid, in the ocean, alone at night, and he'd never had an issue before.

He'd just wanted to disappear for a minute.

To bounce along the waves and let something else carry him, if only for a little while. Maybe he did hold his breath too long before he surfaced, lost in his own thoughts, but he can't remember. "I don't know. Needed to clear my head."

"You could've visited your mom for that. Never swim alone," she says.

He looks away, because if she knew how often he used to do it, she'd be upset. And he hates to tell her that his path in life will be one long single adult swim from here on out.

"Have they any leads on Landon? I was hoping you'd drop by for a beach visit soon, and I could take him," she says sadly. "I can't believe... what's happened." Her voice is sad. She's completely out of touch with the situation at hand, how it's destroyed everything around him.

"They don't have any leads. He's gone."

"How terrible... I'm so sorry, son. We don't know why God puts us through what he does. I wish I could tell you I knew why this was happening."

Wyatt stares hard into the awful hospital lighting above him. He knows this has nothing to do with God.

Devils have his boy.

Marco enters the room, clean and dry now. "Marco, my other son." His mother rises to greet him. He hugs her back but holds a grim expression. Wyatt thinks he knows why.

"Always nice to see you, Barb. Do you mind if I have a word with Wyatt?"

"Sure thing. Please come visit, Wyatt. My door is always open. I can make you dinner."

"Okay, Mom. Talk soon," he lies. She's of no more comfort now than she was when he was younger. The stress of his near drowning and refreshed worry over her missing grandson will likely drive her into an alcoholic bender. Wyatt should be concentrating on his own health, but having her around is more of a liability than a source of support.

"Hey, man. Did you fish me out? I saw you at the beach before I went to the hospital," Wyatt says.

"Yeah, I did. I saw your SUV parked, and no Wyatt. Instinct made me stop. Wyatt, I saw your body floating on the top of the water. That is how I found you."

He closes his eyes and sighs. "I'm so sorry."

"You can't do that to me. You're like my brother, you know that." Marco sounds like he might burst into tears.

"I—I don't know what happened. One minute I was swimming and the next, everything went dark. I remember waking up in the ambulance. I couldn't breathe..."

"Are you sure about that? You've been under a lot of stress. Did they make any breaks with the tests they ran at the station?"

Boy did they ever. "It's bad. Worse than I thought. According to the blood tests, and Landon's medical files, he's not my biological son."

"What! Could there be a mistake? What did Rowan say?"

"She didn't say anything. She ran out of the room. Guilty as hell. But that's not the worst of it. If they took Landon because they thought he shared my DNA, he's useless to them. They've probably already..."

"Oh no." Marco looks an extra shade of white, which is hard to do with his olive skin.

"Yeah. I think we both know what they do to kids who serve no purpose. Especially since we haven't heard anything by now. If we'd known he didn't share my DNA sooner, they could've shifted their resources a bit."

"Did Rowan know? He wasn't yours?" Marco sounds like he's having a hard time catching his breath.

"I didn't have a chance to ask her. She ran away so fast!" Wyatt laughs, a sad strangled cry. "My life is such a mess. I need to find out who the guy is. My only shred of hope is that maybe he is the one who took Landon."

Marco shakes his head. "You said there was a female companion."

"Maybe he has friends. They usually use women when they're trying to lure the children."

"I can't believe this," Marco says.

"Or perhaps the guy Rowan is sleeping with is a fucking creep. He's soulless enough to sleep with a married woman, so who knows."

Marco shakes his head. "It can't still be going on. She's pregnant."

"With whose kid?" A tear leaks down the side of Wyatt's face. "I just want some answers."

"You went into that water without the intention of coming back out," Marco says quietly.

"Maybe I did. I can't take this anymore. Truly. My entire life is a lie. My wife is not who she said she was. My kids may not be my kids. What is this?" he asks hopelessly. "Punishment for all the girls we messed around with when we were younger?"

Marco says more quietly this time, "I think Rowan probably just made a mistake. It doesn't matter who he is. You're the one who raised Landon. He's yours. He'll always be yours. People make mistakes." Wyatt doesn't like that Marco is making excuses for Rowan or how Marco's looking at him.

"A mistake? I met a woman at the bar in Mexico City. She fathered a child with another man and passed it off as my own! She's a horrible human. How can you side with her?" If he had more strength, he'd yell louder. Marco always takes his side. Even when he shouldn't.

"Haven't you ever done something that you'd do anything to take back? Something really bad?"

Wyatt thinks on this. "I wonder if I hadn't met that woman if everything would be fine right now and if I'd be at home with my family."

"Just a drink, come on. Don't beat yourself up. How were you supposed to know?"

"Well, I need some direction to steer my pain or I'm going to be nose deep back in that water. I swear to God."

Marco puts his head in his hands and pulls on his full dark hair. Wyatt used to be envious of it when he was younger. The ladies loved Marco's hair, and everything about him. Wyatt didn't have the discipline to lift weights every day like his best friend. It was just part of Marco's normal routine, and it showed. "The other guy doesn't have Landon, Wyatt. I can't have you in knots over this."

"Quit making shit up! Not when it comes to my son. You don't know what you're talking about." Wyatt shuts his eyes, the pain from his incision nagging at him. He noticed they put a fresh bandage on it and wonders if he ripped his wound back open by how it's pinging right now.

"I'm not making anything up. I have to tell you something.

Do you remember that night Rowan went looking for you when you were in Atlantic City?"

"Yeah..."

"She couldn't get ahold of you and drove up and down the shore in a panic before deciding to go to your hotel room."

"And?"

"And she stopped to see me on the way."

"Why would she stop and see you?"

Marco stands up and he's pacing now. "You know I'm a fuck-up. You know I do stupid shit. Well, that's the one night I did something horrible that I really wish I could take back."

"You're not saying what I think you're saying."

Marco looks directly at Wyatt as he delivers the blow. "Landon's mine."

FORTY-TWO
THE DOCTOR

Playing both sides as the buyer and the broker does have its pitfalls. Wyatt Bishop was the first decent mark they'd had for Walker.

The list Andre's currently on is endless because there have been no compatible donors.

There's no inventory and nothing anyone can do to create it —except them. The Network.

All the worries she had for Andre's father come flooding back. The desperation as Damon grew sicker, the hospital's continual no callbacks when she phoned in to inquire. She won't let her grandson go the same way. She was so much more spiteful when Damon was denied medical help. There were organs available for him.

They were just giving them to someone else.

Andre's in a different boat entirely. Marta should've tried to get Landon's medical records before snatching him, but the cybersecurity precautions on medical records these days are some of the toughest to hack. It's much easier in foreign countries with lax healthcare systems. They weren't able to get into Landon's records and decided to take their chances.

Andre was too sick to travel to the States and it would've looked doubly suspicious to kidnap Landon and try to pull off a surgery somewhere near him. They had to get him out of the country as quickly as possible.

Who could've guessed that Landon was not Wyatt Bishop's biological son?

She thought her chances were at least 50/50. A child with a parent who has an A and O blood type can make a type A or O baby. A child who has a parent with a B and O blood type can create a type B or O baby.

They never had a chance with Landon.

Neither of his biological parents have a drop of O blood. Blood compatibility is only the first step, and they struck out before they even got started.

She wonders if Wyatt or the public know Landon isn't Wyatt's son, and if it will lessen the manhunt any if Marta reveals the child isn't from the perfect all-American family as depicted on television. Maybe the guilt will go back on the mother somehow.

She'll save that card for when and if she needs it.

So far there hasn't been any warning bells that anyone has come close to finding them out. And Marta has all her technological filters on high alert.

But right now she has to endure the painstaking process of vetting the lead on her computer screen. Someone reached out on the dark web that they have a potential child donor that matches Marta's request.

She wonders what this entails. Is it a person who has a child in their custody willing to put them up for this procedure for monetary gain? Marta's not sure she wants to deal with a buyer like that.

They are offering $50,000 for it, but Marta is skeptical because the request came from New York.

As a rule, they try to stay out of the US.

The healthcare system and national security are too highly regulated.

Sometimes individuals in less developed countries in a horrible financial state willingly sell their organs, but no one has offered up a child before. Adults can donate to children, but it's also possible that the organ could be too large, and Marta doesn't want to take that chance. Andre is a very slight, frail eight-year-old. It took them almost two years to find a match for Walker. Finding another smallish adult with all the necessary compatibilities, even for the donor on the Network's screen, seems an impossible feat. But she has to try.

Marta wants to give Andre the best chance for success. And to do that, a child donor is best.

Marta must entertain the lead, for Andre's sake, but she'll do so carefully.

Normally, she'd punt it back to the Network, and they'd qualify the candidate, but because she's the buyer and the broker, Marta's not going to do that. She doesn't want the Network to know Landon wasn't a match for her patient. She has her reasons, although she hasn't shared them with Walker. He won't agree with her at all.

"Miss May." Landon tugs on her sleeve. That's what he calls her—Miss May. She doesn't know how it started, but it works for her.

"I'm working, Caiman." Marta's given him a nickname too, based on the stuffed animal he brought along with him. "Caiman" means alligator in Spanish. She's hoping maybe it will stick, and they can live in this nice little life as Miss May and Caiman.

She won't make the same mistakes she made with her other two boys.

"I want to go home now," he says. "Where's my mom?"

"Oh... I see we never finished our story. About the Bear Prince."

She stops typing and looks down at the young boy's face. He perks up at the mention of the tale.

"No, we didn't."

"You'll understand more once we're done. Let's see... oh yes. The daughter was sold to the bear for misbehaving." *Marta's version.*

Landon looks down at his bare feet, as if remembering why he's there.

"The interesting thing about the bear is that he turns into a prince at night. He was put under a curse by a witch. He has to say a funny phrase before he transforms. Do you want to know what it is?"

Landon now stands on strained calves in anticipation of what it could be. "Yeah."

Marta smiles, wishing she would've had the chance to become a grandmother the traditional way, because she would've enjoyed this part. "Okay. Here goes... Bear so hairy, Bear so alarming. Change into a prince, handsome and charming."

"Bear so hairy!" Landon giggles.

She tickles his tummy. "That's right!" His laughs could fill her halls until she turned old and gray, and she wouldn't tire of it.

"The thing about the prince is that the daughter, Ninfa, fell in love with him and her new place in his enchanted cave. And when she was given the chance to go home to visit, it didn't go well. She tried to break the curse so he could be a prince all the time, and it ruined everything. She lost the prince, and her enchanted cave, and she discovered she didn't want to go back with her family after all. They'd given her away. And the Bear Prince loved her more."

Landon appears very concerned "Did she ever get the Bear Prince back?"

"She did, but she had to give up her old life forever."

Landon's smile spreads slowly across his face.

She looks at him sternly. "As long as you behave, this will be your home. Let's stop talking about the old one and the people there, okay?"

"Okay, Miss May."

She tousles his hair. "Good. *This* is your home now."

FORTY-THREE

ROWAN

Rowan watches as Wes types on his laptop, keying feverishly to keep windows from closing as new ones open.

"Are you a computer programmer or something? How do you know what you're doing?" Rowan asks. She's in sheer shock that she's staring at the very site where her family's life was brokered off like Bitcoin, and that Wes knows how to navigate it so proficiently.

"No... I was an insurance salesman before all of this. Had a normal life. A good life," he says, solemnly.

"Then how do you—"

"Months. Years of purgatory in the same place you're in right now. I learned their system myself because no one could give me answers."

"That's amazing."

Wes continues typing while he speaks. She's sure that if he stops, all the keystrokes he's just made will be a wasted effort. "I'm afraid I won't be able to give you many leads either even though I think I found your buyer. I put in a note that I had a donor for them. Don't get too excited. The Network will vet it and lock me out."

Rowan rocks sideways. "You found the buyer. On there. How do you know?"

"There's a recent post looking for an O blood type, child's kidney."

He shows her the screen that continues to try to block him with pop-ups and warnings.

"That's my husband's blood type," she says. She knows it all too well after the testing catastrophe in the police station. What they must all think of her now. She hopes no one squawks to the news about her infidelity. She's afraid it'll negatively impact the search efforts for Landon.

Rowan sees the request and the username: Geo72.

"Let's call the cops! They can trace it."

Wes shakes his head at her like a man who's stood upon the same hill of disappointment as she's on right now, and not been able to see the other side.

"You could do that. But the cops will squash any chance you have of tracing this."

"Why?"

"Everything moves at a snail's pace when it comes to international affairs. The Network knows when the authorities try to probe their system. The minute they do, they'll change the username to something else. They're constantly altering it so you can't trace it. International web crimes are extremely hard to monitor and shut down."

"But they're stealing people's organs." Rowan can hardly believe her ears.

"You're preaching to the choir."

"I can't believe they can't shut down the site. Have you ever gotten close to figuring out who's behind it?"

"Not while my son still had a chance. Only after they found him..." Wes's face clouds over. "It took me a while to figure out the site and algorithms they used. Months of studying the work around."

"You can help me. My boy might still be alive."

Wes fights the tremor in his hands. He takes a sip of his drink. "I lost everything I had trying to crack this thing, Rowan. I was obsessed. My wife left me. All my friends... My job."

"I'm so sorry."

"Is that what you want, because I'm sure it isn't."

"I think we still have time." Rowan has to believe it's not too late.

Wes doesn't look so sure. "If they took your son and learned he isn't a match as you've said, and they're reposting the listing, what do you think that means for him?"

Rowan stares out the windows caked with dirt and grime at this realization. "I still have to try. You're the only one who can help me. No one else knows their system like you do. No one's even gotten close."

Wes sighs in frustration. "The question you have to ask yourself is, are you ready to lose everything you have left for what's already gone?"

Rowan concentrates on Wes's dry hands, and the table littered with crumbs beneath his laptop, because it's easier than the question he's asking her. "My job will wait for me. For now. I'm on leave. My marriage is over. My husband left me when we learned during our blood-typing session that Landon is not his."

Rowan's had all of a two-and-a-half-hour car ride to realize the weight of what she's done and the devastating consequences. She closes her eyes as she remembers the way Marco breathed into her ear.

He never was one to stick with just one woman...

She's not sure why he betrayed his friend the way he did. Wyatt spoke of Marco's competitive nature in all things, women included, but he had to have known *she* was off limits.

Rowan understands why she did it. It's no excuse, but her upbringing left her with a tangible need to control her domestic life with two firm hands. And the call with Wyatt's flirtatious work crush, combined with his non-response when she tried to confront him, threw her into a tailspin.

Right into Marco's arms.

She felt as if her insides had been gouged out when that woman's voice pierced her eardrums from the receiver of her cell, every promise Wyatt had made to her thrown in her face.

Her actions were out of spite. She did it for control. But when she found Wyatt sound asleep in his hotel room she realized what an egregious error she'd made, and it was too late.

Wesley looks at her, shocked for a brief moment, and then continues typing. "You have another child on the way. You might get him to come around. There's hope for you. Just as long as you don't get tangled in this network. It's toxic. It will kill every bit of hope you have left for yourself and humanity."

The bleakness of his words makes her queasy. She laughs, then cries.

Wes takes a long sip of whiskey and then coughs. "I've made terrible mistakes in a craze to shut this organization down. I've come to the realization now that I cannot do it. I'm just one man. They're ruled by many."

She wipes tears from her face. "But you can help me try to find this person on the dark web? Please. You're all I've got."

Wes seems to soften at this. "I make no promises, but I will try."

FORTY-FOUR
THE DOCTOR

"What're you doing in there, Mar?" Walker calls for her.

Marta's been trying to vet the contact in New York City, but this isn't her area of expertise. She doesn't know much about New York, only that it's big and easy to get lost in, and even easier to hide in. She should roll the dice with this one, and hope it's a match. But that didn't work out so well for her the last time.

She can't let Walker know what she's doing, playing both buyer and seller. She realizes she's compromising their organization, letting her personal life get in the way, but what's at stake is great.

Her grandson.

And her... other child. If she has the Network field the request, they'll know the last one they secured didn't work out. There'll be questions.

"Miss May, can I play with Andy?" Landon's just come in from outside. His hair sticks up on his head in two brown waves. Marta has the realization it's going to need to be cut soon. She can take a pair of shears to it, but it makes her wonder how she'll maintain his other needs. She can handle doctor's visits and homeschool him, but what if he has an emergency? Are they to keep him locked in the compound forever?

Eventually, they'll have to take him out in public.

Marta reasons with herself that children grow quickly at this age. Once Landon sprouts a few inches, he'll look completely different. At least not easily recognizable as the fluffy-haired four-year-old on all the missing person flyers currently posted on social media.

"Did you feed the chickens?" Marta asks.

"Yes," he says, a smudge of dirt on his sweaty face. Their property is so large, Marta requires one of the help to go out with Landon. So far, no one's asked her who he is or why he's there. They probably assume he's a part of their family somehow. "They're not hungry anymore. Can I go see Andy?"

"That's so nice. Do you like Andy? Is he like having a big brother?"

"Yeah..." Landon leans from one side to the next. "My mommy has a baby in her belly. I'm going to be a brother soon."

Marta winces at his comment. She doesn't know how she's going to make him forget about his old life. "She's not going to be your mommy anymore. Remember?"

His face twists with sadness. "I can't believe she said she didn't want me anymore. Just because I didn't listen."

"She said she hopes the new baby listens better."

Landon's lower lip wobbles. She knows it's bad to say things like this to him, but the sooner he can move on, the better.

"Go on and play with Andy. I put Battleship in his room."

"What's that?" Landon brightens a little. He's holding his alligator by its tail. Ever since Marta told him that he wouldn't be returning home, and that his mother gave him to her, he hasn't let it out of his sight.

"A new game. It's fun. Go see!"

Landon darts off toward Andre's room.

Marta was happy to see Andre up and about today. His

health wavers from one day to the next. Sometimes he has so much blood in his urine, Marta wonders if keeping him there is the best plan.

If a hospital could find him a kidney, she'd gladly admit him. But with so few options, she's been forced to care for him there.

However, they are on borrowed time. With Landon, she has more control and their time together feels more like a long-term investment.

You haven't met Caiman? He's my cousin's child. She fell ill and we're his guardians now.

Marta has so many cousins, it's negligible whose it is.

She remembers when life was good, and her family and extended family was large and healthy, and they had massive wheelbarrow races. The winners would break into a happy victory march or play the dancing game, *Jarabe Tapatío*. All the participants sat in a circle, and each child was called to the center to create their own routine until all had performed.

Marta can still hear the happy laughter.

Taste the fresh treats her mother would prepare, flour tortillas filled with meat and cheese. She can see herself with her sisters, spread on a patterned blanket, their bare toes tickling the colorful fringe.

After she married Walker, that close-knit dynamic changed, and her family became smaller.

She was limited to just the family she created with Walker, but she tried extra hard to make it wonderful without her parents. The fact that they didn't want her there always seemed a good reason to take daytrips to the coast. Everyone in the family loved to fish.

What're we going to catch today? Yellowfin? Sailfish? Bass?

All day they'd spend in the sun, casting the line, reeling it in.

Marta can remember her boys with their sunhats and long

shirts to protect them from the sun like it was yesterday. Their beautiful faces squinting into the sun.

If they caught something, they'd cook it that night for dinner. It was tradition.

If they didn't, there was an excellent restaurant the family liked to visit on the water with fried ice cream on the menu.

She swore sometimes Damon would lose his fish on purpose because he wanted that ice cream. He never was good at staying away from temptation.

Marta's afraid Caiman's upbringing will be so secluded, he won't thrive. When school's back in, his socialization will suffer.

For now, he has Andre, and he must survive.

He's the only friend her boy has.

FORTY-FIVE
WYATT

Wyatt trudges into his mother's one-bedroom apartment in defeat. She seems surprised to see him, and immediately starts moving dirty dishes and old magazines from surfaces to make room for him and his duffel bag.

He should've packed more clothes. It doesn't look like he's ever going back.

"I would've fixed supper if I knew you were coming." Mom is still clearing things from the counters of her tiny apartment. Wyatt notices in disgust as she pulls the garbage from the bin and sees a plethora of empty bottles. He assumes that's her dinner most nights, just like the old days.

"That's okay. I don't have much of an appetite. I'll take it out." He grabs the bag from her even though he's wobbly from his near-death experience. She doesn't fight him. He has a need to feel useful. If only dragging a plastic bag to a garbage dumpster.

He checks his phone and has one missed call from Stone. Nothing from his wife or Marco. It's unreal how quickly the most important people in his life have seemed to disappear into thin air. Why is he so easy to abandon? Shouldn't Rowan be begging him for forgiveness?

Or Marco?

Who slept with his wife. *Fuck.*

He doesn't blame himself for not suspecting anything, because there were absolutely no signs this could be a possibility.

Except for his psycho wife showing up in his hotel room at his work event. She said she was just concerned, but Wyatt knows she thought he was with Tatum. Tatum was a terrible flirt and nothing more, but Wyatt never imagined in a thousand years his wife's insecurity would drive her to even the score.

He tosses the bag in the dumpster that reeks of sand and sweat and Jersey shore mischief. He wipes his hands, calls Stone.

"Hi, Wyatt, how're you holding up?"

"Okay... I have some info on who Landon's biological father is." He snaps back into investigation mode. He can feel sorry for himself later. As far as he's concerned, his wife failed their son by lying about his paternity. She had to have known it was a possibility. He won't do the same.

"Good. I heard what happened at the shore."

"Been better, but I'm okay."

"It can't be easy. All you've learned... Who's the guy?"

He sighs. "Marco Lucarelli is the name."

"Do you know him?"

"He's my best friend. From childhood. Still lives here. In Wildwood. He definitely does not have Landon. He had nothing to do with his abduction."

"Jesus. I'm sorry. We'll question him anyway. Please send his contact info. Is that why you went for a swim?"

"No. Found out afterward."

Stone is the one to sigh this time. "I know this is all very difficult. And I'm sorry about what happened in the police station. None of us expected that. But it's placed elevation on the case now that Landon isn't a match."

"I understand. What do we do?"

"First, I haven't been able to get in touch with Rowan. Do you know where she is?"

"She's not at the house?"

"No," Stone says. "Have you heard from her?"

"I haven't." Wyatt leans against the siding, suddenly unable to breathe. He's already lost one child. Is Rowan so distraught by this information that she'd do something to endanger the baby?

"Question. How did you get to the hotel in Mexico City?" Stone asks.

"Taxi."

"Was it a registered taxi or a hired driver."

Driver. The word sparks something within him. "Well, I was supposed to take a car service ordered by my company, but I forgot. And grabbed a cab instead."

He closes his eyes. *Pay attention, Wyatt!* He can hear his wife's voice screeching in his ear. "Do you think that's where they got me? The taxi?"

"Possibly. How well did you know your employer. Apex?"

"I didn't," he says.

"We went to investigate and the building is empty."

"That doesn't surprise me. My boss said the comapy was folding."

"They don't have a registered tax ID number."

"What does that mean?"

"They weren't a legitimate company," Stone says.

"What? They were. They had software they created."

"There're other similar software programs to the one you developed." *What?* They told him it was software they created. It was the whole point of his job—to learn it. To roll it out to the other employees.

"Are you saying the company was fraudulent?"

"Most certainly."

"I don't understand how this is all connected," he says.

"We don't either and please don't share this information, but we're working on it. I need you to find Rowan. We're worried about her. I know you're not in a good place with her, but can you help?"

"I'll try." He means he'll try both physically and mentally, because he cannot forgive her. But he can try to push aside his anger and betrayal to locate her and their unborn child. He has to believe the second one is his. There haven't been any workplace flirtations since Tatum, or romances of any kind. She's had no reason to repeat her actions.

He can already feel a bitterness settling in where love used to live. He would love to hate his wife. But first he has to find her.

Wyatt hangs up the phone and tries tracking hers—nothing.

She either has it turned off or has disabled her location services feature, which is concerning. He's the one who was wronged. He tries to call her again—straight to voicemail.

She should want him to seek her out.

Unless there's something else she's not telling him.

FORTY-SIX
FRANCISCO

Francisco received a note from the Network that his payment should arrive shortly for his latest procedure. The only problem is—Francisco hasn't performed a surgery since his last one.

He doesn't want to alert the Network of this fact, but he also doesn't want to take Corazon's money, the only other surgeon on the roster. That man is ruthless, and Francisco will be the one left without body parts if he touches his cash.

He also doesn't understand how a mix-up could've occurred.

It's never happened before. The Network doesn't make mistakes.

The air in Florida is restless today—raining one minute, bright and sunny the next, matching his internal turmoil.

This can't go on...

He's had the thought more than once recently, like working against a ticking clock. His time to figure out how to escape is running out.

Francisco has enough money to slip away safely.

The only problem is, there's nowhere he can go where they won't find him.

The one time he even thought about leaving them, he was in Brazil on a job. He met a man who told him he was part of the rainforest community where Francisco could retreat. They needed a doctor among their growing society.

The man said they built their houses in the side of trees, and cell towers were too far away to track him. There was nothing but rope ladders to maneuver around the village, and manual labor was the normal way of life there. He warned Francisco it was a farming community and that he'd have to get his fingers dirty. Francisco was fine with that. They couldn't get any filthier than they already were.

He traveled on that assignment with a lot of money in case he needed to pay off the locals for safe passage, especially in the remote areas.

The only regret Francisco had as he was riding by Jeep—deep into the thicket of the jungle, ready to disappear into the rainforest forever—was that he was indefinitely leaving Lola and his child behind. He'd never really been a part of their lives, but Lola would worry when he didn't come around.

She'd suffer financially when her envelope didn't arrive too.

He promised himself that once he was settled he'd try to courier her some cash.

His parents wouldn't know what happened to him in South America, but if he disappeared, he convinced himself the Network couldn't make assumptions, and that they wouldn't immediately kill them.

Anything could've happened there—robbery and murder. A dark fate with a jungle animal. No body didn't mean much in those parts. There were plenty of places to dispose of one in Brazil.

And if the Network made assumptions and they slaughtered his mother and father—so be it. They're the ones who put him in this situation in the first place.

He thinks of that unfortunate moment in time as he calls his mother.

She answers quickly. "Hello." She seems confused. Probably because he only limits his calls to necessity.

"They paid me, but I didn't complete a job."

"Oh." Francisco can hear something in the background. A squeaking. No... a child's laughter.

"What is that noise?" he asks. He wonders if his mother might be at the hospital working.

"It's Andre," she says. "He's having a good day today."

He immediately knows she's lying. Andre doesn't make sounds like that. His nephew never had a normal childhood. Andre's father died before he was born, his mother abandoned him, and he has a rare disease. Kids like him don't giggle like that.

"What's going on, Mother?" He's angry now, because whatever she's up to, she's put him in danger. He can't accept money for an assignment he didn't complete. He can't not accept it either.

"Don't worry, Zo. Just keep doing what you're doing. Think of it as a bonus."

He grits his teeth. What has she done?

"You know I can't accept money for a procedure I didn't perform. They're going to find out. It's going to be bad..."

"It's taken care of," she says. "You'll earn the fee. Don't worry."

"You were working on hacking the medical records of the child you were considering using as a donor for Andre. Were you able to get in? Is he a match? Wyatt Bishop's son? Is that what this is about? Are you waiting for Corazon? Why did they pay me, Mother?"

"He wasn't a match," she says quickly.

"Well, then who is the child in your home?"

"Andre. And a friend, okay. He was lonely."

Francisco leans his head back on the clean white walls of his house. Expensive art from an artist he can't name hangs in the entranceway. He's here so infrequently, he paid a designer to install everything. "You cannot let anyone in that house. They could stumble upon the war room. Figure out what we do. Did you have a parent drop them off? What're you thinking?"

"No, we had Alistair pick him up. It's just for the day. You two used to play all day..." Her voice softens as she says this. She uses Damon's death as an excuse for everything she does, but it's also a crutch for taking advantage of him too, and it's not fair.

"I wouldn't make a habit of it. Any more leads for Andre?" He does feel terrible about his nephew. Francisco doesn't know why he was spared the genetic curse. There's no good solution here, but if they're acquiring Andre's kidney through the Network, they can't have playdates at the site where the surgery is being performed.

"No... and this isn't an everyday thing. It's a boy he used to go to school with."

His mother has the edge in the voice she uses when she's not telling him everything. He just hopes she's not putting the rest of the family at risk to save one of their own—again.

FORTY-SEVEN

ROWAN

Rowan watches as Wes's fingers fly over the computer keys. She's taken to cleaning up his kitchen, washing his dishes by hand, putting them away. It gives her something to do, makes her miss her own kitchen.

Her old life. With her husband.

It's funny how fast her feelings morphed from hatred to regret when she learned the truth about who Landon's father is.

Wyatt called her, but she can't bear to call him back.

What would she even say? *Sorry, I slept with your best friend...*

She received a text from Marco that just read—*He knows.*

She's relieved not to have to explain herself, but she's also wondering what Marco told him, exactly. She can't believe Wyatt is contacting her, and worried he might have an update on Landon that she's missing. But she can't abandon this lead.

The first one she's had since Landon's fingers slipped through hers.

And she can't leave the only man who can help her.

Wes has stopped tapping the keys to take a picture of the

laptop screen with his phone. In the absence of his typing all the windows on the screen shut down.

He takes a second look at his camera screen and appears satisfied he's captured whatever he found. Rowan wishes she knew how to manipulate the system so she could have kept typing for him. Like two paramedics working on a patient, she could've continued breathing life into the laptop to keep the crooked site from arresting.

Wes hasn't stopped staring at his screenshot.

"What is it?" she asks.

He looks up as if he forgot she was there. She's guessing he's been alone for so long, having another human in his apartment feels unnatural.

"There's a wire transfer tag for the first pediatric case. It's back up. Posted. It appears as though the buyer has already paid someone with this confirmation number. It's weird, posting a receipt."

"What does that mean?" Rowan asks.

"I don't know. I've never seen this before. It's not typical of the Network to post any receipts. They don't give up private information on here. My bigger question. Why post a duplicate post for the same thing if they've already received it with the first?"

"Maybe because it wasn't a match. Let me see it," she says.

Rowan takes a picture of the twelve digits with her own phone. She sends it to her sister, with a note that says—*Show Amir.*

It's a receipt for Landon and the hacker I'm with says it's a link to an account.

She immediately receives a message back from Riley.

Riley: *A hacker?!*

Rowan: *That's right. The cops are useless.*

Riley: *Be fucking careful.*

Rowan: *Can you send it ASAP?*

Riley: *He's sitting right here. Says it's a bank account.*

Rowan glances at Wes. "It's a bank account."

Wes raises his eyebrows in surprise. She takes it as a spot of hope.

Rowan: *I need Amir to trace it and tell no one. Time is not on our side! If this is a receipt, my son has already been transferred to another party.*

Riley: *He's on it.*

Rowan knows this could be in reference to a different kid, but what're the chances? Two posts for the same exact thing within weeks. Even if it's not a receipt for Landon, it will likely lead them to the person who has him.

Wes is busy typing again. "Who're you texting?"

"My sister. Her boyfriend works for national security in DC. He's going to try to trace the account."

"Well, son of a gun," Wes says with interest.

"What is it?"

"The whole post is gone. The account number and everything."

"Well, how can that be?"

"The Network is constantly updating it, and once a job is completed, they clear the history. They must've posted it by mistake."

Rowan brightens, holding her hand to her belly as if this

moment is everything. "It's a sign. It's our break. We were meant to find him. I should call Stone." Rowan pulls out her phone.

Wes stands and touches her arm lightly. "Look... this is good. It could lead you to him, but the police will stymie your progress. They'll immediately alert the CIA and international cyber security and tip these guys off. They're very savvy at knowing when the authorities have caught onto them. And if they know we're getting close, and your boy is still alive..."

Wes can't finish the sentence, but he doesn't have to. Because she understands what he's telling her now. "It could endanger him."

"Yes. We don't want to fly flags saying we know one of the buyer's bank accounts, because they'll immediately contact his bank, and it will alert the Network. They'll shut down the account and probably murder the buyer for being careless with sensitive information."

"Jesus."

"You're better off letting your sister's boyfriend work his magic behind the scenes. Do you trust him?" he asks.

"Yes. She's been dating him for a long time. We can trust Amir."

"I don't trust anybody," Wes says too quickly.

Rowan's phone lights up. "The bank account is registered to an Alonzo Firth at First Horizon bank in Fort Lauderdale, Florida."

Wes leans back and types on his phone. She imagines a younger version of Wes with a less sallow complexion, thirty pounds lighter, and she can see how he could've been an attractive man before this organization destroyed him. "There's no one on social media by that name. No LinkedIn. No Facebook. Nothing." He looks at her bleakly.

"Maybe he's a private person."

"It's a ghost account. Not his real name. I'm sure there's

money being transferred to that account for that job. But that's not the real recipient."

Rowan's typing in the map section on her phone. She grabs her purse off the table.

"What're you doing?" Wes asks.

"I'm going there. I'm driving to Florida. I can't fly, the police will be able to track me."

Wes stands up again, and she's afraid he's going to get in her way, so she quickly darts around him.

"Now, just hold on. You can't travel all that way. In your... condition."

She places her hand on her hip. This guy has no idea what she's capable of, pregnant or not.

"I did not mean any offense. It's a long drive. You're chasing a misnomer. What happens when you get there? What's the plan? The bank isn't going to give you any information. What if you do find him? Are you going to run him down yourself?"

She squeezes her phone, angry, because he's right. She has no plan. She doesn't even have her gun. Only the desperation to find the people linked with her son. "And you're certain that if we tell the police they'll tip off the Network?"

"One hundred and fifty percent. Long after my son was gone, I had a clue that there was a buyer in Pakistan. I notified the police. Within fifteen minutes a computer virus had infiltrated my system, took ahold of my controls, and typed in big red American letters that I'd be next if I didn't stop."

Rowan's mouth drops open. "What did you do?"

"My wife hadn't left me yet, although she'd been ready to for a while... But I was trying to hold onto the marriage and I feared for her safety. So, I stopped dabbling in their system."

"And she still left?" Rowan asks, sadly.

"Yeah." Wes's voice is heavy with remorse. "Neither one of us knew how to be together without him. We just couldn't figure out how to work through the loss. It was like walking around an iceberg in the center of the room every day, and trying to pretend like it wasn't there."

"Have you tried to reach out to her, recently? Maybe you're both in a better place now." Rowan is clutching her bag to her side, still prepared to drive to Florida by herself, but she wants to know the answer to this question. It's like looking into a crystal ball of what will happen to her own marriage.

Wes shakes his head. "We never found our way back to each other. Every time we looked at one another all we could see was what we lost. She's moved on," he says sadly. "With someone else."

Rowan looks around at his dusty apartment. "Come with me."

"What? No way."

"This is your chance. To bust them. It's what you've been waiting for."

"My days of chasing these people are over."

"I mean... what... with all that's happening around you." She kicks a pile of papers.

"I have a job."

She stares him down as if she doesn't believe him.

"As an online insurance auditor," he says.

"And you love that job and would hate to leave it."

Wes releases a croak of a laugh and glances out the window.

"You're right. I can't do this by myself. But you know I'm going to try, right? Let's nail these guys," Rowan says.

Wes stares at her long and hard. "Let me grab a bag."

FORTY-EIGHT
THE DOCTOR

Marta has finished a mini-shift at the hospital. She was questioned again by the authorities about the American who was hospitalized after a tourist attack. She gave them the same information she provided before—*he didn't remember what happened.*

It's an isolated incident.

She knows nothing more.

There's a part of her that misses the old Mexico City that would've let this slide. Since tourism has gone way up, so has the scrutiny over their safety policies.

The house is quieter than she'd like when she returns. The hallways glint with tiny white candles. Their low wicks flicker weakly, indicating someone lit them long ago.

Marta waltzes swiftly by Andre's room, and he's resting. So sad for a boy to sleep the day away. He should be on summer break with the rest of his peers. She's losing this battle, sadly. But where is his buddy?

Marta walks into the war room to find Walker hunched wearily over the monitors, a notebook in front of him. "What is it?" she asks.

"I received a call from Enid."

Enid? Uh oh. "And?"

"The pediatric bid had a transfer number attached to it. She traced the purchaser back to you." Walker doesn't look up when he says this. She feels the air leave her lungs and leans back on the desk.

They're locked together for eternity, she and Walker, which makes arguing very difficult. Most of the time when they disagree, they resort to quick snipes and the silent treatment—but this is different, and she knows it.

She's endangered them all. Only Enid could see the purchaser, but if Marta forgot to block the transfer number, it would've not only shown her purchaser ID, but where she sent the money to as well—to Francisco's Florida account.

She's already talked to him about it. She should call Francisco and let him know about the breach, but only those seeking a donor with that specific genetic sequence would've noticed it on the Network. You have to click on the bid to see all of the information.

She and Walker are having an unspoken conversation of horror, momentarily making eye contact, and then fretfully looking away. They're in this together. When one of them makes a mistake, they both suffer. "There can't be another person out there looking for the same pediatric match," she says. "No one else saw it."

"You hope." He goes back to what she can only assume is scrubbing the system. He'll start with the main server and then go back and delete any inference of her post in the history.

"Are we in trouble? With Enid?"

"She yelled a lot, saying she understood that we've never been in the position of being both the buyer and seller before. But... why would you post a wire transfer when you didn't even buy it? There was no procedure," he asks. "I didn't tell her otherwise." After an organ is extracted, a payment is made, but that wasn't the case here. Marta had her reasons for wanting the Network to believe the extraction was successful. This is the question that will do her in. "I knew the Network would be curious if we didn't show a receipt of a surgery. They have to know we kidnapped the boy by now." She looks around, suddenly realizing that it's very quiet in the house. "Where is Landon now, Walker?"

Walker ignores the question. "What about Andre? Won't the Network be suspicious when you place a second order? I saw the duplicate request..."

"That system hasn't provided any results for two years. We're going to have to do better research. We need to make sure we have a match before we... get another donor." She won't inform him about the one she found—in New York. He must've not seen the response to the post, so hellbent on clearing it. He would tell her not to entertain it, but she can't turn her back on it. It could be a lead.

Walker shakes his head. "So, you're trading one boy for another. You just wanted to keep your pet. Andre is dying and instead of putting his needs first and placing all your energy in sourcing him a new kidney, you're busy babysitting the Bishop kid." He sounds disgusted beyond belief.

A sickening feeling creeps up the back of her neck. Marta always felt sorry when they lost patients. She looked up the donors' bios provided by the Network, the families they left behind. Lit candles. There're a few in her hallway illuminated right now that represent the lost souls who didn't make it through surgery for one reason or another.

But Walker was different that way.

He saw them as donors and nothing more. Francisco tried to leave them in a way that gave them a chance for survival, stitched them up, placed them in ice if he could, but if the patient had any type of comorbidity that made their surgery riskier, it didn't end well.

And, if any of the donors posed a risk for disclosure, the Network disposed of them.

Walker may have viewed Landon as a risk now that the transfer was exposed. A big one.

"Where is Landon?" Marta asks.

"I had Alistair take him for a ride. He won't be coming back."

Marta walks over to where her husband is typing and stands there until he stops. "Where is he taking him?"

"Depends on how everything goes. He wasn't being very cooperative." Walker's eyes are frosty and bitter. He's upset with her for putting them in this situation to begin with, but he shouldn't have made this move without her permission.

"Why're you doing this? It wasn't necessary." Her voice is barely audible. She's sacrificed everything for this family. And for this organization. Couldn't he let her have one spot of happiness?

"Your attachment to the boy was unhealthy. It made you distracted. You were more worried about preserving his place here than your own grandson's," he says.

She wants to slap Walker across the face, but she knows he's right. Never could get anything past him. "I was avoiding having to explain myself if they saw Wyatt Bishop's son missing on the news. I just want to know if Alistair is getting him back to the States. What's the plan?"

"We should've done more recon to make sure he was a match before taking him. Now look..."

"Where is he, Walker! Please, just tell me. Promise me they won't hurt him." She's trying not to show emotion. It's dangerous to care too much in their industry. She just wants to be sure he's okay.

"I make no promises." He turns his attention back to the computer screen. "I'm too busy cleaning up your mess."

Marta turns on her heel, runs through the lit hallways, and out the front door. She will not lose another one.

FORTY-NINE
WYATT

At first her communication came in small spurts, a message on social media here and there, something to make him smile in the middle of an arduous workday.

> Hello, friend, I visited this mountaintop in Switzerland today. Reminded me of our time together. When I summit I think of you. Have you done any climbing lately?

An attached picture of Mount Pilatus could be found with beautiful Naomi smiling in the forefront. She always sent pictures of herself alone, and he'd wondered why she'd never coupled up. She explained she had family duties that made it difficult to establish her own family. She admitted that the pictures she sent him were from when she graced him with a rare morsel of her free time.

She didn't ask too many questions about what he did, and he knew even less about her occupation, but work isn't what bound them. Connection was. She'd always reach out when he was having a particularly shitty day or when Rowan was riding his ass about something. It's like she knew he needed that hit of

Naomi. He assumed his messages back provided the same sense of relief.

> That looks beautiful. The only hills I've been climbing lately are the mountains of debt I've acquired by purchasing my new home for my wife. Hoping this job pays off.
>
> Xx,
>
> Wy
>
> Why did you purchase such a large home? That would be absurd to do such a thing over here.
>
> Sich die Wurst vom Brot nehmen lassen.
>
> You forgot to turn your translator on…
>
> I didn't. It's a German phrase my mother used to say. It means don't let someone take the sausage off your bread. Stand up for yourself. If you don't want a house that big, speak up and get a smaller one. There's no need for such extravagances where I'm from.

He thought about that one long and hard. His messages with Naomi had trickled in and increased, especially over the last five years. And in that time, he'd worked more and more to offer Rowan the things she desired, but as a result he didn't see her as much. No matter how much he brought in, it never seemed enough.

There were some weeks he was grinding at the office, his only moment of solace—a message from Naomi.

And now…

The brunette straddles him in the front seat of his Highlander, kissing him, and pumping her hips wildly. He wanted to talk to her first. They have so much to discuss, but his resolve is crumbling.

He's been waiting so long to see her. If all this pain wasn't for her—then who?

"Be careful. I'm still sore." He points to his side. He still hasn't inspected his wound beneath the bandage since his nearly fatal swim in the ocean. It's harder to look Truth in the face these days. It's easier just to bury himself instead—in the waves—and her curves...

"I'm sorry." Naomi's accent is exactly as he remembers it. The lilt in her voice only arouses him more.

When she contacted him online years ago, before he started at Apex, he thought he was dreaming. He confessed to her that when he was stressed, he mentally retreated to their mountaintop and pretended that he was sitting there with her in quiet bliss.

She said she had those same visions. Their mountaintop was her happy place too.

They compared notes and concluded that on two separate occasions they'd met each other in their minds at the exact same time. It was an impossibility, Wyatt realized.

But he did think they were bound together in an otherworldly way; their connection undeniable.

Naomi said she hadn't met anyone else that made her feel the same way as he did since the last time they were together. She'd discovered Wyatt on social media and just had to reach out to him. She said she could feel him through the computer screen—calling out to her like a beacon from across the ocean. A distress signal.

He loved how spiritual she was. Naomi teemed with good energy. She wouldn't cheat on her husband or harass him on a daily basis about his oversights.

If Rowan was better to him, things could've been different.

He might've even found it in his heart to forgive her. But she's not. She hasn't even called him back. Owned her actions. Apologized.

Wyatt and Naomi used to talk for hours about everything from what their favorite bike trails were to their hopes and dreams. Back then, Wyatt told Naomi that he just wanted to make enough money so that he never had to worry about where his next meal was coming from, or that of anyone else in his household.

Naomi wanted a simple life too. Opening a yoga studio was on her shortlist. As was teaching meditation, bringing mindfulness. She said she had a lot of childhood trauma to heal from. So did he, but neither one of them talked about it, because their time together was short, and it would dampen their party.

Being with Naomi was like floating on a cloud. He was at peace in her presence then.

And he's at peace in her presence now.

Except for this moment, where she seems to break character and turn into a sex-starved maniac. She wants him in a way his wife never has. It's why he's traded any chance of a life with Rowan for her. Because if it wasn't over before, he's just sealed the deal.

He's not sure what he'll do about the new baby.

He just has to keep Naomi a secret from Rowan until they're officially divorced. And everyone else too. It won't look good that he's moved on so soon.

She'll make him forget... this angel on Earth.

"*Oh my god,*" he says. Nothing about their lovemaking is a chore as she slips him inside of her. She moans in his ear, and in that moment, he is possessed.

Naomi can have anything she wants from him.

His old life is over.

He wonders if it was ever even real to begin with, any of the relationships he formed, the people he met. It all seems like a contrived paradox now, a part he was playing that he no longer wants.

They have sex like teenagers in the front seat of his car, and it doesn't last long. Their emotional relationship has gone on for years, the build-up culminating to a point of no return now that his marriage has dissolved.

They sit there half-clothed, parked at the beach, smoking a joint, windows rolled down. Neither one speaks as they stare at the ocean. Wyatt was never able to sit like this with Rowan. She was uncomfortable with long stretches of silence.

In a way, Wyatt thinks it's almost as important to be at ease with someone when there's nothing to say as it is when you're talking about the important stuff.

"I don't have anywhere for you to stay. I'm on my mother's couch for now," he says, sadly. "I called the realtor. Once I sell my house, I'll be able to buy us something nice. Hopefully, far away from here." Obviously, he was not meant to be a father any more than his own father.

Naomi smiles. "I was never after your money."

"I know." He smiles back. This is true. He had nothing more than a backpack when he met her. But she has to understand he's made a successful career for himself since then.

Rowan always made him feel like providing for her was his number one responsibility. She criticized him for every mistake he made. He just hopes trusting Naomi isn't one of them.

He wants to believe Naomi. That they'll fly to San Antonio, Texas, meet an anonymous man in a black SUV who says he has his boy, take him back—but that possibility seems unreal. Naomi said that when she heard about Wyatt's plight, she used her resources overseas to help locate his son.

Wyatt really hopes she knows what she is talking about. After all, she did live in Europe, and that was where the Network was located. It was plausible this might all work out.

But he and Rowan were warned about strangers coming out

of the woodwork to try to claim they had information to cash in on the reward money.

But these people weren't looking for a reward. Rowan would be upset if she knew the woman Wyatt used to sleep with is the one who gave him the referral for his job at Apex. A company that's not even real.

But she'd be even more upset if she's the very one to get their son killed.

FIFTY

FRANCISCO

The money has sat for two days and no one's come looking for it. Still, the payment feels "hot," and Francisco isn't comfortable just letting it stir in his bank account. He didn't earn it, and he doesn't understand what his mother means by a work "bonus."

There's no bonuses working in this hellscape.

She's lying about the money's origin and he doesn't understand why. What procedure does the Network think he's performed?

He decides to cash out twenty-five thousand and give it to Lola.

He has an awful foreboding that his days working for the Network are numbered, and his employment is not going to end well. Lola doesn't realize it, but he's left her everything. Every penny in his bank account. His house, which is paid off. The cars. But he's also afraid the government will seize it all once they learn how he's acquired the funds. Best to funnel as much as he can now.

He doesn't care if she sells every last thing he owned or lives in the house herself, only that someone benefits positively from his work and the wealth he created. Even if they have to enjoy it after he's dead.

Surely, that's what's coming next if his mother screwed up the way he suspects she has.

He starts to write the name of the owner of the account on a bank slip, and accidentally scribbles his real first name—Francisco. He crumbles the paper at the station. Picks up another, and writes his fake bank account name, Alonzo Firth. Removes his fake ID to withdraw the cash.

He can't conceive the Network made an error on this payment.

His mother manufactured this. She's the most destructive person he's ever met.

She climbs into the snake pit, rolls around, and then blames everyone else when she gets bitten.

He's spoken to his grandmother infrequently because she hates his father, but she told Francisco once that his mother used to pick fights with other kids in the playground. She was enthralled with the human body even back then. His abuela reasoned she liked to see how body parts became broken so she could examine how to fix them later.

Francisco wonders if there's a small, sick part of her that enjoys what the Network does. The dark magic of sourcing organs for desperate patients, even if that means taking them unwillingly from others.

She should've really become a surgeon if that's the case, because when he learned how to cut during his residency, this certainly wasn't what he had in mind.

He leaves the bank. A ragged-looking couple behind him takes his place. He feels like he's seen them before, but he doesn't know why.

Traveling around the globe, rubbing shoulders with the world, has made everyone look familiar, yet he doesn't feel like he really knows anyone. This subservient life he's been living isn't enough anymore.

Once he reaches Lola's place of work he thinks about the unusual request dancing on his lips.

He shouldn't ask her.

It's a mistake.

He should let her be happy with the ugly dude in the graphic t-shirt he spotted her with in the bleachers at Nico's game. That guy can give her so much more than he can just by being a free man.

But if this is it... if his mother has slipped, given them up, is it so bad to ask to meet his son, just this once? No one knows they're even related. Maybe he can lie and say he's an old friend of his mother's.

He thinks about his boy often.

The story Nico has been told is that his father left before he was born. Francisco wonders if Nico's asked about him, and if Lola's given him a name. He told her not to, so hopefully if she did, it's a fake one.

But years from now, after Francisco's dead, he wants her to be able to say:

"Do you remember that man we met at the park who I told you was my old friend from school? That... was your father."

Maybe, then, he'll have some sense of who Francisco is. Perhaps it will also give him insight into his own self. Francisco doesn't know who he'd be without his father. His childhood was good. They weren't rich, but they were well-off. They didn't have a great relationship with his mother's side because of his father, but they did have a tight-knit family unit of four.

Until Damon went and messed everything up.

Damon was more like Mom. Although he didn't just like to roll with the snakes.

He liked to taste their venom too.

They're at Snyder Park, a good distance from the beach, near the butterfly garden. Lola looks beautiful in a long flowing sundress, light makeup, soft smile. There's the girl he fell in love with—the wife he would've had if the Network hadn't stolen his life away.

And the young man before him, Nico, is nine years old. He's the son in that same life-that-could've-been scenario Francisco often replays in his mind.

Nico stands with his baseball glove on his hand, socking a stitched white ball in the mitt, over and over again.

Francisco bought him a Miami Marlins baseball cap with extra embroidery on the side. He hands it to him. "Do you like it?" he asks.

"Yeah... that's dope. Thanks," he says as he places it on his head. It's almost painful how much his son looks like him. He can see a wild streak in Nico's eyes. Lola grins, because she sees it too.

"Keep crushing it on the field." Francisco pats the bill of his new hat.

"Thanks, man. What's your name again?" he asks.

"Uncle Z. I'm an old friend of your mom's."

"Cool. Thanks... for the birthday cards too."

"You bet."

"Mom, can I go check out the garden?" He points at the butterfly garden.

"Go for it!"

Nico dashes away, his new hat shielding him from the sun, which has grown brutally hot even though it's only morning.

"Still traveling for work?" she asks. Lola doesn't know exactly what he does, only that his parents got him into something illegal right before he finished his residency, and now he can't get out of it.

"Yeah..." He sways side to side, trying to decide how to tell her he thinks it might be the last time they'll see each other. Ever.

"Still dating the guy with the bad Affliction t-shirts?"

Lola punches him in the shoulder and giggles. "Kenny owns his own extermination business and takes very good care of us."

"That's nice. That's what I want. Really."

"I thought you couldn't meet Nico. That it would endanger him. Us. What's going on, Francisco?" she asks.

He turns toward her. "My parents made some mistakes. It affects me. I might not be able to see you again. I have a horrible feeling."

She offers him a quick hug. They both look over to find Nico trying to catch a Monarch with his mitt. The butterfly swoops around the leather, its gold and orange dots and stripes making zigzags in the air, but Nico's too slow, and the insect flutters away.

"Here." He hands her a fat envelope of money.

She takes it and counts it, eyes wide. "This is a lot."

"Take it. I don't know when I'll see you again. I'm so glad I got to meet him. Tell him, someday, I wanted a relationship with him. I just couldn't have one. It's what was best."

"You're scaring me." Tears hang in Lola's eyes, but it's better she realize that he's probably not coming back now than to find his obituary in the newspaper later.

FIFTY-ONE

ROWAN

Rowan and Wes crouch at a nearby bench and watch the family. A dark-haired male and female, and a little boy who is undoubtedly their son. But they're distressed, and Rowan can't understand why. The woman kisses the man, but then she looks as though she's going to burst into tears.

"Who is that?" Rowan whispers.

Wes seems intent on studying this couple, but much like when Rowan was sitting right in front of him at his apartment, it's almost as if she wasn't even there. During the sixteen-hour car ride, Wes was a decent conversationalist, but he would drift off for hours, and Rowan feared she'd soon fall into the same mental canyon of no return if she didn't find her son. This state of in-between, of not-knowing is not living. It's purgatory, a holding pattern in Hell until someone can deliver definitive information on where Landon is.

"Wes?" she says. "Who're we watching?"

He holds his finger up at her to wait a minute.

When the man left the bank, Wes instinctively picked up the scrap of paper he dropped at the bank window as Rowan inquired about opening an account. They didn't have a great plan, only to ask about wire transfers, overseas transactions, hoping to scrounge up a clue about how the Network made its payments there.

Violence was not beneath Rowan at this juncture. If the teller wasn't going to give up the information and some was to be had, she envisioned herself reaching across the tiny window and yanking her through the other side. Wes rushed her out of the bank mid-sentence instead.

The urgency of this mission was felt with every fiber of her being.

The new posting that went up on the Network for another child catapulted her fear off the charts.

What have they done with her son in the meantime?

He's just a little boy. Couldn't they let him go?

She fought to steady her breath for her unborn child, and forced herself to eat, but her stomach felt raw, her chronic headache, one that sliced with the ferocity of a samurai sword between the ears.

Rowan understands why Wes is the way he is now, victimized by an organization that appears invisible to most.

Dealing with the Network is an impossible situation, a private horror only they can understand.

Wes seemed sure from the scribble on the paper that the man at the bank was important.

He whispers, "I think it's Zo. There're two surgeons. Zo, the more merciful one. Corazon is the one who got my son."

She's heard these names before, but has already forgotten what they mean. "Are you saying that's the man who cut open my husband?"

"Yes."

Rowan rises from the park bench to charge him, all the emotions of a woman with a lost child and the one man who can tell her where he is, elevating with her. Wes pulls her back down and shushes her. "You need to take careful steps here. This is as close as I've gotten to them. I understand how you feel, but rushing this guy isn't going to solve anything. He's very dangerous. A trained murderer."

Rowan steadies herself, but she can feel that Delco blood burning in her veins. She could be a killer too if that man had anything to do with her missing son.

The couple are now headed in separate directions.

"I think we should split up. You take the car and follow her, and I'll track him on foot. We want to find out where they live. Get her license plate number if you can. That's it. We can figure out our next move after that."

She nods, and quickly hops to her feet where she keeps a safe distance behind the mother and son. The woman's shoes are too tall, wedge sandals that look uncomfortable to walk in. She wipes at her eyes as her son tosses his ball in his glove. He seems the hyperactive type, like Landon.

It didn't seem to throw her off kilter when she accepted that giant wad of cash he handed her—blood money. She's just as bad as him.

The woman tells her son to wait and walks into a park bathroom.

Rowan used to pull Landon in public bathrooms with her, because he was too small to trust on his own. But this little guy's got to be about eight or nine.

The ball he's playing with slips from his grasp and rolls in Rowan's direction. He scoops it up before she intervenes, and then she gets an idea.

There's one thing that might make a corruptly brutal man like Zo confess to all, and tell her where her son is.

Rowan tails the woman by car and is led to a nearby apartment townhouse community in a nice neighborhood. She notes the number on the door as the woman keys in and her son follows.

She takes photographs of the woman's license plate, as instructed, and her address, and sends it to Amir asking for a quick trace.

She texts the photos to Wes, with a note—*Progress on your end?*

He sends her a pin with a note—*pick me up*—and a license plate picture of a Porsche Carrera. She's assuming it's Dr. Zo's.

Her tongue gets caught on the roof of her mouth as she mentally says his name. He's no doctor. He's a murderer.

She sends the picture to Riley, prefacing that she may be killed if Riley tells anyone where she is, and drives away from the apartment complex. Rowan finds Wes waiting for her on a sidewalk bench, just another lost soul looking for answers.

As soon as Wes climbs into the car, her phone dings.

"Yes!"

"What is it?" Wes asks.

"I got the name of the owner of that Porsche."

"Who is it?

"Francisco Sumner. Grew up in Mexico City. Son of Dr. Marta Santos and Walker Sumner, nuclear engineer. Francisco was enrolled in a surgical residency program in Miami, but dropped out."

"Wow, your almost-brother-in-law is no joke."

Rowan shoots him a sideways glance. "Amir works for the NSA. That's it. Francisco is our guy. He's Dr. Zo. Do I call Stone now? We did all the work. He's the one who cut Wyatt. He knows where Landon is." She pulls her phone out of her purse. Wes doesn't stop her, but he doesn't look nearly as thrilled as she does. "What is it?"

"What happens next, Rowan? You call Stone, and then

what? It takes them two days at least to strategize with the local police. In the process, one of their communications will tip the Network off. No one knows we're here..."

"Two days..." Her voice cracks because she knows they're already on borrowed time. She's known since that blood test in the police station.

"What did that envelope of cash and the tears look like to you?" Wes asks.

"I don't know. Why haven't I hit the send button on this call yet?"

"It looked like a goodbye to me. A long goodbye."

Rowan stares into Wes's bloodshot chestnut eyes, because if she could articulate what she felt in that moment, Wes captured it perfectly. Francisco *was* saying goodbye. That's why he offered a parting gift. Cash.

"Any intel on the woman?"

"Lola Leone. Her son's name is Nico. There is no father listed on the birth certificate of that child."

Wes nods. "They're not married, but he supports her financially because of the kid. It's possible the Network doesn't know that about him."

"So, you think if I call Stone and they intervene, Francisco will be long gone by the time they get here, don't you?"

"I do. I think he's probably always traveling, but maybe something came up... and he won't be back for a while."

"Something to do with Landon?"

Wes shrugs and looks away, and she's only spent a minimal time with this man, but she's already learned his mannerisms. He has a hard time ingesting the pain of others because he's already absorbed an incredible amount himself. But this action, right here, means *yes*.

Wes pats his side, where his gun is holstered to his hip. "Is that car registered to a property around here?"

"It is, but he'll kill you if you bust in there. And he's not even the one who got your son," Rowan reasons.

"They all got my son," he rasps.

"No, you can't." She won't have Wes kill a man out of blind revenge. He'll get himself killed first. She can't have his blood on her hands. She already feels like she has enough dripping through her fingers. She just needs to know where Landon is—dead or alive.

She rubs her belly.

"Are you in pain? Is everything... okay?"

"Yes. I'm fine. I just can't let anyone else get hurt because of my mistakes."

"You did great work getting us here."

"You did all the work. On the computer. I'm just your driver."

"Well, your sister's..."

"Yes, my sister helped."

"We could stake out his house and wait for him to leave and follow him, try to corner him."

"That could work," she says, even though she had different ideas tumbling about in her head. "There's a motel on Sunrise and a convenience store. Let me do a quick ride past the address attached to the Porsche and see if I can spot him. It might be another false lead like the bank account name. You can get us situated? Maybe buy duct tape or anything you think we might need at the store if we catch him. Use cash if you have it." She doesn't want to saddle Wes down with all the expenses, but no one's looking at his checking account.

The police may investigate hers once they find out she's left the state.

The situation has become dire, and she finally has a lead.

This man they're stalking had every intention of cutting open her son.

He might've still done it, who knows. In any case, Rowan wants to hit him where it hurts most and squeeze every last ounce out of him until he tells her where Landon is. It's a brutal thought, but at the same time, it's not. It's just being a mother and doing everything humanly possible to find her missing child. Even if that means taking someone else's...

FIFTY-TWO
WYATT

Wyatt sits on a plane next to Naomi. The police asked him not to leave New Jersey during their pending investigation, and here he is, fleeing the state with a woman who's not his wife. The only thing Wyatt knows about San Antonio is that it's close to the US border, it has a nice riverwalk, and it's where the Alamo is located.

He's praying they don't have their own showdown when they get there.

"So, you said your parents' communication company had links to the Network. How so?" he asks.

"They're in their social sphere, in a similar market."

"Was your parents' operation illegal?"

"No. They reached out to the person who was harboring Landon, and he called me asking for a trade. The trade isn't monetary. I've taken over their operation and my company's services are a needed asset. The people who've taken Landon also want him off their hands."

Relief washes over him at her answer. It all sounds like logic. He just doesn't know if he can trust her, even though he desperately wants to. She's somehow linked up with the

Network to get this information. Then again, she's the only link he has. The cops haven't had a single lead. But this could be a great one.

"Naomi, why don't you let me call Detective Stone? Maybe we could work together. It feels really dangerous tackling this by ourselves."

"That's a quick way to get your son killed. If they sniff a cop, the deal is off and Landon likely... dies. I've been given explicit instructions."

From who? he wonders. He wishes he could speak to these people, but his guess is they don't speak English.

Naomi was the one to give him the job lead at Apex over a year ago. She said she knew the owner of the startup. Naomi says now that she had no idea the Network dabbled in more than tech.

She squishes into her neck pillow. "You know... if you don't feel like you shouldn't risk all for a child that isn't yours, that's okay."

"What?" She can't be serious. She has to know how tormented he's been by all of this. It makes him worried he's made a giant mistake. "He is my child..."

"He's not, though." Naomi shows him her cell screen. A story scrolls across the top—*Father of missing Bryn Mawr boy not the biological father.*

He takes her phone and zooms in on a picture of himself. The whole story is in the *Philadelphia Inquirer*. He agreed to meet with the reporter yesterday at Naomi's advice. Wyatt is not the villain here.

Rowan is. And everyone should know about it.

It would be easier for Naomi to start over with Wyatt if he didn't have children. And if other people knew he was betrayed. They've been connected for years, but their emotional relationship has really blossomed over the past few. He can't help but think she was meant to come into his life at this very moment for a reason. "Good. I'm glad people know," he settles on.

All the secrets were taking their toll on him.

It's not just the fact that his son is missing, it's the extreme danger he's in—and now everyone else will realize it too.

He doesn't understand why they kept the truth under wraps for so long. What happened to Wyatt in Mexico City is his story to tell. And how his son was stolen afterward, and his wife's infidelity, is part of the story. Rowan is a controlling human. She's a horrible person. He didn't fully realize what it was like not to be abused until he started spending time with someone who treated him properly.

All the ugly details about his organ removal, and how they believe Landon's kidnapping may be related have been exposed.

The journalist at the newspaper asked him if he was going to file a lawsuit against the hospital, but he didn't know what the charge would be for. The hospital reported the incident. The doctor there made it sound like it happened all the time, but the reporter assured him that it doesn't. Mexico City has come a long way since the eighties, a popular vacation spot, and acts of random violence on tourists, especially in the nice area where he was traveling, are rare.

Mrs. Bishop had an affair during the marriage...

Wyatt made sure the journalist added that point so readers weren't led to believe that perhaps Landon was conceived with someone else, prior to their marriage.

Everyone in the world would know how vindictive Rowan was to him now.

The opportunities to cheat presented themselves to him over the years, but he'd never betrayed her—not physically, anyway.

It's such a sticking point for him because he knows Rowan didn't have those same temptations. She's not an attention seeker, especially from strange men, and hardly hypersexual.

Going after Marco was a malicious attack on him and nothing more.

When he's not thinking about where poor Landon is, all he can do is rewind his mind, and think about this little piece of power she held over him for so long.

Every time she told him how irresponsible he was or how he needed to pay attention to something, in the back of her mind, he can hear her whisper, *You're so clueless, you don't even know I slept with your best friend!*

The whispers don't end with her, though.

He hears his best friend's too.

I told you she was high maintenance from the get-go, Bro. One slip-up, and she was banging down my door...

He hates them both. They've taken up so much real estate in his life and mind that he wishes he could get it back and invest somewhere else. He just wants someone who understands him. Someone who puts him first for a change.

"I'm here because you need my help," Naomi reminds him. "We've been messaging each other, but I think we both know it's about more than that. Our relationship has grown way past texting buddies, and it's time to take it to the next level." Her lips are plump, and the words that roll off them are everything he needs to hear. Beauty and brains, Naomi's got it all. But is it real or an illusion?

"I just don't understand their incentive to hand him back. Aren't they worried we'll have the police with us?"

He has a terrible feeling, like the kind he used to get from some of the men who hung on the railings of his mother's apartment complex back in the day. He ignored those men, but he had a sense that if he engaged with them, something bad would happen. Growing up in not the best circumstances taught him to follow his gut, and he's not doing that right now.

He's listening to this woman because he's beyond anxious to

retrieve Landon, but he's worried his desperation is clouding his judgment.

"They want him off their hands as badly as you want him back, Wyatt," she says.

"Then why... have they kept him this long?" He hates to say the words. "These aren't nice people. They're animals who rip out victims' organs and leave them to die."

"Don't question it."

"It could be a setup."

"For what? They're not asking for money. They're being paid in other services. I told you this already. Relax."

"That's what worries me. If they were asking for money, that would make this seem legit."

"Do you think they want a dead American boy on their hands? Landon's picture is all over the news. They want to return him."

What she's saying makes sense. He thinks about the Baxter boy Rowan told him about, and how much of a media craze that caused. The Baxter boy is the only other child reported for this type of incident—and he didn't survive.

FIFTY-THREE
ROWAN

In her Delaware County days, after she knocked out Colleen and was sent to a private Catholic school, Rowan gravitated to the other expats there. Students were enrolled at Nazareth for two reasons—either their parents were encouraged by the curriculum and disciplined classroom setting, or they were sending off their holy terrors in the hopes that an education system founded in religion could stave off their child's demons.

Rowan belonged to the latter half, and gravitated to the side of the lunchroom that modified their school uniforms to mimic Britney Spears in her "Not That Innocent" days. Rowan's closest friend there, Kelsey, was a former military brat forced to plant roots in Philly. Turns out, Kelsey couldn't properly settle in any one place either.

Nazareth Academy was Kelsey's third attempt. Rowan was determined to make this hop stick for Kelsey because she seemed to understand her strife. Kelsey was also one of four children, and the other three didn't seem to have a problem just following their parents' lead—*stay, go, stay go...*

Kelsey's real rebellion stemmed from a boy she'd left in France whom she loved and was forced to leave. Rowan confided that she didn't agree with how her parents handled life either, and that's how she ended up at Nazareth.

Kelsey had a nervous energy about her that drew Rowan in.

She had special skills too, like self-defense moves she taught Rowan that would enable her to kill a man with her bare hands. Her strange self-defense lessons with Kelsey were based on a military-style fighting style called Krav Maga. Kelsey had acquired a quick, local boyfriend, Erik, a wrestler at a neighboring school. They used to hang out at his place on Mondays for *WWE Monday Night Raw*.

Private school hadn't calmed Rowan down one bit.

If anything, it surrounded her with other people who had some serious rage issues, only feeding hers.

One thing Rowan learned from Erik on one of the many nights he chose to demonstrate his passion for wrestling, was how to initiate a chokehold to make someone pass out. If done correctly, the action of wrapping one's arms around another's neck can hit on the carotid arteries on both sides, narrowing the blood flow, and causing a blackout.

As Rowan sits in front of Lola's townhouse she's proud of herself for making it this long, in this life, considering how she started out, without having to use violence to get her way. Her childhood seemed shrouded in it. Her parents weren't physically harmful, but their actions instilled anger that led to violence.

Her father's gaslighting lies were the kerosene that lit the flame. *"I swear I was just working late... You're being paranoid."*

The pores on her arm sting with the memory, each lie a minute of her life she wouldn't get back—or give back to her father as he aged.

Her children would never be able to look at her and say the same thing. She'll raise them in a disciplined environment, even if she has to find another partner to help in that endeavor. Maybe if she can figure out how to get Landon back, Wyatt will be so thankful he'll overlook the only single transgression she'd ever made in their marriage.

She glances at her watch. Wes probably wonders where she is. Daylight is escaping into the atmosphere as pinks and yellows darken into reds and oranges.

Nico leaves the front door of his residence, walking a small dog. Looks to be a Cockapoo or Shih Tzu. The dog poses a hurdle, but this is what she's been waiting for. A chance to get the boy alone. Nico and the dog walk toward a nearby park. Rowan pulls the car slowly behind him. He doesn't appear to notice her.

She'd never hurt a child.

She doesn't plan to hurt this one either.

She just wants to borrow him until someone can return hers.

Once at the edge of the park, Rowan places her car into park.

As she comes up behind him, she can see the light sculpt of his frame. She saw the ball he was palming, a little athlete. This might not be as easy as she anticipated, but she tries to channel everything she learned in Erik's basement.

There was one night she put Kelsey in a chokehold where she actually made her go down. It scared the shit out of Rowan, how fast Kelsey went out.

It's a running joke between them. *"We can still be friends. Even though you knocked me the fuck out."*

Rowan starts to second-guess herself. Will the small mound on her belly make a chokehold difficult? It shouldn't because of Nico's size, but the additional hindrance could create extra space for him to squirm away if she doesn't get a good enough grasp on him.

What if he screams and causes a scene? He most likely will.

If she lays hands on this boy and it doesn't go right, she could end up in prison for a very long time. She hates the idea of hurting another child. It wasn't something that was in her DNA before this happened. But if she doesn't at least try, she might never see her son again. She doesn't see a lot of alternatives here.

There was a period of time when she had a sliver of hope. And that timer ran out days ago.

She thinks about the slick, tall, muscular man she saw at the park earlier. She and Wes don't have a chance of taking him down.

Then, she remembers the envelope of cash he held which contained bills earned by selling off parts of her family. And she knows she has to try.

No one else is getting the job done.

The Network has destroyed lives. Wes's life. Her life.

It's all she can think about as she exits her vehicle, makes a quick move behind the boy, throws her right arm around his neck. The air leaves his throat in a squawk. He tries to move, but she holds him fast, squeezes tighter. His body goes rigid. The leash is dropped.

The dog barks and bites at her ankle.

She kicks it away as she drags the boy's limp body into the backseat of her car.

FIFTY-FOUR

FRANCISCO

"Calm down. What do you mean he's gone?" Francisco's packing his suitcase. He doesn't have a new assignment yet, but he's so sure he's going to have to run soon once his payment is tracked that he's already thinking ahead.

"He was walking Coco, and Coco came back, but Nico didn't!" Lola screams into the phone.

Francisco stops lowering a shirt into his bag, fear cramping his arm. "Where was he headed?"

"He usually just walks Coco around the park and comes back."

"You let him go alone?"

Lola's practically spitting fire into the phone, and he immediately regrets the question. "He walks Coco all the time! It helps me out!" He's not blaming her. He's just trying to gather all the facts. "It gets him out of the house. Nico doesn't like to sit still. And it's so hard raising him on my own." She's crying now.

"Call the police. I'm headed to the park by your house." He doesn't tell her anything else before he hangs up. He knows this is related to their chat this afternoon.

Someone was watching them.

His worst fears are coming true.

Francisco dials his mother as he zips down the street.

"This isn't a good time." She sounds breathless, like she's been hiking up the side of a mountain.

"That's too bad. Someone has stolen my son. Do you want to tell me why?" he seethes into the phone.

"Your son?" she asks with a thread of a giggle.

"I had a son with Lola. The waitress I was dating in med school who you didn't like. I didn't tell anyone about him because of the Network, and I've been transferring her money over the years. Today I met him in person for the first time. I had a bad feeling with the off payment... thought it might be my last chance..."

"You had a child and didn't tell me?" Cars honk, and wherever his mother is now, it's highly trafficked. He has an idea of why she was breathless. His father owns a bullet-proof Range Rover that he keeps in a hidden garage on their compound, accessible only by an extensive trek up the side of the property. What has his mother gotten them into now?

"You endanger everyone you meet. I never wanted him to be harmed. Did the Network take him?" Francisco asks. "Just tell me."

"I can't believe you've kept my grandchild from me. I always regretted you didn't have a better relationship with your grandparents."

"You can't be serious..." He's just reached the park. It's mostly empty, and it's hard to believe anyone could've been taken in plain sight here. "As if there's any way this boy could have a normal relationship with you? With the work you do."

"You mean the respectful position of being a doctor."

Francisco laughs. "Get over yourself. That stopped being your real job years ago. What use would they have for him? The Network? Where is he?"

"I don't know! I didn't even know he existed."

And now she has the audacity to be angry he tried to keep his son safe. "Is he a match for Andre? Is that what this is about? If something happens to him, you will be sorry."

His mother gasps into the phone. "This isn't my fault."

"If not yours, then whose? He's been the only thing keeping me going all these years."

"You live a good life."

"I live a damned life! Because of you." She knows he detests her. He's just not sure if she realizes how much. That if someone were to place Nico, a boy he met just today, and her, in a room, and he was asked to choose who lives and dies, it would be the easiest decision he's ever made.

"I wish things could've worked out differently with your brother too," she answers. It's his least favorite excuse.

"You can't keep using Damon as a shield. Your damage goes far beyond what happened to him."

"Well, your son could be a match, I suppose..." She's returned to the land that's most comfortable to her—what benefits Marta. "But I don't think they're aware of him, Francisco. If your son was abducted, I don't think it was the Network."

FIFTY-FIVE
WYATT

Naomi drives further south in their rental car, but he thought they were meeting Landon in San Antonio. They passed the winding riverwalk, with all of its waterfront storefronts and colorful restaurants a while ago, and now all he can see out the window as the sun goes down is a brown desolate landscape.

Signs for Mexico have been popping up everywhere.

Mexican border 43 miles

Mexican border 20 miles

"Where're we going?" he asks. Wyatt asked her about a half an hour ago and she said they were almost there. He doesn't understand how she knows where *there* is. To his knowledge, neither one of them has ever been to Texas before.

"Laredo," she says. Her hair is pinned up in a bun with two bobby pins. She wears a handstitched cardigan even though it's eighty-eight degrees outside. She's not the picture of a woman on a stealthy mission, and he wonders if her absolute naivety about her parents' connections will get them killed. Maybe he would feel more comfortable if he knew what services were being exchanged and if they held any real value. But right now, he doesn't.

Wyatt does a quick search on his phone. "That's a mile from the border."

"It is," she confirms.

Wyatt continues to search on his phone. "It doesn't look like the best area. I'm reading about drug wars right now... Maybe I should drive."

"I know how to drive," she snaps.

"We don't have any weapons. What if this doesn't go well?" Wyatt scans the seat establishments on the side of the road for gun shops or a shady-looking vendor who might have one.

"We don't need weapons. Violence breeds more violence."

He bites his lip. She's obviously never watched *The Cartel*. He keeps reminding himself of the condition the Network left him in at the Marriott. The only reason he's alive is because of his pure will to survive. He's not sure a second stand-off with this crew will have the same result.

But if they have Landon, he has to try.

If they get the cops involved, the Network will know, and Landon will be quickly disposed of. That's the story Naomi has fed him anyway.

"I don't understand why you're doing this for me," he says.

"This is the first day of our new life," she says. "It's as it should be. It just took a long time for us to get here."

He likes that answer, but it can't be that simple.

Laredo comes into view, a town of strip malls, graffiti, and fast-food chains.

Broken-down cars and trash litter the parking lot of what appears to be an abandoned Lowes. As they park, Wyatt can hear a man screaming in the distance. Naomi appears undeterred. He doesn't understand how she can be so cool.

"We just wait here? Do you think it would be better to be somewhere where there's... witnesses? And street lights, maybe?"

She turns to him, sharp, and serious. "Nobody will touch me. I am protected."

He doesn't understand what that means. "Protected by who?"

"I'll explain later..."

"I'm concerned you're not aware of the risks." Is she referring to God when she says she's "protected"? As Wyatt looks around, he's pretty sure God doesn't patrol this area. And what about him? He knows he's not *protected*. If she's referring to her connections at home, does her protection stretch across the sea to the far corners of wherever they are? Does she fully understand how things work here? He would feel better if they had something to offer these people.

She told him not to bring any money. "I am," she says. "Believe me."

He has one hundred dollars in his wallet and a Saint Michael the Archangel charm in his pocket that his mother gave him when he was younger. A customer had left it with their tip one day and she'd given it to him. He'd carried it with him ever since. It wasn't with him when he went swimming.

He's thought about that more than once.

Marco was his angel that day.

A black SUV pulls into the lot.

Wyatt can feel acid rise in the back of his throat.

Is his son really in there? Is it true? If Wyatt dies in this deserted parking lot in Laredo, he hopes everyone will know he did it for him. His father didn't even show up for his birth, but he'll die trying to find his boy. Biological or not, Landon is his.

A tall man with glasses exits the vehicle. He doesn't appear to have anyone else with him, which is a comfort to Wyatt.

"Don't get out of the car," Naomi tells him. "Let me talk to him." She rolls down her window.

The man walks over to the driver's side. "Ali?" she asks.

It's fully dark now, and Wyatt can barely see his beak as he looks in the car. "Yes," he says.

"Do you have the package?" she asks in a tone he doesn't recognize. Less light and frilly, more business-like, assertive.

"In the back seat... Sleeping."

Wyatt's hair stands on end. What does sleeping mean? Alive? Drugged... Dead?

"Go get it now and put it in the back of this vehicle," she commands.

He nods and walks swiftly away. Naomi smiles. Wyatt's body surges with hope and confusion. Who is this woman with the authoritative voice? He looks at Naomi like she's an ethereal being, both literally and figuratively. She returns the warmth in his smile.

Wyatt hears a car door open, but then he also hears something else too. The whizzing of tires behind them.

Wyatt turns around to see headlights. There's someone else in the parking lot, and they're coming in hot.

FIFTY-SIX
ROWAN

Rowan received a text from Wes that he's all settled in at the motel.

When Wes was behind the wheel on the way down, she did some research and read about a case in India where a migrant worker willingly sold one of his kidneys for a large sum of money. His employer had stiffed him on his last manual labor job, while his family was starving, and waiting for him to provide for them.

The buyers took the man to a house with a dirty mattress, cut him open, and removed his kidney. He wasn't given proper care afterward, developed an infection, and died.

Stories from around the world like this were too common, and astonishing at the same time.

Rowan's not sure if the Network was responsible for the one she read about. Where there's dirty money to be had, there's usually more than one person in business trying to make it. But today she holds the Network responsible and uses everything they've done as a reason for what she's doing right now.

Wes texts her again. He wants to know where she is.

He'll be angry with her, but desperate times call for desperate measures.

She can't let another day go by with her son in peril and everyone just waiting around for a break to occur.

Her mother told her once—*you make your own luck*. If you sit around waiting for someone to create it for you, you'll be waiting forever. Rowan's mother had to recreate her entire life after their dad left, and it didn't happen by her sitting on her ass waiting for circumstances to change.

Rowan's making the moves now, a powerplay to put herself in control—her favorite place. Someone's about to get a taste of their own medicine.

She races to the motel, Nico still passed out in the backseat.

She didn't hurt the boy. He's just having a nice nap. But he'll rouse soon and she'll be in big trouble if she doesn't get him detained before that happens.

When she pulls up to the crappy building, a two-story string of doors surrounded by cracked concrete, she calls Wes and instructs him to bring her the duct tape and zip ties.

"Why?" he asks. "What's going on?"

"Just do as I say, please." She tries on her most professional, human resources voice. It's the same one she used when she asked Lynsey Hamilton not to file her complaint. Sadly, after Wyatt's little article was released, Lynsey filed a civil suit against her, claiming she was coerced into not filing a harassment complaint. She felt threatened, she says. Rowan's company has placed her in suspension until further notice.

It's a sin, really, the way people punch you when you're down. First Wyatt with the defaming article, and now this girl.

Well, Rowan swings back. And her hits pack quite a punch.

Minutes letter, Wes is at her window with a plastic bag of supplies. He looks in her backseat and jumps backward, then surveys his surroundings to make sure no one saw his reaction. Night is heavy in the air now, the flickering lights of the motel barely showing Wes's fright. They're practically there all alone, the parking lot mostly vacant.

"What did you do, Rowan?" he asks.

"He's fine. But we have to hurry." She grabs the bag out of Wes's hands and then slips into the backseat where she places the plastic ties around Nico's wrists and ankles. She'll wait to place the tape over his mouth until after he wakes up. She doesn't want to prematurely wake him by cutting off his air supply.

"I need you to hold the door open to the motel," she tells him.

Wes looks like he might lose his lunch. Theirs consisted of roadside sandwiches melded to foil and fountain sodas they snagged from a gas station. "What were you thinking?" he's screaming at her in a hushed tone. "I can't be a part of this anymore. I'm going to grab an Uber to the airport."

"What now... you didn't sign up for this? Well, I didn't ask to have my son snatched from me either, yet here I am. If Zo cares about this boy, I'll get mine back. I understand yours is already lost. But mine isn't, Wes. There's still a chance. Nico's not hurt. We're just borrowing him. Collateral."

"You can't carry him. You're already carrying enough." He points at her middle.

Rowan appears undeterred. She may be pregnant, but this situation isn't about the child in her womb. She promises to double up on prenatal vitamins and go to Pilates to recenter herself after this, but there is no future without her firstborn, and nothing will break her focus. "Are you in or out? This is your chance to help catch them." She points at Nico. "We have one of their own now."

A glimmer of hope flits across Wes's face. Not in a malicious way, but in one where this might bring his son justice. Wes doesn't say another word, he just opens the backdoor of her vehicle and hoists the boy in his arms.

Rowan's thankful, because it did pose a challenge moving Nico into the motel. Carrying him up a flight of steps, pregnant, was going to break her, and possibly harm her unborn child.

She hoists herself out of the car, sore from her brief brush-up.

When they enter the motel room, a musty-smelling place with ancient furniture and thin, floral comforters that appear as though they've been painted on, Wes carefully lays Nico on the threadbare couch. "He's going to be so frightened when he wakes up."

Rowan closes the door and locks it. "I wonder how scared your child was when he woke up on a table with strangers hovering over him with surgical instruments?"

Wes's Adam's apple bobs up and down as he swallows and she wonders if he's almost thrown up. She is not messing around anymore. She's waited long enough for answers.

"What do we do now?" Wes asks.

"I want you to put a posting for him online." She's thought about this idea the whole car ride there and thinks it's the perfect plan. All this time Wes has been scouring this site looking for his child on the flicker of a computer screen.

They should know what that feels like too.

"What?" Wes asks.

"Like the last one. Fuck with them. Place the order for a PED, age eight or nine, a boy, not just the organ. They'll get the drift that we're looking for more than an organ. And whose exactly."

"That's absurd."

"The ones who're watching the site will know what it means. It also keeps it off the police's radar. The police have no idea we have Nico and won't know what this means if they're watching the site. This is between them and us."

"What if the Network traces the post somehow?"

"To Florida? Then, they'll understand we mean business.

Since that's where the boy is from. I will find out where my son is in the next twenty-four hours. If your personal safety is compromised, you can get out of here, but I'm not backing out now. I just need you to do this one last thing for me."

Wes shakes his head, but she can tell he'll do it. He has nothing else to lose. He's already lost the most important things to him.

"Please... Wes. You know their system. You're the only one who can help me."

She notices a six-pack of beer on the counter. Wes cracks a beer. And then he cracks open his laptop.

FIFTY-SEVEN

WYATT

"Who is that?" Wyatt asks Naomi. The other vehicle, also an SUV, is now parked behind the black one. Wyatt wants to watch it to see who's inside, but his eyes are glued to the man approaching the back passenger side door. That's where Landon is.

Behind. That. Door.

"I don't know," she admits.

Wyatt wants to leap from the car and run to his son, but he has a feeling they're in imminent danger. Naomi turns her body all the way around and won't look at him. Then, she does the most surprising thing.

She reaches into her tote bag and pulls out a pistol.

"What in the hell? How did you get that through security? I thought violence bred violence!"

"Change of plans. I didn't. It came with the rental car."

"Excuse me?"

"I had a friend put it in the car."

"A friend?" Wyatt couldn't be more confused. He thought he was her only friend in the States. How does Miss "Stay in the Light and Good Energy" even know how to use a gun? She sure looks secure holding it now. Her story isn't adding up. If her parents were comfortable supplying services to illegal operations, what other bad lessons have they passed down to their daughter? He's afraid he's about to find out.

"Naomi, are you going to tell me what's going on?"

"The driver of that vehicle doesn't seem to be much interested in us." There're shadowy figures hanging around the SUV parked directly behind them. The vehicle that houses Landon. Wyatt feels at a loss that he doesn't have a weapon, but he's so close... to his son.

He's only a few feet away, and he can barely contain himself, but something is off about this situation. Wyatt has his body turned all the way around to watch the interaction between the second driver and the first.

It's hard to make out what's happening, but the tall man, who Naomi strangely referred to as Ali, has his hands up. The other driver, a much smaller person, is waving something in the air.

"Is that a..."

And then the gunshot, loud enough to pierce a hole in the moon, rips through the night. Wyatt jumps, and he's sure now that the second driver was holding a gun and has now shot the man, Ali, at point blank range.

Even in the night, beneath the one working light in the parking lot, Wyatt can see the tall man fall over like a collapsed tower, a pool of blood spread out beneath him in a dark circle.

"Fuck," Naomi says.

"Landon..." Wyatt touches the handle of the car, and Naomi grabs him. "Don't... if he's in there, we'll get him."

"What do you mean, if he's in there?" he asks.

"Things aren't going as planned," she says.

"*No shit.*" Wyatt decides to ditch Naomi. She's lost all control of the situation, even if she doesn't fully realize it.

As soon as his feet hit the pavement, he's running toward the back of the SUV.

"Stop, or I'll shoot you too!"

Wyatt hears a woman's voice and is surprised the shooter is, in fact, a female.

"Is my son in there? What do you want with him? Just give him back. How much money do you want?" It's then that he recognizes the woman behind the gun. "... Dr. Santos?"

"That's right." She doesn't appear like the serious physician at his bedside anymore there to dole out helpful medical and personal advice. Now, she is a malicious older lady holding a pistol, the gleam in her eye undeniably evil.

"No wonder you didn't want me reporting the assault." His shock is bringing his guard down. He doesn't understand how all of these people are connected.

"The hospital did it anyway," she says, angrily.

"So, you're in on it? Take your patients' organs and then sew them up? Fine. You got mine. Just give me my son! You've taken enough from me."

Wyatt hears the click of a car door, and feels Naomi's presence beside him, but he doesn't take his eyes away from the woman holding the gun.

The one who is closest in proximity to his son.

He thinks about different ways he can attack her, wrestle the gun away, turn it on her. Kill her.

"Put the gun down now," Naomi says.

"Look who's making an appearance," Dr. Santos says.

"You know her?" Wyatt asks Naomi.

"Yes."

As he watches Naomi respond, his fingertips tingle at the thought of the gun Naomi must have hidden in the bag clutched at her side. If he can get to it first, he can beat out this older woman. She's the only thing standing between him and Landon.

Dr. Santos waves the gun at Wyatt. "This one catches on slow. Hello, Enid."

"Enid?" Wyatt asks. "Who's Enid?"

"You know the real me," Naomi tells him. "That's the name my parents had me use for work."

Whatever that means. Naomi is going by a different name, but Dr. Santos seems to recognize it. Maybe Wyatt is the one who's been played here.

"Put the gun down. This wasn't the deal," Naomi says.

The deal? His focus bounces between Marta's gun, Naomi's purse, the backseat of the black van where he prays his son sits alive. There's no way Mountaintop Naomi is going to outgun this lady. Although, if she's connected to the Network, which she must certainly be, maybe she does have something extra slithery up her sleeve. In any case, Wyatt is going to have to make some quick moves here.

"Hand the boy over and we go our separate ways." Naomi says this with such confidence, Wyatt's half-tempted to believe her.

"Or, what?"

Wyatt turns his head slowly toward the woman he's been fantasizing about for the last ten years and realizes she might be yet another stranger in his life.

"You know the real me," she tells him, once again, under her breath.

He doesn't believe her anymore when she says these things. She's painted a false narrative of who she is, and he doesn't believe she has the gumption or the power to get them out of this situation. He looks around to where he can run and hide, and to his dismay, there's nothing but a black canvas of pavement in every direction. "You do what I say or that estate you've built will be seized by the Mexican government, and you can go back to working in the ER wiping noses and asses."

Wyatt clutches his side, the one he had cut open.

"It's funny... the way it's always worked where I'm from, is if you want to take someone's position, you displace the person in charge," Marta says.

Wyatt's pulse ticks in his neck. He's sure these two are going to have a shootout and he can't allow himself or Landon to be caught in the crossfire.

Naomi removes her gun and points it in Marta's direction, but she isn't as quick as her opponent. The bullet whizzes by Wyatt's ear as it's fired and launches between Naomi's beautiful eyes, the contents of her head splattered out of the back of her skull. She falls over in a heap of tissue and blood as if she never existed.

Wyatt's exposed arms are littered with goose flesh, his body full of fear as he tries to sprint away. He's toppled over by a bullet that catches his side. All he can think of as he hits the pavement is that it's his good side.

And that he's failed his son.

FIFTY-EIGHT
MARTA

She could hear the sirens faintly in the distance, but she was fairly certain she accomplished what she came there to do. Walker and Alistair are traitors, taking her boy away from her without consent. She dealt with Alistair the only way possible so it wouldn't happen again.

She found a search on Alistair's computer recently about how to barter for immunity with the authorities. He was considering turning them in. Yellow belly whistle blower. Everyone had a price. The only one she could trust was family.

She'd reason with Walker later...

Walker is helpless without Alistair.

She and Ali were the ones who ran the computer systems. Walker was more in charge of setting up the surgeries, the bigger-picture arrangements, but she'll be able to start her own network now.

It was time to put that estate on the market and start over somewhere else anyway. It was growing hotter by the day. The questions at the hospital about the American who'd been victimized in their care hadn't stopped circulating.

She thinks Landon will get along fabulously in Costa Rica.

He'll be able to explore all day with the rainforest backdrop and exotic animals surrounding him. He deserves more for his curious mind than Bean beetles and Spanish chickens.

Costa Rica is a location where no one knows their family.

It's a perfect place to set up shop. Or maybe they'll cash out completely, and she can work at a clinic down there, and Walker will be able to run a fishery.

"Miss May, what happened out there? Where's Ali? I heard a noise."

She looks in the back and Landon has his headphones off. "I told you to keep those headphones on no matter what. Remember how you arrived here..."

"I'm so sorry I didn't listen, Miss May. I heard a very loud noise and was worried."

Worried? Bless that child. "Alistair had to run you to the location for me. I was meeting him there. All the debts for you have been paid. Like in 'The Bear Prince.' So, we can set off on a new adventure now."

"Like the woodcutter and his youngest daughter."

"That's right."

"I'll have a brother or sister soon, so I won't be the youngest."

"I would forget about them too."

"I hope they're better for my mom and dad and they won't have to give them away."

"Me too. Good little boys and girls listen. Why don't you put your headphones back on. We have a long drive..."

FIFTY-NINE
ROWAN

"It's done," Wes says, and pushes away from the laptop.

He appears both satisfied and disgusted that he's successfully created Nico's post on the Network. She hopes once they get to the other side of this, he'll understand what an instrumental part he played in taking down one of the largest covert criminal organizations in existence.

She no longer believes meeting Wesley Baxter was by accident.

Rowan feels almost called, as though she was meant to team up with Wes. It feels more like a mission to benefit the masses now than just a singular cause for her family. Especially since they're the only ones fighting this war.

Even if she doesn't find her son, no one else will have to suffer at the hands of this evil empire if they take them down. She'll expose what they are. Who they are. What they've done.

She won't remain silent and shelled up in a dusty apartment, like Wes. The public will share in her pain once they realize the extent of the Network's terror.

Nico is starting to come to, and Rowan kneels in front of him, hating this part of her plan.

She doesn't want to scare him, but she knows Nico will be petrified once he realizes he's with strangers.

As he wakens, she observes his struggle as he comes to the realization that his arms and legs don't work quite right. Nico wiggles awkwardly with his back against the couch before his eyes flicker open to meet hers.

"What the..." Then he screams, a horrible, terrified, shrill cry and pulls at his restraints with all his might.

"Help!" he shouts.

Wes tosses her the tape, because he informed Rowan he would have no part in touching the child, aside from carrying him out of the car and making sure he arrived on the couch safely. Wes argued with her about taking the boy, but he must also see the brilliance in her plan, because he's still here.

How else would they get the Network to turn over her son, or at least tell her where he's buried, if she didn't threaten them with losing one of their own? What reason would they have to compromise their entire operation if it didn't hurt them somehow? In order to beat them, she has to start thinking like them.

She places the duct tape over Nico's mouth. "Calm down. We're not going to hurt you."

Nico shakes his head furiously, trying to thrash, but his limbs are pinned together in a way that makes it impossible to do so. Rowan pulls up a picture of Landon on her phone and shows it to him. "This is my son, Landon. Do you see him?"

More upset than before, Nico blinks his eyes rapidly, his face turning beet red. He screams beneath the tape, and she hopes he can breathe through his nose.

"It's okay. You won't be harmed."

Tears pour out of his dark eyes, so afraid now. She tries to stroke his hair, and that only makes him angrier. He knocks his tear-streaked cheek at her fingers until she stops.

"Okay, I won't touch you... Your father stole my son. That is why you're here. As soon as he returns my boy, you go home."

Nico shakes his head—*no*—as if that can't be right.

He stops his squealing until he's completely quiet.

"Would you like me to take the tape off your mouth now that you've relaxed? Now that you understand no one is here to hurt you."

He shakes his head—*yes*.

"If I take it off, you cannot make any noise," she instructs.

Rowan glances over her shoulder at Wes who has his head in his hands, second beer at his side, terribly uncomfortable with this situation.

"You have the wrong boy," he says breathlessly. "I don't have a father. He took off when I was younger. You need to let me go!"

"Who was the man with you this afternoon?"

"Uncle Z! He's not my dad." Nico's breathing so hard he's practically hyperventilating. "And he's not even my real uncle. I just call hm that. He's a friend of my mom's, I think. Sends me birthday cards. Shit..." He looks away for swearing. "She's probably so worried. Please let me go. I won't tell her anything about Uncle Z."

Rowan sinks to the ground at this information. *Not his real son. Not even related.*

Wes smacks the table with his fist, drawing Nico's attention.

"It's okay if you made a mistake. Wherever you've taken me, I'll find my way home. Just let me go."

"You look just like him," Rowan says.

"Today was the first day I even met him!" Nico says. "Please just let me go."

Rowan walks over to Wes.

"Where're you going, miss?" Nico asks, so polite to call her miss, even though she's knocked him out and tied him up. His mother must've taught him good manners. She's probably beside herself with worry, just like Rowan was in that visitor center. She wishes she could have a carrier pigeon send the woman a note letting her know her son is just fine, but she can't put someone else's feelings before her own right now.

Rowan tells Wes in a hushed tone, "He could be lying to us. And Francisco knew him enough to give him a hat and pay off the mom, so there's vested interest there."

"Is it enough interest for a trade? To compensate for the situation we created?" Wes asks in a low tone.

What Wes means is—will taking Nico be the bargaining chip we need to barter for Landon's life, or is this child so insignificant to Francisco that it will be the nail in Landon's coffin instead?

Just then, Stone calls. Rowan lets it go to voicemail. Could Stone possibly know what she's gotten into down here? Highly unlikely.

Stone sends Rowan a text next.

Stone: *There's been developments in Landon's case. Call ASAP.*

Rowan shows Wes the phone screen. "I have to call her back."

"You need to put tape back on the kid first."

She looks over at the couch and Nico still appears uncomfortable with his limbs tied behind his back, but he's at least quiet and looks like he's at peace for the moment.

"I'll take the call outside."

Wes nods and sips his beer.

Rowan slips onto the second-floor balcony of the grimy motel. "Hi, Detective Stone."

"Where're you? I drove by your house, nobody is home. Your sister and mother don't know where you are."

Riley didn't give her up. Good. She would expect nothing less. They aren't exactly close, but Riley is a great liar. Riley got into just as much shit as Rowan did growing up, but she was better at self-control and not getting caught; a perfect specimen for the US government.

"I took a road trip. I'm fine. Please tell me what's going on with Landon. Someone saw him?" She's far from fine, but she must stay composed to carry out her plan.

"I'll tell you what I know, but I'd advise you to come home immediately. You weren't supposed to leave the state." Rowan recognizes Stone's phishing tactic to see if she has indeed left the state. She won't fall for it. Her activities in Florida cannot be known. Once Nico is reported missing, it might tip Stone off.

"I understand. Detective Stone, where is my son? Is he in custody?" If he's alive and at their fingertips, they should have him by now.

Please let it be true. If it is, she'll drop Nico off at the park by his house and call it a day, but she doesn't believe it's possible.

"No... Unfortunately, we believe your husband tried to receive Landon from an unknown party on his own." Stone huffs into the phone. "That was a mistake. We explained false claims to extort the two of you was a possibility. We wish he'd taken our strict warning. It always goes sideways."

"What happened? Is my husband okay?" A few hours ago, after Rowan read the article in the paper, quickly followed by an unkind email from her employer, she was fine with never speaking to Wyatt again.

Given that he might be injured, he's all of a sudden *her husband* again. The feelings she has for him are mixed and confusing, and it will take years to sort them out, but he's not her first priority right now. Injured or not. She has to be careful where she places her energy right now.

Nothing can distract her.

"He tried to engage in a negotiation near the border in South Texas. He was found alongside two other people who were shot to death, a man and a woman. Wyatt was shot as well and is in a critical condition at San Antonio Regional hospital."

Rowan places her hand over her mouth and leans over the railing. "No." Wyatt's dumb, rash behavior will truly be the death of him. They shouldn't have split up, but this isn't her fault.

"Who were the man and the woman?"

"Alistair Esquire, a Mexican citizen, and Naomi Chalfant."

"Naomi?" Rowan says out loud. The name rings a bell. It's a girl from Wyatt's backpacking days that Marco dated. Or maybe Wyatt. What was Wyatt doing with *her*?

SIXTY

FRANCISCO

Francisco purchased a one-way ticket to Mexico City. A missing child report has been issued for his son. Someone was obviously watching him yesterday, and he's kicking himself for being so stupid. Not only did he accept a payment that he didn't earn, but he handed it off to someone who means the absolute world to him in broad daylight. And now he's being punished for it.

But there's one person who's really to blame—his mother.

She doesn't even care that his child is in danger. Because it's Lola's kid. She never approved of Lola or her station in life as a waitress.

Francisco promised Lola he'd return her son, even if it killed him.

When he arrived at her home, she smacked him on the chest repeatedly. He held her wrists back and they cried together.

The only thing he could say was, "I'm sorry. I'm so sorry..."

It was such a mistake to meet Nico. He only wanted to do it once...

He's already resolved to this being the last time he speaks to his mother. He will leave the organization and they can hunt him down and kill him, and that can be his end, just as long as he returns Nico to Lola.

He receives a phone call from his father on the way to the airport. Their relationship is fraught as well, but only because his father follows his mother's lead.

"This is Zo." He won't tell his father he's on his way to see them. It has to be a sneak attack when he holds a gun to his mother's head and forces her to give up what he needs to recover his son—or else.

"Your mother told me you have a son, and that he's gone missing."

"Yes. His name is Nico."

"Why didn't we know about this son?"

"Is that a real question?"

"There's a strange posting for a young boy, eight or nine, on the Network."

"What do you mean? They post only blood and organ type on the Network, not descriptions."

"This is a posting for an actual boy."

"We don't sell whole humans, take it down!" They aren't in the human trafficking business, and they won't start. He really will burn his parents' estate to the ground before that happens.

"It's the same poster who claimed to have a donor kidney for Andre. He's been transported to Children's, by the way. A legal match has been found. Andre's surgery is scheduled for Monday."

"Thank God." Francisco does the sign of the cross, kisses his fingers, and points them at the sky to his brother. At least one of his prayers has been answered. His nephew will hopefully survive. It makes him wonder if any of the work he's done is good at all. And if he's interfering with God's plan. He's just glad Andre surviving may be part of it.

He yanks on the back of his ponytail as the pieces slide into position. "What're you saying? Who has Nico? He has to be the one the post is referring to, right?"

"Yes. Whoever the person is who hacked the Network, somehow they know about us. And they know about you, and they know about Nico. My guess is it's a relative of Landon Bishop. Your mother has the boy, she's very attached to him and they're headed south. I don't know where to. I tried to return him to his father via Alistair, and..."

"And what?"

"And your mother shot and killed Ali and the father at the US border."

"Holy shit."

"I'd start with the mother."

"This can't end poorly. I have to return Nico to his mother."

"I know. And I'm supportive of you doing whatever you have to with your mother to get him back. This has gone on long enough... for both of us. She didn't have to kill Alistair. He's been my only confidante for years. The suspicious research Marta found on his computer... was research I asked him to do." His father's voice is drenched with pain and remorse. He clearly feels responsible for the death of the only friend he's been allowed to have for the last decade. At least he had one, Francisco thinks, sadly.

"Okay, thanks for that," he says. Alistair's death is the final straw for his father. He's finally ready to break away from her.

"Zo, one last thing. The posting had a unique note."

"What's that?" He's almost afraid to ask.

"It says: *will accept trade.*"

"I see." That's it, then. This woman wants her son back, so she's taken his. There's nothing stronger than a mother's love. He only hopes his mother loves him enough to make the choice that's best for him.

SIXTY-ONE
WYATT

When Wyatt wakes up, Detective Stone is at his side. He's stopped expecting his wife to be there. She wasn't available when he almost drowned, and if she's been informed of his near-death shooting, it hasn't interested her enough to show up for that either. He knows he lost a lot of blood. He can barely lift his head, the memory of the back of Naomi's blowing out, making him lie right back down.

Why? Why, her?

There's still so much he doesn't understand.

As hospital machines and people materialize around him, there's someone else there. "Hi, Marco."

"Hey, man. I know you don't want to see me, but I thought you might want someone here when you woke up."

"It's nice to see a familiar face," he rasps.

Marco's face lightens with relief, but there must be another reason he's there other than moral support, because he's also on the quiet side, looking up into the dirty rafters of the hospital as if he might find the answer to his problem there.

"Listen, Wyatt. You're not the only person Naomi's contacted over the years."

Wyatt couldn't believe it. Either they had the exact same taste in women or Marco was a much bigger backstabber than he imagined. But this is about Landon, not him, and if Marco has important information, Wyatt needs to hear it. "Go on..."

"And... I thought I could shed some light there."

Wyatt's so exhausted his eyelid twitches, but he can't help but tune in for this part. "What do you have on her?"

"She's the reason... I did what I did with... Rowan. It's no excuse." He places his hands up. "But when we were backpacking, she liked me first, and then you kind of swooped in."

"Seriously?"

"That wasn't what got me. It was after you were married, and settled, and she let me know you two still talk. I think she was looking for a way to diversify here. She started asking me about genetic stuff too. DNA tests. She said she had a kid and thought it might be mine. Wanted a sample from me."

Wyatt gapes at him strangely. "Does she have a kid with you?"

"I don't think so. Every time I asked her for proof of the kid, she never sent it. It doesn't matter. I just thought, here you were, lucky with Rowan, and you had her too..."

Wyatt closes his eyes. "It wasn't like that."

"I get it. Anyway, I'm sorry, she... died."

"I don't know what she was even doing here. She knew the person who took Landon. She also went by an alias. Enid."

Stone chimes in then. "You mean Naomi knew Dr. Marta Santos?"

Wyatt thinks about this. "Yes. It was supposed to be a simple handoff."

Stone looks at him like the simpleton he is. "We could've provided backup. This could've gone so differently, if you'd only gotten us involved."

Wyatt nods. "My son was there. At the scene."

Stone glances up from her notepad. "You saw Landon?"

"Well, no." Tears leak out of his eyes. "But there must've been something in the vehicle worth trying to kill two people for, and I have to believe it's him."

Although he would feel a hell of a lot better if he had seen Landon with his own eyes.

"The woman who shot me was... Dr. Santos... the same doctor who treated me in Mexico City."

Stone is on her cell. "Yes... Dr. Marta Santos. I realize it's in Mexico. I need a team deployed right away." She turns her attention back to Wyatt. "We have someone raiding her home. This is a double homicide and a kidnapping case now.

"It should've been escalated all along," Marco pipes up.

Stone shoots him a dirty look and exits.

They're both silent as Wyatt grapples with how to speak to his friend.

Marco breaks the silence for him. "I don't know what to say to you. I realize an apology is not sufficient, but I still want to help bring Landon home."

Wyatt nods. "You're here. Rowan's not."

It's such a telling statement. Marco rocks back in his chair. "I'm sure she has a good reason for not being here."

"Why're you defending her?"

Marco looks away. "You're right. I just mean, it's probably not because she doesn't care. I'm sure she's tied up."

"Doing what, Marco? I almost died getting our son back. Where is she?"

He shakes his head. "I don't know. But I'm going to find out."

SIXTY-TWO

ROWAN

"It worked. We got something," Wes says.

"What is it?" Rowan crowds around the laptop. They Door-Dashed Nico some fast food and untied his hands. He sits on the couch nervously popping fries into his mouth and watching them.

"The poster said they'll meet us for a trade," Wes says happily.

"What if it's some kind of sicko and not someone who wants to trade for Landon?"

Nico stops eating his fries and stares at them like they're terrible people.

"We won't let that happen, Nico. This is a trade for my son and nothing more," Rowan assures.

He pushes his food away, frightened. "Just let me go, and my mother will help you with this if it has to do with Z."

"We can't. I'm sorry."

"Call the police, then!" he shouts.

"They're no help," Rowan says.

"They've submitted their personal email. We're to correspond that way," Wes says.

Wes shoots a message from a new, freshly created email address with the subject line: Location.

They send a message back right away that they want to meet in Costa Rica.

"Uh oh," Wes says.

"What's wrong?" Rowan says.

"They want us to meet in Costa Rica. We can't travel outside of the US with a minor. That's too far."

"We'll hide him in the back of the car."

Nico starts shouting and throwing fries and other things. "No. No way!"

"That's an unreasonably long and dangerous trip," Wes comments.

"Nico, no one is going to hurt you. I promise. I have a son. I would never let someone harm you." They've left her no choice but to take these dark measures.

Her phone rings. It's Marco. She's ignored Wyatt's calls, and it's strange for Marco to be calling.

"Keep him under control," she instructs Wes.

Wes raises an eyebrow at her. She knows the rules. He will not lay a finger on Nico. Not to mention, their plan is backfiring if they're required to take this boy out of the country.

"This is Rowan."

"Where the hell have you been?" Marco's hot-headed voice screams into the phone.

"Why, what's going on?" Rowan also notices she has a missed call from Stone, her mother, and her sister.

"What's going on is your husband almost drowns and you're MIA, and then he's almost shot to death, and you can't bother to pick up the phone."

She knows she should've called, but she's been busy fact-finding with Wes while Wyatt was literally drowning in his sorrows. She's always been the stronger one in the relationship. She can't have him dragging them down when she's so close to solving this thing. "I'm sorry to hear that. I heard he followed a false lead." She won't make the same mistake.

"Wyatt was at the Texas border. There was a man there prepared to hand Landon over to Wyatt, but a woman called Dr. Marta Santos hijacked the operation. She's the doctor who treated Wyatt in the hospital when he was attacked. Her son is suspected to be one of the surgeons that works for the Network. She shot all the adults. Wyatt is the only one who survived, but he almost bled out."

Rowan understands now that this is a total family affair. Not only does she think she has Francisco's son, but she now realizes she has the kidnapper's grandson.

"You should come here." There's bite to Marco's voice. "To San Antonio. The woman fled with Landon. South. They don't know where."

I know where... South America.

But she can't tell them that. If she does, she'll have to tell them the rest. That she kidnapped a child. That she's bartering for a trade.

Dr. Santos could pull out.

The cops don't seem to have any idea where that woman ran with her son—but Rowan does. And she can't have them screw it up. She shouldn't be farther along than them on this investigative trail. It makes her completely untrustful of their capabilities.

"I don't know if I can make it there right now."

A siren alerts in the distance. She looks up to see that the beautiful sky has turned angry and gray, and the winds have picked up significantly, making the palm trees fan at her like angry slaps.

"What do you mean you can't make it here? What is that sound? And where're you?"

"It's nothing. Someone whistling. I have to go, Marco.

Please text me updates on Wyatt's condition and give him my love."

She hangs up, upset that her plan isn't working quite right, but beyond relieved that she has solid evidence that Landon is alive. And in South America.

She crumbles to the ground in tears, clenching her belly. He's still alive. Her son is still alive...

SIXTY-THREE
WYATT

Marco enters the hospital room and solemnly stares at Wyatt.

"What is it?" Wyatt asks.

"I just spoke with Rowan."

"What? She answered the phone for you and not me?"

Marco doesn't appear happy about this either. "She's up to something."

Detective Stone stops what she's doing and focuses her attention on Marco. "Why do you say that?"

"She wouldn't tell me where she was, for starters."

"She wouldn't tell me that either," Stone says. "I assumed she was headed home the last we spoke, but Schrader says the lights are still dark at her home in Philly, and nobody is answering the door."

"Do you think..." Wyatt has to pause because speaking hurts; the bullet bypassed his kidney but pierced his lung "... she's mixed up with the same people who got me?" Wyatt's still processing that Naomi is gone. She's been such a secret comfort to him over the years, a soft spot to land when life turned cold and hard, and all along she's the ultimate illusion at the peak of his mountaintop—the apex.

"It's possible. We learned more about Naomi Chalfant. She's part of a crime family in Belarus. Want to guess what her family dabbled in?"

Wyatt stares into the fluorescent lighting at this information until his retinas burn and he sees tiny fireballs in the room. "They ran the Network?" Wyatt asks.

"As well as many other illegal trading businesses," Stone says.

"Naomi said they were in communications. I had a feeling it wasn't the legal type." He shakes his head.

"We think she was looking for a way to penetrate the US market. That's where you came in."

"She said she wanted to move somewhere remote..."

"She was trying to make you the new kingpin to her twisted domain. She just needed to take a piece of you so her best broker didn't die in the process."

Wyatt's eyes roll to the top of his head in disbelief.

"What a scam," Marco says.

"What about Rowan? How will you find her? Them?" Wyatt asks. He feels so naive for believing Naomi. It had more to do with his hope that he'd find his son than his trust in her and their relationship—but that part hurts too.

"I'm going to put out feelers for her. Marco, did you hear anything on the phone line? That gave you any idea of where she might be?" Stone asks.

"There was noise in the background. A strange whistle," he says.

"What kind of whistle? Like a kid's whistle? Was she at a park, maybe?" Stone asks.

"No. Not that kind of whistle. Like... a warning whistle."

"A... storm whistle?" Stone clarifies.

"Yes," Marco decides.

"She must be on the coast," Wyatt says. "Like the Jersey shore?"

Stone is on her phone. "There's no storms off Jersey or New York. Coast is clear."

Stone receives another phone call and excuses herself.

Wyatt closes his eyes, but every time he does so, he sees the back of Naomi's head explode through her skull.

She was supposed to be his second chance.

He realizes the fact that he is alive is his second chance. Or his third.

When Stone reenters the room, she has questions for Wyatt.

"Do you think your wife is capable of causing harm if it meant she thought she'd get Landon back?"

Wyatt fights the fog of mental and physical exhaustion overshadowing everything he sees, and thinks back to Rowan's simmering anger, and the fact that she severely beat up a girl in high school for simply mouthing off to her. "Yes," he answers simply.

"We ran a report on Dr. Marta Santos. She's the mother of two sons. One is deceased from kidney disease. He needed a transplant but died waiting on the organ donation list."

"Shit," Wyatt says. This is her motivation. "She must actually think she's providing a viable service to others," he says, as if to himself.

"The other son is a man who never finished his surgical medical training and has seemingly vanished. His name is Francisco Sumner."

"Dr. Zo," Wyatt breathes out.

"We believe so."

"Francisco has an address in Fort Lauderdale, Florida. There was a missing child alert issued there today for a nine-year-old boy, Nico Leone. His mother is also the former girlfriend of Francisco Sumner. Sources at her work have witnessed Francisco around from time to time. They think he floats her money."

"What're you saying?" Wyatt asks.

"Marco heard a whistle, like a storm warning in the background from his phone call with your wife. Guess where a storm is rolling in right about now?" Stone asks.

"Florida," Wyatt says. He lays his head back down this time because it's swimming with confusion.

"You think Rowan has Nico?" Marco surmises.

"Possibly," Stone reveals.

"How would she communicate with the person who has Landon? If her intent is to hold him as ransom?" Wyatt asks.

Stone shows Wyatt her screen. *PED, Boy 8-9, healthy, dark hair and eyes.* "We think she's using the Network. And if they find her before we do... they'll kill her."

SIXTY-FOUR
MARTA

Marta has set up shop at a lovely little cottage on Coco Beach until Walker can meet her there. She's letting him sort things out with the realtor and the movers. Soon, they will have their new start here.

She watches the boy frolic along the beach, a solid and brown packed surface, not as lovely as the pure white sands she's used to, but the beautiful mountains in the distance and lush greenery certainly make up for it.

Soon, they'll buy an extravagant property like the one they had, reach out to their brokers and surgeons, and announce their new organization. She's decided to change the name to give it a fresh spin. They'll name their version of the Network, the Fountain. *New life springs from unlikely places.* She'll brand it differently. It won't sound as nefarious as "The Network."

She barely hears the man as he approaches, but that's the human she created; a stealthy being who can slip in and out of undisclosed hotel rooms and spaces, complete his job, and sneak back out. Francisco places a firm hand on her shoulder, and as she looks up at him, she relishes his touch for just a moment. He remains staring straight ahead.

"My... you must've drove all night," she says.

"Caught a flight as soon as your tracker stopped."

Her lips form a straight line. "Walker had a tracker on the Rover?"

"He put one on it the last time we had trouble. Just in case you took off." He's referring to when the man showed up at their door and pressed a gun to her head when Francisco wouldn't complete the heart surgery. Has he taken all her sacrifices for granted?

"I see."

"It has to be over now, Mother. Dad is ready to cash out too. He'll move down here and be with you. But no more network. I'm sure they won't have us anymore anyway after your last stunt."

She shakes her head. "We're going to start our own network. We don't need them. We've learned enough and can start our own. That's what smart entrepreneurs do. We're calling it the Fountain. Newfound youth and vitality."

"You sound delusional. It's not a spa."

"I'll run it differently. No pressure. If someone doesn't want to take a job, they don't have to. You can have a family. Even with the waitress," she says with distaste.

"You can't contain an organization of that sort this way. There's no guarantee your workers won't rat you out if there's no fear they'll lose their lives. The work is atrocious."

"I'll pay them very well."

"It could never be enough. It's over. Let it be over. You've stolen enough years of our lives. Damon is gone. Andre still has a chance and needs parents. It's time to let it go. While you still have your freedom."

"Nonsense."

"Landon's case has heated up. You've gained a lot of attention with your murderous tirade at the border."

"They don't know it was me."

"Wyatt Bishop survived and told all. It's all over the news. You're a wanted fugitive now. Congratulations."

Oh, that is not good.

She thought she'd fired that shot directly at his heart, but it was dark, and the sirens from the police had started to wail. She hadn't had time to double check and make sure he wasn't breathing. "That one's like a cockroach. He just won't die."

He ignores her. Killing Wyatt Bishop was never the plan. "I will let you live down here in solitude as long as you'd like, until they catch you, but in exchange, I have to take the boy."

Marta stands to face her tall, handsome son. He's grown his hair and it's pulled back in a ponytail. She'd like to cut it off. "You don't negotiate with me, dear son."

"They know he's still alive. They won't stop until they find him."

"Let them search."

"Mother, I can't get my son back if you don't return this boy unharmed."

"You can start over with someone new. There. I've released you of all your duties. You don't need the boy and the waitress. She's trash anyway."

"I was done working for the Network regardless."

"There you go trying to change the rules again."

Landon has plopped down in the sand and is carving lines with a stick.

"There are no rules," he says.

She turns to him. "What do you mean?"

"It will take a lot of pressure off you if I return him. He needs to go home. He misses his real family. They miss him too. Beyond miss... they're stealing other people's kids to get him back. The situation is dire."

She flinches as if he's smacked her. "No. He's mine."

"Have you lost your mind? How did you even convince him to stay with you?" Francisco asks.

"I told him the story of the Bear Prince. I changed it a bit, but he sees now that life is best with me."

Francisco's eyes widen at her insanity. "What did you plan to do with him? Why do you want to raise a four-year-old boy?"

The sun begins to set on a beautiful day. The first of many, Marta thinks. Her old life, the characters in it, are blackened and dead to her. In her mind, she's taken a Sharpie and blotted them out.

They've all turned their backs now that she's no longer of use to them. *Users.* Francisco would leave his aging mother down here to die to run off with some cocktail waitress. "Andre will get better, and then we'll ship him down here. They can be like brothers, Andre and Landon," she explains.

Francisco shakes his head. He thinks she's gone mad, doesn't he? Everything she's done is for her boys. It's time to put the last of the naysayers away. Alistair was first.

Francisco is a traitor too.

"No, they can't, Mother. That time in your life is over. You have no more sons. This boy belongs to someone else. I'm taking him home." Francisco turns away from her as if she's nothing and walks away down the beach toward her boy.

She cannot let Francisco take him away. It'll ruin all her plans. She tries to remind herself that she lost Francisco long ago anyway as she pulls out the gun.

"Francisco, you cannot take him. I will not let you. You may leave, but not with him."

When Francisco turns around, he has something shiny in his hands too, and it has something long and pointed on the end of it—a silencer. Marta squints through the sunset, but not in time to duck from the quiet bullet as it flies toward her head.

SIXTY-FIVE
FRANCISCO

Francisco buckles Landon into the back of his SUV and hands him a stuffed alligator. "Who're you, and where is Miss May?" Landon asks.

"My name is Zo. I'm sorry, but Miss May did not tell you the correct story of the Bear Prince, and for that reason I must take you back to your real home now. In Philadelphia."

Landon's reddened face is creased with confusion. He looks like he might unbuckle himself and try to run, but Francisco shuts the door fast, climbs into the driver's seat, and child-locks the doors.

"What do you mean? Where's Miss May?" the boy asks, scared.

"Landon, as it turns out, Miss May did not tell you about the evil witch in the fairytale of the Bear Prince. The one who cast the spell on the Bear Prince and made him a bear by day, and a prince by night. That's a very important part of the story."

"It is?"

Francisco needs Landon to trust him in order for this transport to work. His mother was manipulative enough to use a fairytale to gain his favor. He'd do the same, only he'd tell him the real story.

"Yes. What did Miss May tell you about your real parents?"

"That... they gave me away because I was bad."

"That's not true. You were stolen away. And, in this scenario, Miss May is the evil witch. Did she give you anything to get you to come with her?"

He puzzles, and Francisco is taking a risk with this question, but there has to be something.

Landon inhales sharply like he has the answer. "Her helper gave me a painted flute! Like the one my dad promised. I followed her and then I fell asleep and woke up. Miss May was there and told me the magic flute carried me through a secret portal."

"Ah, the flute was spelled," he says. Francisco pulls onto the highway toward the airport. Despite not being around children since his own younger days, he's always enjoyed them. When he's stayed in foreign countries, even when he can't understand what the civilians are saying, there's a universality to how adults speak to their children.

"It was?" Landon says with wonder.

He's observed many adults teach a child how to kick a ball, read a book, noted the light inflection in their voices he's trying to emulate now. "I know the story of the Bear Prince well. The youngest daughter wasn't given away because she was bad. Is that what Miss May told you?"

"Yes."

"She was given away because the woodcutter needed to pay the bear for using his woods, and she was the daughter who volunteered to marry him in exchange."

"Oh..."

"Yes, and the daughter begged to go home and see her sisters, and when she did, they told her to gag the prince so he couldn't say his magic verse that turned him into a bear each day. Did Miss May tell you what it was?"

"Yes!" He giggles. "Bear so hairy..."

"Right. Well, that backfired. The Bear Prince broke up with the daughter for messing with the curse, which made things worse, and he ended up with a different girl. The marriage was cursed by the witch, and eventually, the Bear Prince realized that, and went back with his true love. The daughter. You've been under a spell this whole time, Landon."

"I have?" he asks with wonder.

"Yes. I know you never *really* believed your parents would give you away. Right?"

"You're right."

"Well, I am the wizard who broke the witch's spell. She's been cast away and now you finally get to go home."

"Thank you." Landon clutches his alligator happily in the back seat. And Francisco speeds along trying to figure out how he's going to pull this off. His father won't likely be happy about what he's done, but it would've never ended if he didn't kill her.

It would've gone on and on.

She would've somehow roped him back in, controlled his life, hurt more people. Even if his father couldn't see it now, he did the right thing.

He thinks the person who has Nico is Rowan Bishop. It's a matter of safely handing off these children now. They both have a vested interest to do this the right way.

When he looked up Rowan Bishop online her picture looked like the furthest thing from a dangerous kidnapper. She could be his first-grade teacher, she was so innocent-looking, with her slight frame, straight hair, thin-lipped smile.

After reading the articles on their family, he's learned she's also pregnant with her second child. It seemed, Nico, the busy kid he met yesterday, could've outmaneuvered her, but Nico was probably terrified an adult was attacking him.

And if he was walking his dog, he might've put the dog's safety before his own, like a good owner.

There are so many scenarios as to how she got a hold of him, but what she's done with him since is the question.

The woman on his cell phone screen looks harmless. He's comforted she's not a convicted felon with a rap sheet a mile long. Maybe they can all come out of this with two healthy boys.

That's his greatest hope.

There's a number across the screen for anyone who has a lead to where Landon Bishop is located. Francisco sighs. He's tired of running. If the Network is going to come after him for what his mother's done, maybe he's safer in the police's care.

He'll try to negotiate a lighter sentence and police protection in exchange for the boy and any information they want on the Network. He'll serve time, but maybe if he does the right thing, he'll have an opportunity later to develop a relationship with his son. First, he has to get Nico back from the people who've taken him.

Francisco dials the number.

SIXTY-SIX
WYATT

An urgent call comes in for Stone regarding Landon, and Wyatt is woken up by Marco out of his drug-induced haze. "They've got something."

"This is Detective Stone." Wyatt watches her intently.

"You have Landon Bishop? And who're you?" Stone asks.

Wyatt tries to listen closely, but he can't stretch his body with it strapped down with all the wires and tubes.

"Francisco Sumner, this is Detective Stone, head detective on this case. Where're you? You took Landon from your mother who stole him in the first place... Yes, of course, we'll work with you if you return him, but where're you? Yes, we're aware your son is missing... We can't advise you to travel with the boy. No. No!"

Stone looks at her phone line, dead.

"What is it?" Wyatt asks.

"He wants protection for an exchange arranged when they arrive in the States. He won't say where he is. He said he knows Rowan has Nico, and he's setting up the swap. He'll hand Landon over, and in return he wants a lighter sentence for giving up the Network. He wants out."

Psh. "That motherfucker carved men up like a Thanksgiving turkey and then stole my son. He's not getting a lighter sentence," Wyatt says.

"You can testify against him. I think his mother enlisted him long ago. He was an A student in med school. Top of his class, and then he just disappeared one day."

"I don't care if he was *summa cum laude*. Those people are monsters. I won't believe Landon is okay until I see him."

"Of course, but you can't fly to Florida in your condition. We're pretty sure that's where Nico is."

"I'll go," Marco says. "In your place, Wyatt. And I'll make sure he's recovered. I won't let you down this time. I know it doesn't make up for what I did."

"Well... he's *yours* too. I can't tell you not to go. Get him back for me, Marco."

Marco's large brown eyes melt like caramels. He offers Wyatt a sympathetic grin for the acknowledgment, kisses him on the forehead, and then walks out the door with Stone.

SIXTY-SEVEN
ROWAN

Rowan and Wes are researching ways to transport Nico to Costa Rica.

A new complacency halo has formed around Nico where he doesn't talk to them at all and just stares straight ahead. Rowan thinks he's either realized that he's going to come out of this okay, even if that involves a little field trip, or he's plotting something of his own.

They've had to keep him overnight, which means they've resorted to changing his ankle zip ties to a rope so that he can walk to and from the bathroom. She and Wes have been taking shifts watching him.

They've decided flying is out of the question. They can't get fake passports in the limited time they have, and if they could, Nico would do something to give them away.

The Network is currently down for some reason.

Wes's tried to log on several times and it says the website is inoperable, which is peculiar, but the buyer has Wes's email address. Wes requested a meeting spot closer to the border, but they have not received a response yet.

"They're probably just securing a spot," Wes says.

"Or they've backed out," Rowan says nervously.

Her mother and sister have called incessantly, but she won't pick up. She's seen the recent news report about the doctor and her murderous tirade. This is the woman who has her son. She can't be talked out of this, and they will try.

This woman tried to kill her husband—twice. She murdered her own personal assistant of a decade.

And now she may kill her son if they don't act appropriately.

Rowan concentrates on the map. They've come up with a few different exchange points.

Her cell phone rings and this time it's Stone. She lets it go to voicemail. Then she receives the text.

Stone: *We have confirmation, Landon en route. Call ASAP!*

Rowan flashes her screen at Wes quickly. She dials the contact number. "What's going on?" she asks Stone.

"Dr. Zo has Landon. We've received confirmation."

"Great." Now she knows the person she's been messaging is Zo and not Santos. Zo will be harder to overpower, though, if it comes down to it. She's glad they have Wes's gun. "How do we get Landon back from him?" she asks, although internally, she's reeling.

This was not the plan. She had a connection before that the police did not which somewhat excused her behavior. She may have some severe legal consequences to face now because of what she's done to get this ball rolling, but all that matters is that Landon is safe.

"We know, Rowan... And we think the Network knows too."

"What do you mean?" She clenches her cell and looks

through the windows of the motel, paranoia settling in, but there's hardly any cars in the parking lot.

"We know you have Nico Leone."

Shit. "Why do you say that?" She shuts the blinds, locks the door, then deadbolts it.

"We understand your thought process, but you need to tell us where you are and let the police handle it from here. We'll help with the handoff. Nico's mother needs to know he's safe, and maybe, just maybe, after she understands why you did what you did, she won't press charges."

Rowan gnaws on her lip. She's being bated here. They'll charge her with kidnapping either way. Stone's trying to trick her.

Stone's also done absolutely nothing to bring Landon home. She organized a press conference and a ransom, but Stone was handed the Network on a platter, and they were told the police couldn't crack it.

If Wes, an ex-insurance agent, was able to figure it out after countless, dedicated manhours, surely, someone on the police force could've done it too. They just didn't want to invest the time.

Now, Rowan doesn't trust Stone.

Not with her son's life. If she hands over Nico she loses her leverage.

Wes is mouthing at her—*Tell them.*

She realizes her decisions implicate Wes as well, but he can leave her now. The Network is down. No one ever has to know he was involved. It was one of her goals for Wes to post Nico on the Network, and he did. Message received. Wes has done his job here.

"Detective, with all due respect, my main goal is to get my son back, and so far you haven't been helpful with that effort..."

"Don't do this, Rowan. Your husband tried to handle things on his own and he almost died. You're making a mistake."

"I'm not. You've made many. When you decided to disregard a website that was your number one key to finding my son, you lost me. You didn't want to use your time or resources to break it down and countless people have suffered because of that action."

"I don't know who you're working with, but you're in danger. These people will come after you! We can help. Let's work as a team," Stone says.

"I will not turn this boy over until I have mine." She slams down the phone.

Wes closes his eyes and rubs the bridge between his nose.

"Go!" she tells him.

"What?" he asks.

"You've done your job. You don't agree with what I'm doing. They don't know you're involved. The Network is down. We helped crash it."

"But..." Wes is hesitant.

"Our little post must've been behind it. That was a big part of this endeavor. To take them down. Right now, no one can make a transaction on the dark web for an organ, and that's victory."

Wes stands up and straightens his back. The six-pack of beer is gone, and she's guessing it's the alcohol speaking when he says, "I don't think I can let you finish this on your own. What if the Network comes after you before you can hand off the boy?" Up until this point, he's been like an unfeeling, subservient counterpart, and she can't have him getting emotional now. This all must go smoothly.

"What're you going to do in that case, Wes? Fight them all off with your single gun? Why would it be worth it for you to stay?"

"I want to see them go down too. With my own eyes," Wes says.

He'll never know how much she'd like to be the one doing the shooting. She wonders who's a better shot. "You can leave at any time," she decides on, because she doesn't really want him to go. But she doesn't want him to be there unless he's 100 percent invested in this operation either.

Nico finally emerges from the bathroom. His face is ruddy with sweat and his legs are blistered from where he apparently was trying to tamper with his restraints.

"Don't do that to yourself, Nico. You're going home soon," she says.

"Don't tell me what to do." Nico plops on the couch.

"Your dad is on his way. You'll be free soon," she says.

"He is not my father," Nico says, frustrated. "I told you that."

Rowan and Wes exchange a knowing glance. Wes shakes his head at Rowan. It's not her place to tell Nico life-altering news right now. He's been through enough.

"Your Uncle Z is fighting to get you back for your mom. It's happening. Just a little more patience," she says.

"Whatever." Nico sinks back into the crummy couch and closes his eyes.

Just then, Wes receives an email.

Meet at Crooked River State Park. Kingsland, GA. Tomorrow at 2 pm. Email when you arrive. Come ALONE.

She emails the man, who she hopes is Francisco, back, letting him know she'll meet him there, but if he arrives with any "friends" the deal on her end is also "off." She has skin in the game too, in the form of a nine-year-old boy, and she can't lose sight of that. It's the only bargaining chip she has to get Landon back.

"What if that's the Network, trying to get you alone to kill you? I'm still going with you, but I think you should tell Stone," Wes says.

"The instructions are clear. Come alone."

In the morning, Rowan packs for the five-hour drive up the Florida coast to the Florida-Georgia line. She wonders why this man's chosen to meet them there, exactly. Kingsland is near many waterways, including the Okenfenokee Swamp.

"There's still time to call Stone," Wes says.

"She had her chance. She didn't do her job. This could've been over a long time ago if she had. I don't trust her to finish what we started."

"What happens if this guy takes Nico and shoots us?"

"He'll be shooting me, not you. Let's just hope this family doesn't want to increase their body count."

"What if he's not who he says he is?" Nico peeps from the backseat. "My mom tells me not to trust people I meet on the Internet."

Rowan smirks at this.

"He doesn't have a bad point..." Wes says.

"Given the circumstances, I'd say chances are really good it couldn't be anyone else. I'll take Wes's gun. Wes stays in the car with Nico. Nothing happens until I see Landon, alive. If they shoot anyone, it'll be me."

"I don't think so," Wes says. "Reverse that."

"I don't want you to get hurt. I set this up. It should be me who takes the risk," she says. "He's expecting me."

"You have two lives at stake." He points at her belly. "I have one. And mine... has seen its best years."

"Don't say that. After we put these guys away, you can start over. You'll be a hero."

Wes snorts. "I hardly think anyone will think that."

"You'll be *my* hero," she says.

Wes offers her a slow, spreading smile, and they're caught in a special moment until Nico says, "Yuck. Get me out of here."

No one else has stepped up to the plate for her and Landon like Wes has. She just hopes it's all worth it for both of them. Wes couldn't save his son, but he can help save hers.

SIXTY-EIGHT
ROWAN

Rowan watches in astonishment as the stranger from the park lifts her little boy—*Landon!*—from the backseat of a vehicle and practically runs with him to the end of the boat dock. Her body tremors with happiness and fear.

"There he is..." Emotions overcome her, rationality leaving her body in a desperate rush. She touches the handle of her car.

"Stick to the plan," Wes coaches. "He might do something slippery. You have no idea."

Wes has his hand on his firearm, very tense. They all are.

Rowan has to remind herself to breathe. To think. Not to ride on her mother's instinct, which is to throw open the door, tear through the parking lot, and scoop up her son.

Her stomach is upset, and she has heartburn from the black coffee she's just consumed.

"It has to be tempting seeing him... I never saw mine alive again, not even on video footage after he was taken," Wes says. "But we have to do this right."

"Okay." Rowan exhales and listens. *Exhales and listens.* What else can she do?

"He'll probably get jail time, work out a deal because he

handed over the kid." Wes's face fills with anger. "It's not fair. All the people he's hurt. He doesn't deserve to just walk away with his child after the way they found mine." His voice cracks.

Rowan turns to Wes, uncertain. Is he the one losing it now? This must be hard. They found his child disemboweled. It would've ended her. Best-case scenario, she'd be living on top of a pile of papers in a dirty apartment too if that were the case.

But how is Wes's mental state now? Can he pull this off?

She turns around to face Nico, and he has tears streaming down his face. "It's going to be okay," she tells him.

He shakes his head. "You're all bad people."

She turns back around, not debating the point. "Sometimes when you're dealing with bad people... you become bad people," she says. Although she's not sure that's when it started. It's always been a fight to survive, in her small hometown, in her million-dollar home. In her marriage. But there's nothing she'll fight harder for than her child.

A message populates Wes's phone.

"It's time," he says. "I'm going to retrieve him. Be ready with Nico."

She couldn't be more ready.

Rowan parked in a place where she has a good view of the dock and her son. The man and Landon seem almost peaceful, watching the birds, the herons, a pelican Landon points at. Rowan leans in with tears in her eyes.

The man holds his hand.

Her son's hand.

Wes exits the car, walks swiftly up the dock.

The man turns but doesn't appear happy to see Wes.

Francisco sees a scrubby-looking man walking toward him. He was expecting Rowan Bishop, and for a moment thinks maybe he's just a guy out for a morning walk, but his expression speaks otherwise. "I'm here to receive Landon. Once he's safely in our possession, I'll release Nico and let him run down here to you. We're parked..." the man points to the parking lot "right there."

"That wasn't the deal. We were supposed to exchange them at the same time," Francisco says.

"My client didn't feel comfortable doing that because of the circumstances of how Landon was taken."

Francisco doesn't like this answer at all. How can he be sure this man even has his son? This is how people end up hurt. He won't release Landon without his son.

"Who're you?" he asks. "I want to see Rowan."

"You've been corresponding with me," the man says.

"What's your name?" Francisco asks. Landon stands behind him, fearful. He won't go to this man unless Francisco tells him to. Francisco explained on the way over here that the witch can sometimes play tricks and send messengers who take on evil forms, and that he should only go to his parents.

"My name is Wesley Baxter," the man says.

Francisco's hand drops into his pocket in fear.

He recognizes the man's name, of course. His little boy died at the hands of the Network in a most heinous way. Francisco can see the fury rise in the man's body first. He watches as Wesley's hand dives into his own pocket.

Wesley withdraws a gun and points it at Francisco. "Give him to me now, you son-of-a-bitch."

Landon squeezes Francisco's leg.

"They didn't provide me with the right tools for your son's surgery. It wasn't my fault he died." He tries not to think back to the little boy who died on his table, but it haunts his dreams most nights.

Wes's hand wobbles. "*What?* I thought it was the other..."

"I don't know what the Network did with him after I left.

Don't do this, sir. Just stick to our original arrangement," Francisco says.

"You don't call the shots here. *You.*" His hand quakes as he points it at Francisco. He seems to be losing focus, too unsteady on his feet for Francisco's liking. "Your mother... the Network..." he rasps and then refocuses. "Come with me, Landon. Your mother is waiting for you."

"No," Landon says. "You're a witch."

"*You*—" Wesley seems to lose his focus again "killed my son. It was you," he seethes.

Francisco can see a woman running toward them now.

Her arms are outstretched, but she doesn't have Nico with her. This is a setup and he's been had. Rowan Bishop hacked the system with the help of this man, who now understands Francisco killed his son. Have they done the same to his?

Wes turns to see what Francisco's looking at, and then swears under his breath.

Francisco backs toward the end of the dock. There's a boat bobbing in the water there.

"You aren't getting away! You killed him!"

Wes points his gun and fires a shot, narrowly missing Francisco's foot. Landon hops away from the gunshot and almost falls off the dock.

Francisco pulls his gun from his pocket and fires two shots back and hits Wes square in the chest. Wes topples over. Francisco shields Landon's eyes, grabs his stuffed alligator before it tumbles into the water, and he drops into the boat with the boy.

Police descend from every corner of earth in space. Men in black vests with drawn guns surround the area.

Francisco can see a woman in black waving at Francisco to come to her on the opposite side of the lake. He fires up the engine of the little fishing boat and takes off, but not before he sees that the woman who was running toward them is kneeling beside someone much smaller than who he was aiming for.

Francisco's second gunshot—hit his son?

Francisco docks his boat on the opposite side of the lake and twenty cops are there to receive him. He hands Landon to an officer and points to his guns, which are laying in the boat.

"Help my son!" he pleads. "He's shot!"

"We have an ambulance on the way. Step out of the boat with your hands up, Mr. Sumner," a stern-looking woman, who he can only guess is Detective Stone, says.

Francisco does as she asks.

A man in plainclothes flies from around the corner and punches him in the face. "Fuck you, you piece of shit!"

"Mr. Lucarelli..." That man is dragged out of the area. He's taken to Landon's side, and Landon curls up in his lap with his stuffed alligator. He must be family, or Landon would've recognized him as a "witch."

Francisco's face throbs with guilt, hands behind his back, as the cuffs are placed around his wrists, and he weeps for his son.

He deserves this. For hurting all those people. Killing his own mother. This is his punishment.

"My name is Detective Stone and I'll be taking you into custody." She reads him the Miranda Act and places him in the back of a cop car.

Francisco sees another woman running over—a pregnant woman. He searches her body for blood—his son's blood—but doesn't see any. He searches her eyes for recognition. He has so many things he wants to say to her.

They make brief eye contact through the car window, and he's tormented by how this could've all been so different if she'd only done what they decided on in their messages and delivered Nico herself. He made it clear that no one else was to come with her, but maybe she was afraid because she's pregnant.

Couldn't risk putting the other child in danger. Francisco gets it now, but it doesn't make the situation any better.

He didn't trust the cops to make the exchange—not until he saw his son. They could've lied and said they had Nico just to get Landon back, or to bust their operation.

Francisco can see another ambulance arrive on the scene, and he wants to stay and observe and see how Nico is, but he's whisked away.

SIXTY-NINE
ROWAN

They allow Rowan more time than they should before they arrest her.

She collapses at Marco's feet. He steadies her from her shoulders as she shakes uncontrollably, but is stable enough for Landon to climb on top of her lap.

She breathes in his entire being, in a way she hasn't since he was born, pressing her nose close to his hairline, inhaling him. Her boy—is alive.

He returns her embrace, burying his little face in her chest. The tears come next, a torrent of tears, falling so hard, she can barely breathe.

Mr. Crackers is dirty and bedraggled, but she's happy he was able to make the entire journey too. She'd forgotten about him. It means Landon had a little friend to help him through his ordeal.

"Oh my god, I've been so worried about you," she cries. She rocks Landon on her lap. This moment is all she's dreamt about for the last month.

Landon pushes himself away from her, offering some space between them. "I knew you didn't give me away," he says. "I was under a spell. The woman got me to leave with a magic flute."

Rowan gazes at Detective Stone with profound recognition. "It was a flute. That woman had in her hand on the video. Wyatt mentioned it when he was on the phone... with his boss. She must've overheard. The phone call from work. At the visitor's center. That's how she got him."

Detective Stone shakes her head like she understands none of what Rowan is saying. Rowan knows she'll have time to explain it all later—when she's in Stone's custody.

Rowan returns her attention back to Landon. "Of course I didn't give you away. Is that what they told you?" Landon thought they'd abandoned him on purpose.

He nods as if he truly believed that.

He smiles and sobs into her chest. She rocks him on her lap like he's a baby. "We can't wait to get you home."

Marco sits back in wonder, inspecting Landon, and she can't imagine how difficult this must be for him—taking in his son for the first time. She's thankful he's here but wondering what will happen now—with all of them. Certainly, she'll have to serve some jail time.

She looks up to find Stone waiting for her. "Is Wes..." she whispers.

Stone shakes her head that he's gone.

Rowan sighs, then cries some more, losing some elasticity in her arms. Landon remains on her lap, even though he holds himself there, because she's lost control of her limbs. Marco takes over holding Landon for her.

"Wes is gone," Stone says.

Rowan shakes her head. No one was supposed to get hurt.

"We warned you of this."

"But why did Wes try to shoot him?" Rowan asks.

"We questioned Zo..." Stone says lightly. "He revealed that Wesley Baxter drew his firearm because Zo revealed that he was the one who had worked on his son. He thought Wes knew that."

Rowan looks up, horrified. "No!"

"Yes. When Zo revealed it was him, and with his son's murderer right in front of him... he couldn't resist taking his shot."

Rowan understood the rage, but she's so sorry Wes gave into it. He'd thought the other surgeon had killed his son.

"These are the unpredictable circumstances that happen when you try to handle things yourself," Stone says.

"And... Nico?" she asks, although she knows he's okay. Nico ducked when he saw the gunfight break out, but it didn't come close to hitting him. Rowan threw herself over his body just in case. She knows Zo saw her hover over his body, and probably thought the worst.

"He's fine. In the care of an officer who is personally escorting him home right now."

"Thank God." She's beyond relieved he'll be returned unscathed.

"Now what?" she asks, although she thinks she knows.

Stone kneels beside her. "Now... you have to come with us, Mrs. Bishop. You're being charged with kidnapping and child endangerment. The court will decide your fate."

Landon glances at her like he's so confused. "Where're you going? I just got you back."

"Mommy had to do some bad things to find you. I'm so sorry, Landon. But it was the only way to break the spell. Your daddy is getting better and..." She looks at Marco to see if she can count on him.

"And Uncle Marco will be taking care of you until he's all better," Marco says.

"Yeah! Can we go back to the beach?" he asks.

"You bet. I think your Grandma Barb might like to come too," Marco says.

Rowan grins, because she knows everything will be okay. Maybe not today, but her babies are finally safe. "That sounds nice, honey. Just remember, no matter how long Mom has to go away, I'll come back for you. And when I do, you'll get to meet your new little sister."

SEVENTY

WYATT

"Were you administered a blood test when you accepted your position at Apex?" Detective Stone asks Wyatt.

He's alert and feeling much better. The only thing he understands when he wakes up in the morning is that his son is alive, and in Marco's custody. *Thank God.* Rightfully so, Wyatt thinks. He's decided to let Marco have an active part in raising Landon. He'll need the help now that his wife is in prison.

Wyatt made a mistake in trusting the wrong woman to intercept his son, but he didn't break the law.

Rowan lied to the police, kidnapped a child. Thank God the boy was not harmed.

But Wyatt will never be able to reconcile with Rowan. Not after how she endangered Landon by not working with the cops when she had the chance. Wyatt never had the opportunity. Naomi held all the cards and wouldn't let him see any of them.

"Yes," Wyatt answers. "My wife thought the request for the test was odd, but I interned for a pharmaceutical company in college, and I also had to take a blood test for them, so I didn't think it was an unreasonable ask, especially for a foreign company. Different rules."

Stone offers one of her grave expressions. "They were casing you from the beginning. Your blood type and genetic makeup is the reason you got the job."

A mix of confusion and anger bubbles to the surface as Wyatt processes this statement. "There were over twenty thousand applicants on LinkedIn for that job," he puzzles. Even though Naomi had recommended him, he still had to apply through LinkedIn and stick her name in the "recommended" category. He thought it was merit that'd pushed his application to the top.

"Yes, but they qualified the candidate based on the blood test."

He frowns at the information. Naomi never loved him. She needed a man that was a match for her sick broker, and a new love interest in the United States, and when she found him, she probably thought she'd hit the jackpot.

Stone continues, "They were looking for a male with O blood, your professional skillset, but that's not all. Other tests were submitted to their lab for a crossmatch test and other genetic factors. Among all the job applicants, you're the one who met all the criteria."

"How lucky for me."

"You were lucky. You were also supposed to take the car service they ordered for you that day. Where you would've been taken to a remote area, and the hotel never would've gotten involved. They helped save your life. It's a big reason this unfolded the way it did."

My lack of detail has finally come in handy. But wait...

"So Apex was not a real company at all? I created software for them. I don't understand."

"We looked into them as well once we couldn't find a tax ID number. That software already existed. You were recreating a preexisting wheel. It was an elaborate scheme, to set up a fake company, and post it on a job board site, but the patriarch of the

Network's largest broker was dying. They were pulling out all the stops to find a donor for him. The only way to find a donor after traditional methods failed was to post a fake job and require blood draws."

"What about... my boss?" Wyatt is still trying to fully understand how a rug of this size could've been pulled from beneath him.

"Irina was a hired hand, and Apex wasn't the only fake company of this sort set up. It was a global scheme they pulled off to gather private information, for a very long time. The Network posted its patients in need and then the Network sometimes used these fake companies, in areas where they could, to screen them. When people are desperate, they'll pay."

"Holy shit. What about the Santos family? The brokers."

"Walker, the man who has your kidney, is in jail. Francisco, the son, who you'll never believe was also somewhat of a victim in all of this, is in jail, and cooperating with us. Dr. Marta Santos... is dead."

Wyatt nods, not happy the man who cut him up will likely get a lighter sentence for giving up the organization. Maybe, someday, Wyatt will find a place in his heart for forgiveness, but today isn't it.

"Oh, and Rowan wanted me to tell you... She got the results back from her most recent bloodwork. You're having a girl."

He grins. It's what she wanted. Too bad she'll have to deliver the baby in jail. Stone said they're trying to fight for a lighter sentence for her too, but prison time is inevitable because of the kidnapping. She should've left the Delco behind her. It got her into a world of trouble this time, and it's daunting to think he'll have to move forward as a single father of two children, one an infant.

Some things still aren't adding up, and it will be a long while before they do.

"The woman I was with, Naomi, gave me the lead for the job."

Stone sighs. "We think the authorities were starting to place a case against her overseas. Naomi is also known as Enid in the Network, and her parents are part of a Belarus crime gang. She ran the Network since her parents passed away. She was possibly trying to move her operation here using the only two men she knew in the States. You and Marco."

That's what she must've meant by—*I'm protected.*

"Her parents are both dead and the Network dies with her," Stone explains.

Wyatt glances up at Stone and realizes that something very good has come of all their pain. He played a small part in a much bigger plan. They took a piece of him, but they won't take the rest.

A LETTER FROM CARA

Dear reader,

I want to say a huge thank you for choosing to read *Never Come Back*. Please note: although a lot of independent medical research was conducted to write this novel, there were also creative liberties taken in its completion.

If you did enjoy it, and want to keep up to date with all my latest releases, just sign up at the following link. Your email address will never be shared and you can unsubscribe at any time.

www.bookouture.com/cara-reinard

I hope you loved *Never Come Back*, and if you did I would be very grateful if you could write a review. I'd love to hear what you think, and it makes such a difference helping new readers to discover one of my books for the first time.

I love hearing from my readers—you can get in touch through social media, Goodreads or my website.

Thanks,

Cara Reinard

KEEP IN TOUCH WITH CARA

www.carareinard.com

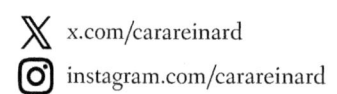

X x.com/carareinard
⊙ instagram.com/carareinard

ACKNOWLEDGMENTS

I started this book after reading a true crime article about a foreigner who was a victim of organ harvesting. I was shocked to discover 10 percent of the world's organ transplants are illegal. My first iteration of *Never Come Back* came next. Oftentimes I'm inspired by true crime, and sometimes in cases like this, reality is truly stranger than fiction.

I did a lot of independent research for this book, and due to a quick deadline, I didn't have many eyes on this novel other than my fabulous team at Bookouture—editors: Natalie Edwards, Ellen Gleeson, and Ria Clare. A shout-out to copyeditor, Donna Hillyer, who contributed to the finer details of cleaning up some of the medical research quandaries in this book. And to Jon Appleton for proofing my grammar blips.

And a special thank you to my colleague and friend, Laraina Lake, a Philadelphia native, who helped me fact check my setting. I've never seen her Delco attitude at work, but I'm sure it exists!

To my family, for the extra support as I wrote on a tight deadline, I couldn't do it without you—thanks for seeing me through another one!

PUBLISHING TEAM

Turning a manuscript into a book requires the efforts of many people. The publishing team at Bookouture would like to acknowledge everyone who contributed to this publication.

Commercial
Lauren Morrissette
Hannah Richmond
Imogen Allport

Cover design
Emma Graves

Data and analysis
Mark Alder
Mohamed Bussuri

Editorial
Natalie Edwards
Charlotte Hegley

Copyeditor
Donna Hillyer

Proofreader
Jon Appleton

Marketing
Alex Crow
Melanie Price
Occy Carr
Ciara Rosney
Martyna Młynarska

Operations and distribution
Marina Valles
Stephanie Straub
Joe Morris

Production
Hannah Snetsinger
Mandy Kullar
Jen Shannon
Ria Clare

Publicity
Kim Nash
Noelle Holten
Jess Readett
Sarah Hardy

Rights and contracts
Peta Nightingale
Richard King
Saidah Graham

Printed in Great Britain
by Amazon